D0429523

Also by Victoria Scott

VIOLET GRENADE

Dante Walker series

THE COLLECTOR
THE LIBERATOR
THE WARRIOR

Fire & Flood series

FIRE & FLOOD
SALT & STONE

TITANS
FOUR HOUSES
HEAR THE WOLVES

VICTORIA SCOTT

Entangled Publishing, LLC
2614 South Timberline Road
Suite 105, PMB 159
Fort Collins, CO 80525
rights@entangledpublishing.com

Entangled Teen is an imprint of Entangled Publishing, LLC.

Visit our website at www.entangledpublishing.com.

Edited by Heather Howland
Cover design by Anna Crosswell
Cover images by
Depositphotos/Alebloshka
Depositphotos/Andrey_Kuzmin
Interior art by
Reed Timmermann and Jeremy Howland
Interior design by Toni Kerr

ISBN 978-1-64063-422-0
Ebook ISBN 978-1-64063-421-3

Manufactured in the United States of America

First Edition February 2019

10 9 8 7 6 5 4 3 2 1

entangled teen
an imprint of Entangled Publishing LLC

For Wayne, who we lost but will always remember.
And for Reed, who I found.

PART I

come as you are

NOW

"Cobain," the police officer says. "What are you thinking about?"

"Nothing."

Actually, I'm thinking about Molly's hands. How small they were in mine. Not nearly large enough to hold my heart inside them. And yet they did.

But now she's gone.

So why am I here, still breathing?

The woman, Officer Hernandez, leans back in her chair and adjusts the red-framed glasses on her nose. Her thick eyebrows furrow as she considers me in my black leather jacket, black T-shirt, dark jeans, and black boots. I bet she's wondering if I always dress this way.

I do. And so what?

"I figured you'd be thinking about Molly," she says.

I scowl. "She is *all* I've thought about."

"What makes you certain she ran away?" she asks.

Molly could read this woman in a matter of seconds. She'd size her up and deliver the perfect response. Something that'd feed a need the woman wasn't aware she had. And the woman would bend to her will like a ballerina, thinking she'd never seen a girl quite as lovely as Molly Bates.

But I'm not a master manipulator like my girl is, so I trace the crow tattoo on my forearm, try to remain calm. I want out of here. I hate talking, but I'd say anything to get onto the other side of these walls. Then I can return to searching for her, just like I was doing before they scooped me up outside the locker room, Coach Miller demanding to see a warrant. But I said, *It's okay, Coach. It's okay.*

And I touched his arm.

And he was so surprised by my hand there that he seemed to forget about the two uniformed officers.

I knew why they came for me. I *knew*.

They think I did something.

Suspicious, the paper said. *Suspicious, suspicious, so wonderfully suspicious!*

The idea that I had anything to do with Molly going missing is ludicrous. The mere *thought* of her gone causes the room to spin.

When my breathing grows too shallow, I focus on Molly. She brings me back. Centers my feet on the floor, toes curled with determination. Molly and her wide, infectious smile. Molly and her hands, forever reaching for me. Molly and her deceptively soft eyes, so green they'd sit beside a crocodile on the color chart.

Where are you, Molly?

"The paper said she took some of her things with her when she left," I say at last.

Officer Hernandez purses her lips, probably frustrated that I know this. Frustrated that the news leaked at all before they could make an arrest and file everything squarely away. Dust their hands off, go out for pizza and beer to celebrate, and pat themselves on the back.

"People only do that when they run away, right?" I prompt.

She ignores me. "Molly is underage, as you know." *And you're not.* The unspoken words float between us. She flips open a notebook and poises a freshly sharpened pencil over paper. I can smell the lead from where I sit. "Regardless of where she went, or what happened to her, it's important that we find her and bring her home safely."

My brain catches on her words—

Or what happened to her…

I shudder.

I hope she's somewhere with those stupid weeds she likes to blow that tickle my nose and make her laugh. I hope she's somewhere she can dance the way she did that day in the park, her face tilted toward the sky. I hope she's somewhere her mom can't reach, so she only thinks of herself the way I do.

Please, *please,* don't be elsewhere.

I run nervous hands through my hair, wish I had something to tie it back in. Molly always said I should grow it out long enough to make a proper ponytail. I was getting close before she…

"You're a big kid," the officer says. "You lift weights, is that right?"

I frown, confused by the question.

"Tall, too. Aren't most weight lifters shorter?"

I fidget, not liking this. I wish she'd get to the point. "I'm not on the team."

She gives a half smile. "I was just curious. My son is in middle school. Thinks he wants to get into powerlifting."

I wonder why a kid in middle school wants to lift weights instead of hang out with friends. For the same reason I did? To protect himself? I wish I knew her son. I wish I could stand between him and whatever, or *whoever*, might be making him feel unsafe.

She shakes her head. "I don't know, though. All that aggression. And some of them take pills, right? Makes them bigger, but also makes them erratic…"

She watches me closely, probably trying to read my body language. I know what she's thinking. What they are all thinking. They believe Molly might not have run away. They believe she may have been taken by someone close to her.

But no matter what they think, that person wasn't me.

Officer Hernandez softens her approach. Lays her pencil down on the table, and looks at me with kind eyes. Eyes that say she wants the same thing I do.

She has no idea what I want.

"Tell me about when you met Molly," she says, her voice gentle.

My heart clenches, thinking of that day. Of how she defended me, a butterfly rousing a bull. Did she hold me in her hands that quickly? Was there anything I wouldn't have done for her from that moment forward? I was easy. One act of kindness and I belonged to her. I was thirsty for it—that compassion. Thought of little else, though I told myself otherwise.

"We were in the hallway," I offer.

"At school?" she asks.

I nod and fold my arms across my chest, feeling myself soften. The truth is, I *want* to talk about her. I need to go back through every moment we shared and figure out where things went wrong. Why not start there?

That pencil again, scribbling. "What day was this?"

The answer fires out of my mouth like a confession.

"Friday. First Friday in October."

THEN

*D*on't make eye contact.
    My head was down, my hands shoved into my pockets. I was watching my feet move, quick. *Get out of the hallway. Into the classroom. Don't look anyone in the face. Don't interact.*

But I looked up anyway.

I looked up because I heard your voice.

When someone talks as little as I do, their ears overcompensate. And I could tell, without seeing you, that you were new. My eyes met yours, and I thought, *Damn, damn, damn*, because I knew how you'd react. Because every last part of me was assembled so that people would leave me the hell alone.

I was so focused on you that I bumped into a freshman, knocking the books out of his hands. I lunged toward the floor and grabbed his things. Put them back into the kid's arms and muttered an apology, avoiding his nervous eyes as he took in my frame.

When I glanced your way again, you were looking at me.

Looking at me…and smiling.

And I looked down because I'm an asshole and I thought maybe you were smiling at someone else.

I'd like to say I didn't think about you while I sat in American History, but my mind replayed every part of you round and round like a turntable. Your hair, so blond it was nearly white, parted down the middle. Your eyes, so intense they pulled me inside out. Your mouth, pink and shiny and curving upward on one side like the sight of me amused you.

My God, your mouth.

I didn't like you at first, did you know that?

Every time I thought of you and that damn smile, I frowned.

And then I thought of it again.

I may have wondered what your name was.

I may have hated you for smiling at me because it opened this horrendous *hope* inside of me, and it was impossible to push it back into place. It was a hernia, that hope. A rabid animal that needed trapping. But it'd already fled so far, so what could you do?

I saw you again after lunch. You were coming in, and I was leaving.

My heart raced, and I told myself—

Don't look at her, you fuck. Don't you dare look at her.

But I did anyway, and you narrowed your eyes at me and tilted your head like you were trying to figure me out. A chick with dark hair—Rhana—was talking to you. She was pointing out the table she wanted you to sit at, but you were looking at me.

And I was looking at you.

And I definitely hated you then.

Because now I was going to think about you all night, even though those two rubbery cheeseburgers the lunch lady slid me had almost gotten you off my mind.

I thought briefly about raising my hand to wave, because really, where were my balls? But then Jet Davis spotted me, and my jaw clenched because I knew what was coming. I knew, and you were still watching me, and you were going to see this all go down.

Jet, like the predictable prick he is, raised his arms in front of his chest, widened his eyes, and started walking like Frankenstein.

"Uuugh," he said, acting like he'd just been raised from the dead. "Uuugh."

He rocked his weight back and forth, his unseeing gaze set on me, while his friends laughed and laughed. And you looked back and forth between him and me, waiting to see what I would do.

Did I disappoint you then?

Because I did what I always do. I put my head down and stormed toward my next class, my bag thumping against my back as I put distance between him and me, between you and me.

I was humiliated.

I wanted to find Jet and beat his face in because even though he'd done the same thing to me a hundred times, it'd never been when someone who had smiled at me was watching.

When I saw you for the third time that day, I was frustrated. Why did you have to be *everywhere* I was? Why were you looking at me?

Stop looking at me, goddamn it.

You were on one side of the hallway, walking toward me. Rhana was there again, talking your ear off. And then, because I have the best luck in the world, Jet came around the corner, and he got right up behind me, and he was going, *Uuugh, uuugh,* and I was ignoring it because I was afraid if I reacted, I wouldn't be able to *stop* reacting. You were coming closer and closer, and Jet was getting louder and louder, and then finally, your eyes left my face, and you looked at Jet instead.

You looked at his *crotch*.

You covered your mouth and snickered, and you elbowed Rhana and nodded toward Jet's crotch. I looked, too, because anything bad that happened to Jet was cause for celebration.

But his fly was up.

His micro penis was properly covered.

So what were you looking at?

Doesn't matter, I guess, because when Jet realized you were laughing at him, he said, "What the hell you looking at, butter face?"

I shoved him, threw my entire self into it, and Jet flew backward and hit the wall.

Before he could react, your hands were on my face, cupping my cheeks. And you said something I will never forget, your pink, pink lips smiling wider than ever—

"There you are."

I breathed hard, knowing I shouldn't have shoved Jet. Wanting to shove him again. But I couldn't do anything besides stand there, frozen between your hands. Jet was yelling and pointing, and his friend was pulling him along, and a teacher was sticking his head outside his door, and you were still holding my face.

You released me then and walked away without turning back.

Did you know it, then, that I already belonged to you?

Because I did, you beautiful, wicked girl.

NOW

*T*he detective leans back in her chair. "So you two met in the cafeteria at your school? She spoke to you first?"

I nod. The real story doesn't exactly paint me in the most stable light, shoving Jet for talking to Molly. The last thing I need is the police suspecting me.

"You parents like Molly okay?"

I shrug.

The detective reads into my indifference. "It can be hard for moms to see their sons take an interest in girls. What's that saying? A daughter is a daughter for life, a son is a son until they take a wife."

"My mom isn't around a lot," I say with more venom than I mean to.

The detective makes a doodle on a notepad. I wonder if it's code for something.

"And you have a brother? He get along with Molly?"

I frown, not liking that they looked stuff up about me before I got here. Still, at the mention of my brother, the muscles in my body relax, and I breathe a little easier. "They haven't met yet. But he'd like her if he did."

The detective taps a nail on the table. I glance at it and realize it's painted red. She is a woman who carries a deadly weapon, who interrogates suspects and slams drug dealers onto hoods of cars and handcuffs prostitutes—*Come on lady, I'm just trying to make a living*—she does all this…and then goes home at night and gives herself a manicure. For some reason, this eases the tension in my shoulders.

She accepts my altered story and writes down *First Friday Oct.* on her notepad.

I crane my neck, trying to see what else she's got there, when a knock comes at the door. A man comes in carrying a McDonald's bag and drink. He was with Detective Hernandez when they came for me at school. Back when I thought of them as *cop* and *officer*, not *detective* and *sergeant* and all those other titles that I'm sure exist solely to intimidate people.

The guy has arms that are far too long for his body and thick black hair. He looks and speaks like he'd make killer Italian food. Is that racist? I'm not sure.

Detective Hernandez sits up straighter when he comes closer, but I'm not sure whether it's because he might outrank her, or if she's into him. He's an all right looking dude, I guess.

Or maybe it's just the McDonald's he's carrying.

"Chicken nuggets, fries, barbeque sauce." He sets the bag down in front of me. "Coke." He pops the cup down beside the bag.

My mouth waters, and my stomach clenches.

When's the last time I ate a full meal?

Molly's been gone three days. Three days past when we were supposed to meet. When we were supposed to run away and start our lives over together.

Detective Hernandez and the dude stare at me, and I stare at them.

The McDonald's feels like a test.

If it is one, I'm going to fail.

I grab the bag and tear it open, lift the nuggets' lid and jam two into my mouth.

"Glad you're eating, kid," the guy says. "You've been really good about staying and helping us out. It shouldn't be too much longer, but I figured you could use a break."

I cram salty fries into my mouth and search the bag for ketchup.

Stop when I remember what Molly said about the stuff.

Stop when I remember Molly.

"I'm Detective Tehrani, by the way. Didn't know if you remembered."

So, no Italian food, then.

I don't respond. He knows my name.

There's a second knock on the door, and a woman sticks her head inside. Her black hair is cut close to the scalp, and she has bright red lipstick on. "Ferris wants you two."

Detectives Hernandez and Tehrani stand to follow her out.

"One minute," Detective Hernandez says to me, and offers an apologetic smile.

I'm about to tell them I'm not waiting around. That they need to be questioning anyone other than myself, but then Detective Tehrani grabs the door and says, "Hernandez, you tell him we found her car?" He doesn't wait for her to answer before turning back to me and saying, "We found Molly's car outside a strip mall in Leesport. Do you know what she was doing there?"

My ears ring, and the food stills in my mouth.

A strip mall?

What *was* she doing there?

Questions fire through my mind as the dude says to someone outside, "What's that? All right, coming." He looks at me, and even though I'm clambering to my feet, he says, "Be right back. Eat, kid."

My heart pounds inside my chest, and I lean against the back of a chair to calm myself down.

Molly was never supposed to be at a strip mall.

We were supposed to meet at a gas station.

But she was gone when I got there. Or maybe she never showed up in the first place.

I pick up the McDonald's bag and throw it against the wall. I know they're watching, and I don't care. Molly is gone, and they're in here talking to me when they should be combing the streets, the woods, the mountains. There should be search parties and helicopters and dogs that can smell a single drop of blood from a half mile away.

But instead, they're looking at me.

Why are they looking at me?

I hate myself for doing it, but I grab the fast food bag from the floor and shove my hand inside, finish eating the fries, the cold nuggets. I open the barbeque sauce and slurp some into my mouth. Then I suck down the Coke. I pace the floor—back and forth, back and forth—and then go for the door.

I take a step outside the room.

Phones ring, and someone—an officer—walks right past me with a folder. We almost touch, and yet he doesn't even look in my direction. Should I run for the exit? No, that'll make me look guilty.

Then it hits me—*why do I care what it looks like?*

I have to find Molly!

"Hey, there." Detective Tehrani strides toward me, holding a drink of his own. "One of the officers said you might be upset. Everything okay? You need to go home for a while? Take a breather?"

"Molly's car. You said you found it. Did you find her, too?"

Detective Tehrani motions back inside the room, inviting me to take a seat. I go in, jerk a chair away from the table.

"No, she wasn't there," he says. "Did you think she would be?"

"I...I don't know. How would I know?"

He looks confused. "You two were dating, right? I figured if anyone would know you would."

"Were her things in the car?" I ask. "The things she took from her house?"

Detective Tehrani hesitates, seemingly deciding whether to provide this piece of information. "No, they weren't."

"Well, that's good. If someone had taken her, they wouldn't have taken her things, right?"

The man leans back. Clasps his hands on the table, his drink forgotten. "You think someone might have taken her?"

"What? No...well, I don't know...the other officer said—"

Detective Hernandez sweeps into the room. "Sorry about that. Was the food okay? I hate it when the fries go cold on you and—"

I pound my fist on the table. "I don't give two fucks about fries. Tell me about Molly's car. Did it seem okay? Was there any sign of a...I don't know...a struggle, or whatever?" I watch them watching me. "Why are you two just *staring* at me?"

Detective Hernandez is looking, specifically, at my hand. The one I hit against the table. My fingers are still clenched, my knuckles white.

She sits down slowly, and her brown eyes meet mine. She pulls in a long, patient breath. There is pity in her gaze, and I feel a surge of guilt for my outburst. "Talking to you, talking to *everyone,* Cobain...that's how we are going to find Molly. That's what you want, right?"

I nod, remembering we're on the same side, even if it doesn't feel that way.

"Now, if you don't mind staying a bit longer," Detective Hernandez ventures, "Tell me about more Molly. Did you two share the same friends? Did she ever meet your parents?"

The fight I experienced only a moment ago leaves my body.

I think about Molly driving her mother's car, heart-shaped sunglasses on her face, window down, hair whipping around her head, fingers tapping on the steering wheel.

A bag on her empty passenger seat.

A seat I was supposed to fill.

THEN

I'd never been one to bounce from bed in the morning. I'd rise, sloth-like, to flip off the day. But that morning, in particular, I had trouble getting up. You'd invaded my mind, a welcome parasite. I wanted to lie in bed forever, let the thought of you keep me in a dreamlike state.

But my mom had turned on the radio. She turned it progressively louder the longer I stayed in bed in a passive-aggressive maneuver to get me up. I knew she'd already have breakfast on the table. Pancakes maybe, or French toast. She wasn't a Pop-Tarts kind of mom, though sometimes I wished she were.

I wondered what you were eating for breakfast, Molly.

I liked to think it was strawberries.

Is that weird?

I pressed my pillow over my head and groaned. Counted to ten and then threw the thing across the room and got up, because Foreigner was growing unbearably loud. I stretched, feeling my muscles ache in a good way, and thought about what Coach Miller said. How I should really consider joining the team. How it would do me good to hang out with some of the other guys.

I'd rather bathe my dick in honey and lie on a bed of fire ants, I'd replied.

And the dude had laughed.

That's why I liked him. Anyone who could take a joke was gold in my book.

I pulled on some clothes and padded down the hallway. My dad turned from the table, a newspaper held stiff between his hands. "Welcome to the land of the living."

"Welcome to the twenty-first century," I replied, and nudged the laptop on the table toward him.

My dad looked at my mom with amusement. "He speaks."

"And to make fun of those stinky newspapers," Mom added. "I like it."

"The smell of newspaper ink is invigorating," he said and took a sip of his coffee.

"That's one word for it." Mom dropped a plate of fried doughnuts dusted with powdered sugar in front of me.

I sighed.

"Don't sigh at me, child. A couple of doughnuts aren't going to hurt you."

She kissed the top of my head, and I popped the first doughnut into my mouth.

"Says here this seventeen-year-old just got a scholarship to Duke for shot put. You could get something like that with your weight lifting, I bet," my dad pressed, though I hadn't been awake fifteen minutes. "If you joined that team, you could—"

"Bruno," Mom warned, though she already had her nose buried in her phone. "I have to leave early this morning. They need someone to cover the early shift."

Mom worked at a center that supported social workers. She couldn't stomach working with foster kids directly, but she did all she could to support the people who did. Sometimes I thought she did too much, especially when she had two sons of her own that hardly saw her.

She quit her paying job when I was a kid. When I got sick.

So I guess it was kind of my fault.

She kissed my dad on the crown of his head. "Go easy on him. Actions speak louder…"

Dad stared at her.

She stared back.

"I'm not finishing that," he said.

"I'll remember that." Mom gave Dad a flirtatious look that made me want to vomit doughnuts everywhere.

Mom grabbed her purse and looked at me. Stared in my direction for a moment too long.

"What?" I asked.

"Nothing." She shook her head. "Just miss you."

"You could *stay*," I mumbled.

Mom's smile faltered. "I can't. They really need—"

I waved my hand and grabbed the second doughnut from the plate.

As she walked toward the door, I made my way toward my bedroom.

"Cobain?" my dad called, but I kept walking.

I pushed the door to my room open then jumped when I spotted movement. When I realized it was only my brother digging through my closet, I grinned and kicked my discarded pillow at him.

"Oh, go on and help yourself to my crap," I said.

Holt abandoned his search and fell back on my bed and, after flicking a pair of my boxers away with a disgusted face, smiled. "Miss me?"

I went to my closet to rummage for my bag. "It's been a while." I glanced at him sideways. "When did you get in?"

Holt shoved his hands behind his head. "Somewhere between last class and last call."

I rubbed my foot into a pink stain on the carpet, wishing, once again, that I were more like Holt. Smart enough to go to college. Thin, because he's not compensating for being socially awkward. He's twenty-one to my eighteen, only three years older, but it feels like more than that. Always has.

"Hey," Holt said, pushing up on his elbows. "Remember when Dad took us to that amusement park when you were like, I don't know, eight, and we dug those wristbands out of the trash? I was thinking about that mess the other day."

I grinned. "We rode almost every ride until that lady ratted us out."

"I'll never understand how she knew we'd snuck in," Holt said.

I thought about all the times my dad brought me with him to repair rides. We didn't have the money to go on the Zipper and Tilt-a-Whirl and Gravitron, and we had to eat crap from home instead of the sticky, fluffy, overpriced snacks offered there. As Dad worked, I could only listen as kids passed by, laughing and linking their arms and running ahead when they saw a ride they'd been looking for.

But one day, instead of hanging out with his friends like he always did, Holt came along. And I said, *I wish I could ride the stupid rides. Just once.*

And Holt looked at me and said, *Then, why don't you?*

As if it were the easiest thing in the world.

I thought about that park, then, and how I'd love to bring you there, Molly, with your white-blond hair and green eyes and mouth that said, *There you are.*

I'd thought about it for days but hadn't yet summoned the courage to ask you out. But I would. I just needed to figure out where I would take you since I didn't have more than five bucks to my name, or the words to keep a conversation going. What did a guy like me have to offer?

That's what I had to figure out.

"What's going on there?" Holt said, drawing a circle in the air, referencing my face. And damn it all, I grinned, because Holt always knew exactly what was in my head. "You grow a third nut? Or a third nipple?" he asked. "God, which would be worse? Nipple, for sure. A third nut would be like a magic source. You think anyone has one?" Holt pulled his phone out of his pocket, probably to check.

"I met this girl," I said, maybe to surprise him. Maybe so he wasn't the only one with something interesting to talk about.

"Hot?"

I laughed. "She's weird as shit."

"Weird and hot. That's a good combo. Honestly, little brother, weird outweighs hot. I've dated pretty girls, but if they don't come a little crazy, I get bored."

"Cobain?" Dad's voice echoed down the hallway.

Holt stood up. "I'll go. I should tell them I'm here. Is Mom going to shove food into my mouth hole the second I get out there?"

"She's already gone," I said. "And I've got to get going, too."

"In that case…" He flops back on the bed and gives an exaggerated smile.

I didn't want to ask him, but I had to.

I had to.

"Will you be here when I get back?"

I sounded so hopeful that it made me sick.

Holt sighed. "I don't know, man. I was just hanging out with some buddies for a night. And seeing what was up with you. I got class tonight, though, so I'll probably drive back soon."

I shrugged like I didn't care, but I wanted to hug my brother. That's all I wanted right then. A goddamned hug, and so what?

"K. See you next time."

"Don't wear a condom," Holt called as I walked away. "I'm ready to be an uncle."

"Idiot," I muttered.

"Who were you talking to?" Dad asked.

"Holt is here."

Dad glanced down the hallway, but Holt was probably already halfway asleep on my bed. That's what he used to do when he came home—partied with old friends and used our house as hangover headquarters. I doubted anything had changed.

Dad's eyes slid to mine. "Did you need a ride to school?"

I shook my head and made for the door.

"Cobain," he said.

I walked faster, but when he called my name again, I turned around.

He looked at me for a long time, like he wanted to tell me something important. But then he just shook his head and said, "Have a good day, all right?"

I nodded and left, gritting my teeth. Despising the hopeful look on my father's face, like maybe when I came home from school today, I'd do so with a load of friends, a B plus on my chem test, and an application for the wrestling team.

I didn't know why I was the way I was. Why my brain ticked a little differently. But it hurt to feel the dreams my father harbored, day after day, as if he were holding his breath, waiting for the moment when I'd be the son he always hoped I'd be.

THEN

For five days, I'd tried to make my way to you, Molly.
I'd tried to cut through your pack of friends and single you out. But they formed a wall around you, leaning their heads forward, searching for an answer to the question even I had to ask—

Were you beautiful?

Or just odd?

Looking at you was like watching a sphynx cross the street. It's not that you're surprised to see a cat in the neighborhood, it's that you didn't expect to see a *hairless* cat. A pink, wrinkled, wide-eyed cat that's so strange looking that at first you think, *That thing just isn't right.* But then you can't take your eyes off it. And you find yourself following it, and smiling at it, and pretending to hold a bit of food to see if it'll come closer.

You were like a hairless cat.

No way would I tell you that.

It was Friday, two days and one full school week after you'd touched my face. I couldn't go into another weekend without talking to you, but I needed a plan. I was still working through what to say to you when I spotted you standing outside the glass doors. You had your phone to your ear, and your face was pinched.

You turned, briefly, and our eyes connected.

There were tears in them.

I wanted to kill whoever put them there. Finding the words to talk to you was like having my molars ripped from my jaw, but fighting? That's something I understood well.

You lowered the phone and put it in your pocket. Hugged your arms around your stomach.

I pushed through the doors. Your eyes locked with mine, and you held my gaze like a challenge.

"You okay?" I asked.

You smiled and raised your chin. "I'm right as rain."

I didn't understand what you meant.

You sighed. "It's just my mom. She's being difficult. This move has been hard on her."

"But not for you," I said.

You frowned. "Yes, for me, too." You hugged yourself tighter, and I noticed how painfully thin you were. You'd look better with more weight, I decided, and something told me you could easily gain it if you allowed yourself to eat.

"Who are you?" you asked.

You asked this like you'd forgotten me—like you'd never grabbed my face and looked at me like you were the only person in the entire world who saw me. Your dismissive words stung more than my mom's constant preoccupation. More than my dad's hope.

I realized then that I'd been making up a relationship with you in my head. That I had pretended all weekend that you'd thought of me. I'd pretended you'd lain in bed and wondered what the rest of me felt like.

I'd committed every detail of you to memory.

Even a few I'm not sure you wanted people to see.

My brain had skipped a hundred steps and fast-forwarded to the point where we could lie down beside each other, hold hands, and not say a single word as the clouds crept across the sky.

You weren't there yet, but I wanted you to be.

"Wanna go somewhere?" I asked.

"Yes."

That quick.

Yes.

I nodded toward the fence that surrounded the school, and you and I jogged toward it. I started to crawl up so I could help you from the other side, but you were right there beside me, scaling that chain-link fence and throwing your leg over.

You were wearing a skirt.

And I wasn't about to look away.

I'm not sure you wanted me to.

You dropped on the other side and said, "I saw you look."

And I said, "Yep."

And you threw your head back and laughed so hard it made me ache all over just to hear it.

"Come on, Cobain," you said, like you were suddenly running this show.

I followed you.

At General Wayne Park, I pushed you on the merry-go-round. You laid on your back, letting your head hang off the side. Your hair brushed the ground as you swept by.

"That guy is scared of you now," you said as I stepped back to avoid decapitating you.

"Jet?"

"Whatever his name is."

"You knew what *my* name was."

You smiled up at the sky. "I asked around."

"Why?"

"Because I chose you."

A chill rushed across my back. You chose me. You could have picked anyone, but it was *me* that captured your attention.

"What did you choose me for?" I asked.

"That doesn't matter," you replied. "What matters is you protected my honor."

"I don't think you have much honor."

You spun around and shoved your feet into the dirt, stopping yourself from going around again. "I have loads of honor."

I smiled and shook my head.

You frowned. "What makes you so sure I'm honor-free?"

"I don't think you're a bad person or whatever. But you're not a saint, that's for sure." I pulled you up. "You made me shove Jet."

"Excuse me. I didn't make you do anything."

I walked toward the swings, and you walked after me. I could hear your feet shuffling from over my shoulder. I heard because I was listening for the sound of you.

I plopped down on the swing, and the chains groaned from my weight. "Yeah, but you set it up. You set up a lot of stuff. I see how you are with your friends."

You narrowed your eyes and sat in the swing two down from me. "How am I with my friends?"

I rocked back and forth, breathing in the tang of rusted metal. "You manipulate them. I saw you do it to Ms. Kimball, too. You put on an act in order to get what you want, and you leave people thinking they're doing themselves a favor by helping you."

You smiled like me seeing through your charade pleased you to no end. "You think I'm manipulative?"

"And without honor."

"Well," you said, leaning your head against the chain. "*I* think you've got demons. A decent guy, with demons." You hesitated. "I saw you pick up that kid's books when you bumped into him."

I felt the smile on my face flicker, and I stood up. Watched as a mother packed up her two children into a stroller and headed for their car.

"Don't act like I discovered some secret. You're announcing to the world that you have demons with your silence and your black clothes and that weird crow tattoo you've got on your forearm." You smiled to tell me you'd noticed it. "You want people to think you're this scary dude. The real secret is you're not."

"Who *are* you?" I asked suddenly, and I heard the defensiveness in my voice. "You're so weird."

"And you're fucking broken, man." You shrugged. "I like broken people. I'm attracted to them. If you wore polo shirts and played varsity basketball and had a bunch of jerk-off friends, I wouldn't be out here swinging with you."

"Yeah, because swinging together is a pretty big deal," I muttered.

You laughed, and I glanced over at you, pleased that I'd made you laugh again. And that I was somehow keeping up with you. You made it easier to talk. Maybe because you seemed to expect me to be exactly as I was.

You pulled a pack of peanut M&Ms from your pocket and ripped the top off. Stuck the trash into your back pocket and then poured candy into your open palm. You held the bag out to me in an offering, but I shook my head.

"We might not hang out after this," you said around the

candy, and my heart clenched a little. Because you could say something like that. Because you were the kind of girl people were drawn to, and you didn't need me. But you know what? I didn't need you, either. I'd grown accustomed to doing things alone, and maybe I didn't want you getting all clingy and calling me and making me shove dudes just to see if I would.

"But I thought you looked interesting," you finished.

You had nothing else to say, it seemed. So you stood up and lay down in the grass. I chewed the inside of my cheek and then went to lie down beside you. We didn't say anything as you popped more chocolates into your mouth and then stuffed the bag inside your jacket.

My eyes darted to where your hands were, fingers interlocked on your stomach. I thought about what you said—

We might not hang out after this.

So I thought to myself, *Fuck it.* And I reached out and took your hand as if I knew you'd accept it. But I couldn't have known, and so my heart pounded so damn hard, and it seemed the earth made three full rotations around the sun before you squeezed my fingers in return.

As my breathing returned to normal, and the chill of the ground seeped through my clothing, I thought, *we should probably go back.* You probably had a mom and dad at home who would be worried.

But we didn't move.

We just lay beside each other, holding hands, not saying a single word as the clouds crept across the sky.

NOW

*D*etective Hernandez grabs her phone from the table. "Okay, great. So the day you two skipped, that would be…" She taps open an app, scrolls. "October eleventh. That's seven days after you two met. So if we call the school, they'll show the two of you were absent that afternoon?"

I nod.

"You guys get in trouble for taking off?" Tehrani chimes in.

"Saturday school," I reply. "Just one day."

"Seems worth the cost to get a pretty girl alone for a while."

I glare at him.

"All right," he says, leaning back. "When did you and Molly see each other after that? Did you call her? Did you guys make plans at school?"

There's a knock at the door, and a girl sticks her head in. It's the same girl from earlier. Her gaze darts around the room until she spots Detective Hernandez. The girl waves the woman over, and I can tell by the way her dark eyes widen that whatever she has to say is important.

Detective Tehrani stands, too, and the threesome shut the

door behind them. I can't hear a word of what is said, but I find myself rising and moving toward the door anyway. If they have new information on Molly, I need to know it.

I have my ear pressed to the crack when the door swings open, sending me flying backward. I catch myself on the table, and Detective Tehrani clips, "We're going to end our chat here. Thanks so much for coming in. You've been very cooperative, and we're grateful. Davea will show you out."

I freeze, not sure what to do, terrified they've found out something bad about Molly's disappearance.

Detective Hernandez strides away, not even a backward glance in my direction. Detective Tehrani walks after her, snatching his jacket, grabbing his phone, headed somewhere Molly might be.

"Wait. Did you find her?" I ask, but it's not loud enough.

"Hey," I try again. "Did you find her? Did you find Molly?!"

Now it's too loud. So loud other officers are turning in my direction and the girl, Davea, is taking my arm and saying, *Let's go. Come on, this way*, but I don't like the way she's saying that. Like she's afraid if I discover what they've found, I'll lose my mind.

"Did something happen to her?" I shout, pulling away from Davea and racing after Detective Tehrani. "Answer me. Tell me what happened!"

An officer I don't know steps in front of me and grabs both my arms, shoves my stomach over a chair, and pulls my hand toward my upper back so that if I move, I risk breaking my arm. "Calm down, kiddo," he says. "Everything's all right."

He pulls me backward and guides me toward the place we came in earlier this morning, but I'm still yelling for Detectives Hernandez and Tehrani to answer me. *To goddamn answer me!*

Detective Hernandez glances back at me once before pushing through a door in the opposite direction. In her eyes,

I see sympathy. It feels like a sucker punch to the gut. I don't want her sympathy. I want anything *other* than sympathy. I'd take suspicion over it. I'd take handcuffs and metal bars, even if someone else deserved them. Because then I'd know that what happened to Molly is still a mystery. That they haven't found something that has them running for their vehicle.

The dude manhandling me leads me toward the front by the shoulder — careful to keep my arm behind my back in case I try something — and then releases me. Davea is beside him, and she points me toward a window, saying I need to sign some paperwork, but screw that.

I burst through the double doors in time to see Detective Hernandez speeding by. Her lights aren't on. That's good, right?

No, that's bad.

She pulls onto Northwest Highway and speeds away, and I'm left jogging toward the bus stop. I need to get home. I need to form a plan. If they won't tell me what's going on, then I have to finish my own search. I have to keep sifting through my memories of Molly to look for clues.

THEN

There was a carnival in Reading, Pennsylvania.

It was the most exciting thing to do on a Saturday night, and so that's where I planned to take you. We'd been out twice since that day in the park, and Halloween was lurking around the corner, impatient.

I didn't have enough money to get into the fair, and so I'd intended to sneak you in. When you discovered my plan, you delivered a smile so devilish I could have speared it with a pitchfork. You floated toward the ticket stand alone, and when I went to follow you, you held a hand out behind yourself.

Stay there, okay? it said. *Let me work.*

And so I pretended I was waiting on someone, and I watched you. You asked for two bracelets and then fumbled inside your purse for your wallet. As the balding man in the booth reached beneath the table, you pulled out your phone. You clenched it between your cheek and shoulder and continued to dig through your purse.

I couldn't hear what you said, but I saw the man lean forward with interest. He pulled his bottom lip back and then flicked his eyes around like he was searching for someone to rescue him. You put the phone away, stared at the ground for an uncomfortable moment, and then pulled out your wallet.

It was empty.

Once again, you reached into your purse as if searching for cash, or a credit card, in a daze—your eyes staring at nothing—before turning to go.

The man called out to you.

Held out two wristbands and nodded toward the buzzing lights and rattling Zipper cages and crackling speakers that filled the fairgrounds with pulsing music.

You smiled at him and nodded. Clutched the bracelets to your chest with such gratitude that the man swelled with pride. You strode toward me, a painted smile on your face. You held your hand out, and a thrill shot up my spine as I took your fingers in mine.

"What did you tell him?" I asked.

"To him?" you said with a smile I wanted to lick clean. "I didn't say anything at all. Not a word."

But you had changed him somehow. Maybe you'd pretended your grandmother was sick, or that your dog had cancer after all. Whatever it was, he bent to your will. I could tell, though, that to do it didn't make you happy. The truth was in the shape of your shoulders—rounded when they were normally square.

We walked around as men called out to us, holding out balls to knock down milk jugs or darts to pop swollen balloons. Smells wafted from vendors selling pink cotton candy and sugar-dusted funnel cakes and caramel-dipped green apples. My stomach rumbled as we passed the food. I was hungry. I was *always* hungry.

I couldn't afford the forty-dollar bracelets we now wore, but I still had a few bucks from when Dad gave me a ten spot. With my dad's shitty paychecks and my mom insisting on volunteering her time, the best I could ever manage was pocket change, but I couldn't imagine spending the last four dollars I had on anything better than a red and white carton of nachos drowning in cheese sauce.

You squealed when I offered it to you, and ate far more than I expected. It filled me up—doing that for you. Providing. It made me want to give you more. To make sure my wallet was never empty if it meant you would keep smiling like that.

When we'd finished eating, you tugged on my hand, a grin on your face. I captured that moment in my mind—the Tilt-a-Whirl cars whipping past behind you, your hair over your shoulders, your lips glossed pink. Your eyes were too far apart, I realized then, making you appear otherworldly.

"Follow me," you said, and I recognized that you were about to do something you shouldn't. It was your favorite pastime, and you knew I'd do it beside you without question. Would I have been as attracted to you if you followed the rules? If you wanted to watch a movie instead of climbing a water tower or breaking into a graveyard or stealing a Butterfinger from a convenience store?

I knew the answer.

You led me to the haunted house with a line of red cars squatting on a track. People waited in line, ready to jump inside—two to a car—and experience false fear. What better way to get into the Halloween spirit?

I figured you wanted to ride.

I should have known better.

You led me to the back of the building and motioned toward an unlocked door. We slipped inside, and—with your hand still holding mine—we lurched into the darkness. The rusted red cars clicked over the rails, and as they turned corners, scenes meant to frighten riders lit up and buzzed. Girls screamed, and I imagined guys draped their arms over their girls' shoulders, thrilled to feel like men.

"Follow my lead," you whispered in my ear. And then you bit me there, on the lobe, quickly, and my body reacted instantly.

You snuck closer to the tracks, your body hidden by the dark but not from me. When the next car chugged by, you were waiting. On your knees, hand raised, you brushed the guy on his neck.

"The fuck?" he yelled, and I had to bite down to keep from losing my shit.

The couple rolled by, and the dude swiped at his neck until they were out of view.

"My turn," I said, and you backed away, your devious eyes sparkling.

Another couple came by, two girls this time. I waited until they'd passed by before leaning between them and whispering, "I see you."

The girls' giddy squeals turned to silence.

"What was that?" one asked.

"There's someone in here," the other said.

I dashed behind the wall before they saw me. Sure enough, the next horror scene that lit up made them scream twice as loud as it should have.

You hooked your finger into my belt loop and hauled me backward. Still laughing, I grabbed you around the waist and pulled you close. My pulse stilled as I moved one hand onto your cheek, fingers slipping into your hair.

"What are you going to do to me?" you whispered.

Kiss you, I thought, but that didn't seem to be enough for Molly Bates. So I said, "Scare you."

"How?" you asked, leaning closer.

I lowered my head, my lips dangerously close to yours. It seemed fitting, I thought, to kiss you for the first time to a soundtrack of screams, as images of dismemberment and mayhem were illuminated by dusty bulbs needing replacing.

I raised my opposite hand to cup your face, to keep you from running. Because you always felt so close to fluttering off like a butterfly you could only watch for so long before it flew away.

I couldn't let you fly away.

"Cobain," you said, so quietly that it rippled through me.

I brought my lips closer.

You lifted a hand to my face, and that's all it took.

My mouth met yours.

You wrapped your arms around my neck. I kissed you gently at first, my stomach clenched with nerves, my skin electric from the feel of you so close. From the taste of you. Your tongue touched mine, and my body pressed into you. You were there to meet every part of me, your hands moving into my hair, tugging. My hands moving lower, grasping. Our breath came faster, and our fingers became desperate there in the dark with the sound of those buzzing bulbs. With the smell of the oiled tracks and the perfume of your hair.

Our kiss deepened, and then suddenly, you stepped back.

You caught your breath, and I caught the conflict in your eyes.

"My turn," you said, and I could hear the playful smile in your voice.

But there was something else there, too.

Fear?

A guy and his girlfriend rolled closer, and you crouched down.

I watched you, bewildered. Still feeling you on my lips, against my body. I may have frozen after you pulled away from me.

You waited until they'd passed and then drew your finger up the guy's spine.

"Hey," he yelled. "What the hell?"

He reached back and grabbed at you. He must have gotten

your shirt, because a surprised sound escaped your mouth. The guy leaped out of the car and blindly reached for you with his other hand.

I stepped in front of him. "No. Get back in the car."

He narrowed his eyes, making out the height of me. The width of me.

"Ash," the girl called from the retreating car. "Get back in."

The guy glanced over his shoulder and then said, "Carnie trash," before jogging after the car. The lights buzzed, and I saw the guy in detail—the leather jacket he wore, the backward hat, the designer jeans…the confidence that said he came from money. A confidence easily recognized by people who had little of it.

I turned back to you, ready to laugh, but you were staring at your feet.

"Hey," I said. "What's wrong? He scare you?"

Your eyes rose to mine. "What? No," you said. And then, "Let's get out of here."

But I pulled you into a corner, anyway, sensing something was off. Worried you regretted kissing me. "Did you know that guy?"

You shook your head.

"Was it what he said?"

You paused, and I thought maybe you'd confess a secret, but then you smiled in the dark and tilted your head and said, "I'm just messing with you. I wanted to see if you'd care if I was upset."

"Course I'd care." I returned your smile, but I saw through your act. That guy *had* bothered you, and for a moment there— just for a moment—I'd seen Molly uncut. I sometimes glimpsed a layer beyond what you showed the rest of the world, but now I'd seen your core.

And I wanted more.

"You like protecting people, don't you?" You laid your hand on my chest. "It makes you feel connected to the person you're defending."

I didn't respond.

"That's so messed up, Cobain." You moved your hand to my cheek. "What happened to you?"

I'm glad you moved your hand away from my chest, because if you hadn't, my heart would have clawed its way out just to be held by you before it stopped beating.

You looked into my eyes and narrowed your own.

Your playfulness fell away, your false confidence crumpled at our feet, and you leaned in close. I wrapped my arms around your waist, my fingers interlocking so you couldn't escape me. So you wouldn't change your mind.

But you weren't going anywhere.

Only closer.

And closer.

Until a man beat something against the walls and yelled, "If there's anyone back here, you better get out before I call security."

As we ran, Molly's laughter ringing above the screams, I thought—

Goddamn it.

And, *What security?*

And, *I'll kiss that girl again if it kills me.*

If it kills us both.

When we left the carnival, you gave our bracelets to two kids sticking their noses between the chain-link fence, their wide, eager eyes watching the rides rotate. They looked at you with such adoration, but you walked away before they could even thank you. You wouldn't even look at *me*. Most likely, I thought as we walked up the hill, you were afraid I'd discover you had a heart.

NOW

I take my dad's car and drive straight to Leesport.

It isn't difficult to find the strip mall where her car had been discovered. When I see the cops, my entire body feels ready to detonate.

There—parked in front of an abandoned fabric store—is Molly's Toyota Camry. Four police officers stand around it, and as I watch, a German Shepherd leaps into the vehicle. My stomach drops as the cadaver dog searches for the smell of a corpse.

I glance around, searching for Detectives Hernandez and Tehrani. I don't see them, which makes me wonder where they *did* go. Did they rush off to question a new suspect?

Worried the other cops will see me, I pull away, my stomach threatening to empty itself as I drive. I feel helpless. Small. I have to do something. I have to go through my head and figure out who, if someone did take Molly or hurt her in some way, it could have been.

As I drive, I make a list of names.

And when I get home, I put those names on paper.

Her mom
Rhana
Nixon
Jet

THEN

*T*his was your kingdom, not mine.

A fire lit the forest clearing, and people from our school swayed to music that blasted from truck speakers. Joints passed hand to hand, and warm beer poured down eager throats.

I held a drained beer in my own hand. Wanted to get another to obliterate the sensation that I didn't belong here. But you'd invited me. Said you wanted to see me there, so damn it all, I had come.

Why couldn't we have come together, I wanted to know. But you'd touched my nose, like there was a hidden button there, and said to find you.

You were talking to a dude I didn't know.

I wanted to dismember him.

Another guy walked by then. He had a girl on his arm, and his hood was pulled up over his head, though it was unseasonably warm for late fall.

"Hey, man," he said. "You good?"

He nodded toward my beer can, his shaggy, reddish-blond hair flopping over his freckled forehead, and I shook it to show it was empty. I was grateful someone was speaking to me. The tension in my chest incinerated, and I felt myself smiling at this guy even though I had rules against smiling.

"You want another?" he asked.

"Yeah," I said, too quickly. "Do you know—?"

"Better go get one, then," he said, and laughed.

The girl laughed, too, and the twosome sauntered off toward the fire. He was just messing around. He might have said the same thing to his friends, but it felt personal. I made things personal. If I could acquire one secret power, it wouldn't be to fly or turn invisible or tell the future. It would be an impenetrable shield that protected me from anything feeling personal.

You need thicker skin, dude, someone had said to me once. *Don't be so damn sensitive.*

But my skin was made of paper. Maybe that's why I had to compensate with muscle.

I'm too quiet?

Get bigger.

I'm too weird?

Get bigger.

I'm fucking Frankenstein?

Get bigger.

I thought about turning to go. Maybe I already was heading toward my dad's car. I can't remember. What I do remember is my name on your tongue.

You walked toward me with a smile.

You were drunk, a little. I liked it, a lot, but it also made me want to catch up, like your mind was in an alternate state and I didn't want your head and mine to be in different places.

"You made it." You grabbed my hand, squeezed, and then released. "Come on. Let's get another drink."

I started to walk after you and then froze when I saw the

dude who'd laughed at me standing at the cooler. You noticed I'd stopped, but I wished you hadn't. It made me feel weak that you noticed.

"What's wrong?" you asked.

It felt odd that you had to ask that as music swept between the dancing bodies and people laughed and kissed and slipped their hands beneath skirts and under shirts. Everyone was happy, and yet you had to ask me, *What's wrong*?

"Nothing," I said. "Thought I forgot something in the car."

Your eyes darted toward the dude. And the guy lifted his beer and shook it at me. Why couldn't I just laugh? Get in on the joke?

Because I *was* the joke, that's why. People knew when they were in on the joke and when they weren't.

Your face changed then—a flash of something undeniably dark.

Your mind spun in that brain of yours. I could see it happening, and it was as beautiful as it was terrifying.

"Listen to me," you said. "You want friends?"

I bit down. Shook my head. "I just want people to leave me the hell alone, Molly." Pause, pause. "I don't want to fucking be here."

"Well, too late," you said. Your eyes ran over my shoulders, my chest, my abdomen. "You want to be seen. Just look at you. You're literally growing so that you *can't* be ignored. So put an end to the invisibility. Right now."

I licked my lips, felt my stomach clench with excitement and dread. "How?"

"You want to know the fastest way to make a friend?" you asked.

I searched your face for the answer.

"Make an enemy."

My brow furrowed in confusion.

You leaned in closer, your breasts brushing my chest. "No one feels more vulnerable, or more upset, than when they're a target. So target someone."

"I don't get it," I said. "How will targeting someone make them a friend?"

You dropped your head to one side, smiling. Your lips were so close, more intoxicating than the beer charting a course to my brain. "You don't target the person you want to befriend, my wolf. You target the enemy of the person you want to befriend."

I found myself smiling, too. "There is something really wrong in your head."

But I was already searching the crowd, looking for an opportunity. Wondering if it could be so easy.

"You *like* my head," you said, but I noted the uncertainty beneath the confidence. So I grabbed your face like you did mine that first day, and I brought my lips down, down, and for a moment your head fell back and your mouth parted and pleasure relaxed every last muscle in your face. Our lips touched, and in an instant, I remembered why I came here. But then you stepped back, abandoning our kiss, remembering yourself. Remembering something you kept hidden, even from me.

"I'll say when." You strode toward the party, leaving ripples in your wake so that I had to fight to keep my feet steady on the ground.

I crushed the beer can in my fist and tossed it away, said, "Screw it," beneath my breath, and walked after you. But it was clear you didn't want to be followed, and so I found a place beside the fire and sat in a lawn chair. I didn't care whose it was. I kind of hoped it was the guy's who laughed at me.

I kind of hoped he said something else to me now.

I picked up an upright half-empty beer from the grass and raised it to my lips. I didn't know what was gonna go down, but something told me I needed to be drunk for this.

I waited for twenty minutes or so—enough time for the music to change from alternative to rap. Enough time to watch you across the fire, swaying your body to the beat, Rhana's hands on your hips. I wondered then if Rhana was jealous of you. She was prettier, you know? In the traditional sense. Her short blue-black hair cut to her chin, her skin several shades darker than your own. She was seventeen, maybe eighteen, but she could have walked into any convenience store, plopped a six-pack onto the counter, and her figure would say *I look old enough, don't I?*

And whoever was standing on the other side of the counter would want her to be old enough. So that maybe he, or she, could smile and ask where she was going with that beer.

But still, I saw the way Rhana looked at you. The way everyone looked at you. Your knobby knees, your elfin ears, your freckles splayed across your cheeks. I didn't want anyone else to see you besides me. But then, I'm not sure anyone did see the real you.

I heard a booming laugh from across the fire and spotted a guy I didn't know doubled over, laughing. Another dude, the bigger one who'd been talking to Molly earlier, laughed too, but it didn't reach his eyes. The first guy popped upright and slammed his beer bottle against the second guy's. Almost immediately, the beer shot up and over the top, and the poor dude had to rush to drink it to keep it from spilling.

First Guy laughed.

Wasn't he funny?

Wasn't he so damn funny?

I glanced at you then, and you raised one slender finger from your drink and pointed at what I'd already noticed.

I stood up, dropped my own drink, and walked toward the two guys. The second guy was still pounding his beer when I said to the asshole, "Nice move. You learn that in fifth grade?"

My muscles clenched, waiting for both of them to tell me to go fuck myself. And what was I doing there anyway?

But that's not what happened. The second guy stopped drinking and laughed, said to Asshole Guy, "Seriously, cum wipe. Who does that anymore?"

"He does," I say. "In between wet dreams and spontaneous hard-ons."

Second Guy laughed too loudly, and Asshole Guy said, "Whatever. Who the hell are you?"

I froze.

"Cobain," Molly sang from a few feet away, "I've been looking for you. What, too good to come say hello?"

I shrugged, but my insides sang. "Just grabbing a drink."

"I'll get you one," Rhana said.

"Nah, he's coming with me," Second Guy said and pulled out a joint. "I'll bring him back."

I looked at Asshole Guy and said, "You coming?" Because it didn't feel great to rag on him, even if he had been dishing it out himself.

"Go fuck yourself," he said.

"I'd rather fuck your mother," I replied.

And thank the gods, Asshole Guy laughed and choked on his drink. "Uncool, man. Funny, but uncool."

"Come on," I said, because Second Guy was saying, *Let's go already*.

Asshole Guy tossed his drink and said, "Whatever, man," and followed after us.

"Cobain?" Second Guy said, raising a lighter to the joint.

I nodded and took the weed when he passed it to me.

"I'm Nixon," he said, and then nodded toward Asshole Guy. "That's Brian."

I could tell Nixon didn't like Brian.

I could tell Nixon liked me because I called Brian on his bullshit.

I could also tell Nixon was a dude who girls liked. They clung to his dark eyes and dark skin and biceps meant for the weight-lifting bench.

I sucked on the joint and glanced at you from across the flames. You looked like a demon standing behind that wall of fire.

I cocked my chin at you—*what's up?*—and that smile of yours stretched until it touched your hairline. Then you caught yourself and replaced that smile with the carefully manicured one you served the world.

Did the pretending ever exhaust you, Molly?

NOW

*A*fter a sleepless night, I turn down my dad's offer to drop me off at school, opting instead to walk the two miles alone and avoid being pressured to talk. I know I'll have the school weight room to myself for an hour before students start arriving.

I load a barbell with weights and then lie on my back, wanting to get straight to the point. Wanting to feel my muscles strain. I unrack the bar and bring it down, breathe out as I push it back up. I keep my feet flat on the floor, keep my back pressed against the bench, keep Molly squarely in my mind as I do two reps. Four. Eight.

Already, I'm starting to sweat.

How much muscle have I lost since Molly vanished?

I'd been doing so well since she came into my life. It was all I'd been able to think about—her, and getting even bigger. Making her smile. Making her *happy*.

I've moved on to squats when I spot Nixon through the glass doors. I'm happy to see him, which shocks me because I'm happy to see no one. Because when you're made fun of every single fucking day for not opening your damn mouth, then your *I-don't-give-a-damn* armor is the only thing that stands between showing up, day after day, and having a world-class breakdown.

He opens the door and says, "Hey. Jet's right behind me with some of the other guys, so..."

This isn't going to end well.

When Jet walks in and sees me, he pauses in the doorway as if he's thinking about doing an about-face and leaving. His hesitancy gives me strength. But as three of his friends file in behind him, he remembers he has a reputation to uphold and that the last time news of the two of us circulated, he came out looking like a chump.

Jet walks to the other side of the gym, and I track every step he takes. It's not that I'm afraid he'll say something.

I'm afraid I'll kill him if he does.

"So, uh, how you doing, man?" Nixon asks, pulling his ankle behind himself to stretch. He's wearing his weight-lifting jersey, and I'm kicking myself for not remembering that it's Thursday. On Thursday mornings, the team can choose to come before school or after.

I shrug and pick up a dumbbell that's heavier than I should be using.

"I heard the police talked to you," he adds.

Again, I don't respond because, quite frankly, he's more Molly's friend than mine. He's got an easiness to the way he stands, talks, acts, and it's so utterly different than the tenseness that infects every proton in my body that I can't help but envy him. He's cool to me, even now, even after the tidal wave of friends that followed Molly saw that she was gone and, as a collective unit, turned and walked, zombie-like, away from me.

"I think she probably just took off, man," Nixon says nonchalantly, stretching his arm across his chest. "I mean, she seemed the type to just, ya know, decide she was tired of this place. There's no point in looking for her, right?"

I don't like the way he's eyeing me. It makes me itch to get out of here. But there's only one thing I was afraid of, and that shit done happened. So what do I have to fear now?

"Anyway," Nixon says, fumbling for something to say to someone who isn't participating in the conversation. "I'm sure you miss her and shit. Molly was a cool girl."

I flinch because it's the second time he's done that—talked about her in the past tense—but this time, it feels like an admission.

Nixon doesn't think she ran away.

I look at him with fresh eyes.

"When's the last time you saw her?"

Nixon releases the weight he was about to lift from the rack and says, stupidly, "What?"

"When did you last see her?"

"Oh, umm…" He glances at the ceiling. But I don't want him looking there. He needs to look at me. "In class, I think. English?"

"Are you asking or telling?"

"Dude, come on." Nixon pauses like he's deciding whether to add something. Finally, he says, "They questioned me, too, you know. The police."

Alarm bells go off in my head, and now I'm definitely looking at Nixon as someone other than Molly's friend. "Why? Do you know something?"

He lowers his voice, but his words have lost their friendliness. "No. And I didn't tell them anything about you, either. So, yeah, you're welcome."

What the fuck? "There's nothing *to* tell."

He eyes me again. "You sure about that?"

A riot of emotions flood my system, and I'm ten seconds away from shoving him when Jet comes over with one of his meathead friends. "Dude, what's your deal?"

I point at him. "When's the last time *you* saw Molly? Last time I remember, you were throwing shade her way, isn't that right?"

Jet steps toward me, but his friend grabs his arm.

"Why you in here, anyway?" Jet snaps. "What? Don't have a gym to go to now that you got fired from Steel? My cousin told me you threatened a guy there."

Steel. The gym I'd worked at while trying to save up money for Molly and me.

I grab my bag from the bench, thinking I need to get the hell out of there. Needing to get a hold of myself. And definitely not wanting to remember what went down at the place I'd grown to love.

"You sure do lose your temper quickly," Jet yells at my back. "Probably lost your temper with her, too, huh? Did she sleep with someone else or something?"

My blood boils. I knew it. These guys think I hurt my own girlfriend. But I would *never* hurt her. I would kill every last person in this weight room before I touched her with anything more than a gentle hand.

I turn and charge him.

I've got him on the floor and am just pulling my fist back, ready to deliver a blow that's been coming for two years, when Coach Miller throws open the glass door and roars for me to get my ass up. *To get my ass up or he'll do it for me.*

Before I can get to my feet, Coach grabs me by the shirt and hauls me backward. "The hell you think you're doing?" he says, right in my face. "You wanna get expelled? Because that's the opposite of what you need right now."

"Coach, he was—" Jet starts.

But Coach Miller holds up his hand, stopping him, and looks at me. "I don't want you coming back in here for a while, got it?"

His eyes scorch holes into my skull, and my face burns with embarrassment because he's one of the good guys, and there's something wrong with me if I'm pissing off a levelheaded guy like him.

"Go on," he says. "Get out of here."

I put my head down and march toward the door, feeling the way they're looking at me. Not really blaming them. I'm so messed up that I'm acting crazy.

I've made it half the length of the hallway when I hear Coach's voice ring out.

"Kelly," he says.

I turn around.

He waves me toward him, and I shuffle back over. He plops a long-fingered hand on my shoulder and raises his chin so we're eye to eye. "Molly's a nice girl. I always liked seeing you two together. She pulled the good out of you, hard as that must have been."

He offers a half smile, and my insides try to piece themselves back together.

"I know you must be worried about her, but I'm sure wherever she is, she's okay. Can you imagine that girl being unhappy in any situation?"

Yes, I can, I think. *Because I know Molly in a way the rest of you don't.*

HER MOM

RHANA

NIXON

JET

THEN

I stood, with good intentions, outside your house.

I knew it was wrong. I knew the police had a word for following someone without their knowledge. But I didn't care. I convinced myself that you knew I was behind you. That you'd stopped to tie your shoe so I had a moment to catch up.

Your house was smaller than I expected, with yellow shutters and an overgrown yard. My dad mowed every Sunday morning. It was his own private worship hour, because as far back as I could remember, he'd never believed in God.

I wondered, as I followed the ivy crawling up your walls and the weeds taking over the front lawn and the overfilled garbage cans near the street, what your dad was like. I'd pictured someone like Coach Miller. Someone who let you dance on his feet when you were little. Who picked you up and put you on his shoulders, above the rest of the world because that's the pedestal his little girl deserved.

But now I wondered.

You saw me as soon as you opened the door. Your eyes went wide, and I caught the vulnerability there, and the fear.

Fear as raw as rotting meat. You recovered quickly, offered that same smile you bestowed on your friends, and I said, "Stop it."

That smile fell away.

"Why are you here?" you clipped. At least I knew you were being honest then.

"Because I know something is going on."

I knew because I saw the lie crawling across your bare shoulders. The lie you projected that said you lived a perfect life.

Your eyes darted to your house. "So it's not actually that big. Okay?"

"Okay," I said.

"And my dad took off a while ago."

"Dads can be jerks."

A flicker of amusement.

"And my mom…" you started.

"Probably spends more time at home than mine does."

But you didn't seem convinced, so I took your hand, laced my fingers through yours, and said, "I know you have broken bits, Molly Bates, and I like them. I like them, and I want to see them."

I squeezed your hand tighter, and you sighed and said, "Fine. You can come in."

You walked slower than I'd ever seen you move. As if you were dragging death behind you and not a two-hundred-twenty-pound teenager.

You pushed the door open, and though I expected darkness to stretch toward us, the sun was everywhere. It shone on everything, illuminating the sheer quantity of *stuff*.

You turned and gauged my face as I inspected the mountains of furniture and boxes and clothing. The piles of magazines and the towers of books. The champagne bottles and wineglasses littering every available surface. There were no framed photos of family that told me this was a home, and enough accumulated belongings to tell me your mother might be a hoarder.

You pulled me past stacks of electronics and throw pillows and lamps decorated with feathers and crystals. In the kitchen, where polished utensils and expensive equipment covered the counters, we found your mom. She wore a red robe, and it draped open to show her long legs. I wish I could have stopped myself from looking, but I couldn't. She oozed flesh and sex.

"Well, hello there, handsome," she said, and I could tell she was stoned.

"This is my friend," you said, and though I wanted to be so much more to you—though it felt like a knife to the heart to be labeled *friend*—I'm not sure I'd ever been as drawn to you as I was in that moment.

Your shoulders sagged.

Your teeth bit into your lip.

I saw you then, Molly. I really saw you. Did you feel me looking? Because I sure as hell did, and later—much later—you denied that I'd been there at all.

Your mother stood up and strode toward you, feet bare on the linoleum floor, and then she wrapped her arms around you. "My baby," she said. "Are you going to stay with your mama today?"

Your arms hung by your sides, but your mom didn't seem to care. She looked at me and said, "I never get enough time with her." She dropped one arm away from you and held out her hand to me. "I'm Samantha."

I shook it but didn't say a word.

Your mom hugged you again, like she was afraid you'd suddenly vanish. I wondered how hard it had been for you to get out the front door today. How hard it was for you to leave any day.

"Sit, sit," she said, and guided Molly to a table overflowing with cloth napkins and punch glasses and a blender that looked like it cost more than our rent. "Did you guys meet at school?"

"Yeah," you said.

Your mom glanced back and forth between you and me. "Maybe you two would rather go into Molly's room and talk."

"Yes," you said, and started to stand up.

But your mom remembered herself and grabbed your hand. "Or. Or you could stay out here with me for a little while. I'm feeling... I'm feeling kind of down today."

She made a frowny face then, like a child.

"I could make something." She looked at her kitchen as if seeing it for the first time. As if she couldn't quite remember its purpose. Her gaze popped back toward us. She grinned. "Or we could just talk. How are your classes, Molly? Do you have any classes with...? I'm sorry, I forgot to ask your name."

"Cobain," I offered.

She reached across the table for your hand, but you moved it into your lap. I resented your mom for putting that look on your face. But I felt sympathy for her, too, because I knew the deep, unrelenting sensation of wanting company. The difference between us was that she reached for it, and I pushed it away, too afraid of rejection to try.

You bore your mother's questions with one-word answers— *yes, no, maybe, sure*—until I could tell you couldn't take another moment.

"We have to go," I said. "We'll be late."

"Oh. Where are you two off to?" she asked. "Need a ride?"

"No. Thank you," I said, and reached for you.

You pulled your arm away, but you did follow me out the door. When I came here, I'd imagined spending time in your room. Of seeing your things. Of feeling grossly inadequate in comparison to your lavender bedspread and built-in bookshelves and your antique writing desk. I just knew you'd have a writing desk.

But what happened instead was an awkward twenty-minute exchange before frustration infected every part of your body, draining you of life.

Your mother drained you.

"You can't just show up at someone's house," you said, walking past me once we were outside. "I didn't tell you where I live, you know. I *know* I didn't tell you."

"No, you didn't." I jogged to keep up. "I followed you home one day."

You stopped on the sidewalk, a safe distance from your house. From your mom.

"That's creepy, Cobain. It's…disturbing."

I leaned back. "You don't really think that."

You pressed your lips together and glanced away. "Most people would find what you did weird. Just showing up like this. It's weird."

"You aren't most people," I said calmly. "You wanted me to see where you lived. You wanted me to meet your mom, too."

"What the hell do you know?"

I took your elbows in my hands. "I know *you*."

You laughed then, and I won't say it didn't hurt me. "You've known me a month. You don't know shit."

"I know you paint your nails just to chip off the polish," I said. "I know you like trees best when they've lost their leaves. I know you want to cut your hair, but you're afraid no one will notice you once you do. I know you love blue mascara and panda bears and covered bridges."

I tightened my grip on your elbows.

You didn't pull away.

"I also know you're desperate for someone to figure you out. And I think that starts with where you come from. I came here to figure you out, Molly."

"Why?" you whispered.

"Because I want to show you that I don't care. That whatever it is, I'll still be here."

You raised your eyes and looked at me. The hardness in your gaze softened. The cunning in your mind relaxed.

You said, "He let me go."

And tears filled your eyes. You bit down on your anger, your entire body shaking in my hands. You weren't mad at this memory you were holding, I don't think. You were mad because you didn't want me to see the emotion on your face.

But I saw it anyway.

And though I didn't know who you were talking about or what had happened, I said, "I won't let you go, Molly."

It was the right thing to say.

I could see it in the lift of your shoulders.

I raised my hands to your jawline. I couldn't wait a second longer, Molly. I just couldn't. My thumbs drew circles on your cheeks as I pulled your face closer. If the world had split between our feet, asphalt falling to the center of the earth, I would still have found a way to hold on to you.

"You'll be sorry," you whispered.

I brought my mouth to yours.

You pushed your body against mine, and I wrapped my arm around your waist, and we just kind of...fell into each other. It was the first time we'd kissed slowly, my thumb tracing your jawline, your hands warm against my upper back. Our lips moved softly, tongues softer still, and when our kiss ended quietly, we kept our arms around each other, your cheek on my chest, my chin resting on your head. In that one perfect moment, we could have crashed into the sun and I wouldn't have noticed the heat.

I released you at last, and you said, "Say it again."

And I said, "I'll never let you go."

And you laid your head against me.

I thought of myself as an animal then. As your protector. You held my leash in your soft white hands. If someone upset you, all you had to do was release me, and I'd have torn them to pieces just to see you smile.

Mom,

I'm okay. I just need some time away. My compass is broken. I love you.

Molly

NOW

I sit on the edge of the couch, digging my fingers into the fabric.

My dad is at work. My mom, picking up unwrapped toys from neighbors. And so I am alone when I learn what happened to Molly.

"The letter was found this morning at approximately nine fifteen a.m.," the TV reporter says. "We're told there's no return address, but there was postage, and it's believed the letter was dropped at a free-standing mail receptacle. It was postmarked at the distribution center in Allentown, but we've learned that all mail in the area is processed here, so that doesn't necessarily mean it was sent from Allentown. It could have been mailed from anywhere within a hundred-mile radius."

Get to the point, I think as my pulse races.

"We're told Molly's mother has handed over the letter to authorities, and we do have the contents of that letter to share with our viewers."

The man raises a piece of paper.

Is that the letter? No, he said they just had the wording.

He did this to make the moment more dramatic.

He begins to read—

"Mom, I'm okay. I just need some time away. My compass is broken. I love you."

The reporter lowers the paper, giving his audience time to take that in.

Giving me time to put my head between my legs and breathe.

"It seems that, for today, Molly Bates is okay, and her mother can rest a little easier. But I'm sure she's eager to have her daughter home safe. Molly will not turn eighteen until June eighth, and so police will continue to search for her until that time. But all signs point to Molly being a runaway. If you or someone you know sees Molly—"

A picture of Molly then.

Smiling.

Wearing a pink sweater though she despises pink.

"—call the police, or you can contact us at KGTV.com/bringhomemolly."

My stomach rolls. Is the local news station really so desperate for a story that they've set up a page for a seventeen-year-old runaway?

I sit upright. Struggle to regain my composure. Molly ran away. That was the plan, wasn't it? But who did she run with? And why leave behind the car?

It was supposed to be me with her.

There was never supposed to be a letter.

What happened to our plan, Molly?

WHAT HAPPENED TO OUR PLAN?!

My compass is broken.

Why does that ring a bell?

"I heard," Holt says from where he leans against the doorway.

I'm relieved he's here. Molly being gone is shredding me,

and it's nice to feel like someone cares enough to stick around to make sure I'm okay. At least, I hope it's because of that and not just because he's tired of campus life.

I furrow my brow and look back at the TV, which is showing Molly's mother, dressed in that same robe. I can't help noticing that her hair is fixed and her makeup is on. She seems awfully put together for a woman who hasn't seen her daughter—who she can't seem to breathe without—for six days. But she *is* vain. And if that letter had said Molly was dead, her mother might have still smeared on lipstick and a smile for the cameras. And then promptly downed a fistful of Percocet and a bottle of vodka and kissed this life goodbye.

Holt walks into the room and stands beside me as we watch the TV.

He shakes his head. "Always the last to know."

"Who? The parents?"

He points at the TV. "No, our news station. They reported it on the Pittsburgh stations an hour ago."

My heart wrenches. I hate thinking of all these people knowing about Molly. Of them praying for her or her mom. I like to believe I'm the only one who sees her. But now all these people do. They're staring at her photo and saying, *That poor girl. Her mother must be a monster. That's why she ran away, you know?*

And she was, sort of, but not in the way they're imagining.

Holt slaps me on the shoulder. "How you doing?"

I shrug.

"Do you know why she ran away?"

"You know I don't."

Holt looks at me a while longer, as if he suspects more than what I'm telling him. "Cobain," he says softly.

I look at him. I can feel the anger boiling behind my eyes. Can he see it?

He sees it.

"When you were younger…"

"Don't," I warn.

Holt sits down on the coffee table. "It's just…do you think it's possible that, I don't know…that Molly was ever uncomfortable around you?"

"What?" I say, genuinely surprised. "No."

Holt glances back at the TV. "She was definitely running from *something,* don't you think?"

"Well, she wasn't running from *me*. Christ, Holt, you're my brother."

"Yeah, I know. I *know.* I'm sorry. I was just thinking how you used to get really stressed about things. Sometimes that was… It was hard to be around." When I open my mouth to defend myself again, Holt raises his hands in surrender. "I'm just wondering why she would take off, that's all. Is there anything that might have spooked her?"

That question presses on me.

And presses.

Until I can't stand it for a moment longer. Until I can't *stand* a moment longer.

Holt gets to his feet and throws his arms around me. Claps me on the back. "It's all right, man. I'm here. I'm not going anywhere."

I hug him back so hard I'm afraid I'll crack his ribs. Because I'm afraid if I lessen my hold by even a fraction, he'll desert me the way Molly did.

Molly.

My Molly.

Where did you go?

It doesn't matter, I suppose.

Because I'll find you.

I will.

HER MOM

RHANA

NIXON

JET

MOLLY
RAN AWAY?

E

PART II

about a girl

MOLLY

The callous could say Molly Bates made herself a victim the night she stopped for peanut M&Ms.

She parked in the farthest spot from the convenience store doors. The only spot the camera didn't quite reach. She blocked herself in on one side by pulling in next to the dumpster and didn't pay any mind when an unmarked white van parked on her opposite side. And then...well, then she walked right by the driver, failing to notice how he slouched in his seat. How he wore sunglasses and a baseball hat pulled low on his head, despite it being dark outside.

Molly was in her own head—thinking about her classes and the hole in her rainbow-colored tights and whether, just for kicks, she shouldn't get a Sprite to complement the candy. Most importantly, she was thinking about who should have been there with her at that very moment.

She was a thinker, her brain constantly puzzling through problems long before a solution was due. And that evening, she was lost to the delirium of love. And so, when she returned to her Toyota Camry, that first green M&M already popped into her mouth, she didn't notice him stepping out of his van.

Her key was already in the door when he wrapped an arm around her chest and yanked her against him. A rag went over her mouth, and her heart shotgunned in her chest, and her mind sizzled and cracked with fear. But try as she might, Molly couldn't focus. Couldn't think past anything but the sound of the van door opening and the feel of being lifted into the air. Her mind went fuzzy even as her body raged with terror. The last thing she remembered before lying down in that field of poppies was her bag of M&Ms. He had that yellow package in his hand. Tipped his head back and filled his mouth, stealing both her candy and her body with the same amount of consideration.

THEN

You demanded to see my house.

I had seen yours, you reasoned, and it was only fair you see mine, too. And so I strategized. Waited until I knew my dad would be working and my mom would be off helping children that weren't her own.

When you arrived, you walked straight down the hallway like you'd been there before and found my room. My eyes flicked to my bed, and I thought of how many times I'd lain there thinking of you, my hand slipping beneath the covers. And now you were here, the real Molly Bates.

You seemed to know what I was thinking and sat down on my bed, patted a spot next to you.

"I like your posters," you said.

I glanced at each one in turn.

An illustration of a beheaded Mickey Mouse.

An illustration of a young girl holding a balloon string made of her own intestines.

An illustration of a crowd of people, their eyes hollowed out, their hands open to a silver sky.

I'd found them at a flea market. The artist was so pleased that I liked them that he gave me the beheaded Mickey Mouse for free. They were signed and numbered, and I felt like an art collector every time I looked at them.

Sometimes, when I allowed myself to be so stupid as to dream, I imagined opening a shop of my own one day. Discovering macabre artists and hanging their work for sale on my walls. I'd have shows for the artists, and instead of champagne and tiny inedible foods, we'd encourage people to wear costumes like it was Halloween. I'd smoke meats on a grill and tap a keg and people would get wildly drunk on beer and wonderfully disturbing art. There is something weightless and freeing in accepting death. That's what I'd tell them as they shopped. If I believed in dreaming, that is.

Then again, I'd dreamed of you being here, in my bed. And here you were. So who knows?

"Are your parents here?" you asked.

I shook my head. "My mom's doing some volunteer stuff."

"And your dad?"

"Working."

You frowned. "It's Saturday."

"Lots of people work on the weekends," I said.

You glanced around my room and out into the hallway. "Your house is nice."

I laughed. "We live in a shoebox. An *old* shoebox."

"Yeah, but it's...clean. And cozy." You nodded toward a bookshelf that used to be in my brother's room. "What are those?"

"Pictures," I said, as heat flooded my face.

You looked at me conspiratorially. "I'm gonna have to see this."

"No way."

You lunged for them, but I was quicker. I grabbed you

around the middle, and we crashed to the carpeted floor. You army-crawled toward the shelves as I grappled for your legs.

"All. Most. There," you said, reaching, fingers brushing the album.

You made it another few inches before I grabbed your ankle and stopped you from going any farther. I clasped your hips and turned you over, pushing my weight on top of you so you couldn't move.

"You've been caught," I said, feeling my body react to having you so close.

"I could get away if I wanted," you said, your voice low, eyes roaming across my face.

"Try and move, then," I challenged, lowering my face to your neck.

You tried to break away from my hold, but I was too heavy, too intent on keeping you beneath me. Besides, you didn't want to escape.

I bit down on your neck, and you wrapped your legs around my waist as if to prove my point. A soft moan escaped your mouth. I pushed my hips toward you, and you were there to meet my movements. If I didn't get off of you right then, I wouldn't be able to stop myself from tearing away your clothes.

Would you have wanted me to stop?

"Is that your brother?" you asked.

I swung my head around and realized you had the photo album open. You were staring up at it from the ground, a victorious smile on your face.

"You used your womanly ways to distract me," I said.

"Yep."

"So, you don't want me to kiss you right now?"

"Nope."

"Not even a little?"

"I despise kissing."

I brought my mouth to yours, and you dropped the album. Looped your arms beneath mine and grasped my back. I slipped a hand beneath your rear and gently squeezed as I traced your lips with my tongue, my teeth. As I trailed kisses down your neck then back to your mouth. You tasted like chocolate, and I smiled against your mouth, knowing I'd find the top of an M&Ms bag in your pocket if I looked.

How many times had we kissed like this? A hundred? A thousand? With your arms around me and my lips on your skin, we were alive as two people could be.

I slid my hand into your hair, and though it unnerved me to do it, I pulled on it. Just a little. Just to see what you might do.

You pulled me closer. You rocked against me harder.

Your hands slipped beneath my shirt, and you dug your fingers into my shoulders.

You gave another intoxicating moan and let your head fall back. Excitement rolled through me, wondering what else I could try that'd cause you to make that sound.

"We should stop," you said.

I rolled off of you but kept my arm beneath your head. I didn't want you to move too far away. I still needed your warmth.

You flipped onto your stomach, and I moved my arm so it draped across your back.

"You're not going to leave it alone, are you?" I said.

You grinned and pulled the album toward you. "I'm curious."

"Curiosity skinned the cat."

"Killed the cat. Not skinned. You are so disturbing."

"Whatever."

You opened the album, and the first picture I saw was one of Holt and me. We were in our soccer uniforms, standing on the field. I had grass stains on my shirt, and he had dirt smudged on his cheek. Holt had an orange Popsicle in his hand, its tip pointed toward the ground as he smiled for the camera.

I was looking at Holt.

Smiling at him.

"You idolized him," you said.

I tried to hide my smile, but I couldn't help it.

"When do I get to meet him?"

"He usually comes home on the weekends," I said. "But he's got finals coming up. Maybe during winter break?"

You nodded and looked back at the album, flipped through page after page of me sitting on my dad's lap. Of me making cookies with my mom. Of Holt and I opening Christmas presents. Of Holt and I waving from bunk beds.

You flipped to blank pages. "What? That's it?"

I got up and moved to my bed. Sat on the edge and avoided your gaze. "Mom stopped taking pictures after a while."

You sat up, crossed your legs. "Why?"

I shrugged.

I didn't think you'd understand, so I didn't want to tell you. Not yet. But I felt the words boiling inside my chest anyway, working their way up my throat, sizzling on my tongue with the need to be exorcised.

"Cobain," you ventured. "Your home is nice enough. You don't have any major problems with your family. So something else had to have happened to you. Something made you...the way you are."

I looked directly into your too-green eyes. "How am I?"

"Quiet," you offered. "You block people out. You dress in head-to-toe black. You have that giant tattoo on your forearm. The music you listen to, the art you like..." You motioned to my wall. "It's pretty dark."

I lowered my gaze, but you were there to grab my chin. To lift my eyes back to yours. "I like it," you said with a nod of your head and a fiendish grin. "But I also want to know why."

I pulled away. Blurted it out. "I got sick."

Your forehead furrowed. "Sick how?"

I shook my head, and you must have seen it then—the shadow of something more. You could sniff out the darkness, find people's weaknesses. You didn't use that knowledge against them, exactly, but you *would* use it to get what you needed. It sounds the same, but it's not.

You pushed yourself up from the floor and moved toward me like a predator. You wanted what was in my head. Wanted to clasp it between your hands and inspect it up close.

"What happened, Cobain?" you whispered. You put your hand on my knee. Laid your head on my shoulder. Said, "Tell me."

I laid my head on yours and closed my eyes. "When I was nine, my parents said I got messed up in my head," I told you. "I just remember having panic attacks and night terrors." My jaw clenched. My breath caught in my throat. "They said I was 'confused' and needed to take a break from everything, so they pulled me out of school and sent me to a psychiatrist for a while. Less than a year."

"Must have been hard when you went back," you said softly.

I shrugged. "The other kids didn't know what happened, but they had fun making up stories. Shitheads."

I felt my eyes burn, but goddamn it, I would not cry over that shit. That was a long time ago. Over eight years now. I wouldn't think about how, back then, my parents never asked me about my therapy sessions. How they never asked me how I was feeling at all.

How they only smiled.

Smiled and pretended everything was fine.

I won't think about how when Dad dropped me off at school and I asked him, "Will my friends know what happened?" he only hugged me and said he was so proud of me. So, so *proud*.

I won't think about how my mom—who, before, always had time to read me a stack of library books, or sit beside me and play Super Mario, or take me to the pool at the apartment complex at the end of our block—suddenly felt a calling to help people less fortunate.

All I would think about was that I moved past that episode. I was better now.

I *was*.

"I think you need me," you said quietly.

I didn't speak. I'm not sure I could have.

"But you know what? I think I need you more." You threw one leg over mine and wrapped your arms around my middle. "Now, there's a surprise."

MOLLY

*H*er head swam with thorns and roses.

She could feel the flowers inside her, taking root within her stomach, stretching up her throat, pushing against the backs of her eyes. She could smell them, too.

Wait. She could *smell* them.

Molly opened her eyes.

She didn't dare move, only stared at the cement ceiling, allowing her mind to catch up. Where was she? What happened?

Her head throbbed.

She went to lift a hand to her forehead but stopped midway.

Her wrist was encircled by a zip tie, which was attached to a rope.

No.

She bolted upright and found both her hands bound, the ropes extending to hooks in the ceiling. Below her was a metal floor drain, above her were a hundred hooks driven deep into a concrete slab like tiny glittering insects.

Her heart pounded in her chest, and she grew dizzy.

"Help me," she whispered.

Her throat burned, her words struggling to find their way out.

She tried to push herself up, but her knees gave out, and her palms hit the concrete floor. Her hands stilled when she realized what she was touching.

Stains.

Red stains.

She jerked her hands away and shoved them between her knees. Rocked back and forth and searched the room in a panic. She saw a twin bed with a white sheet, white pillow, and patchwork quilt. There were two doors. She rushed toward the first one, grabbed the handle, and twisted.

Locked.

She ran to the other.

This one opened easily, and Molly's heart leaped with hope. Inside the small room was a toilet and sink. And a window.

A window!

She threw herself toward it but was jerked backward by the ropes that held her.

She threw herself forward again. Stretched against the ropes. Bit down against a scream she wouldn't release. Whoever took her could be nearby. And if she started screaming, if she let herself succumb to the fear that itched to explode inside her, she'd never stop.

After scrambling to the center of the room, her eyes flicked back to the window. No bars. There were no bars, only blue, blue sky and red, red trees and impossible amounts of freedom she'd always taken for granted.

She inspected her wrists. Tugged on the zip ties. Tugged on the ropes attached to them. They were circled, over and over again, by some sort of wire. She pulled at the material until it cut into her flesh. Until she spilled blood onto the floor, those forgotten stains revived, the drain stretching its tongue toward the salty red droplets for a taste.

"Oww," she moaned.

She sounded like a child.

She felt like a child.

Molly wanted her mom. Her mom couldn't get enough of her. Couldn't breathe without her. She pressed her lips to Molly's and sucked the air straight from her lungs. Right now, if Molly could just be with her, she'd give her anything she wanted. Sleep in her bed. Stay by her side. Do anything, anything.

She wanted her daddy, too.

No.

She wouldn't think of him.

She couldn't.

So she tugged on the ropes one last time and then collapsed to the floor.

"Think," she said to herself. "Think first."

Those were her father's words. She shouldn't use them. But desperate times called for monstrous resurrections.

She put her head between her knees and thought.

What did she remember?

A man. No, a boy. Somewhere in between?

A van.

A hand over her mouth.

The yellow bag. He took her candy. He ate it.

What did he say to her? Something. Nothing. Everything.

He wore a baseball cap. She saw his face!

No. She saw the sun shining behind him.

Was he big? Small?

She couldn't remember.

So what did she know?

A man took her from a gas station parking lot.

He wore a hat.

He spoke to her.

She was in a room with a bed. She was bound, but not so tightly that she couldn't move around. There was a bathroom with a window.

What else, Molly?

WHAT ELSE?!

Her eyes shot across the room, and when she saw it, her gaze narrowed. She put one hand on the bed. Then the other. Pushed herself up and crawled across the squeaking mattress until the entire night table came into view.

There was a vase.

There were flowers.

Roses.

Molly grabbed the vase and threw it across the room. Jumped toward the pieces and gripped a shard in her hand. She started sawing at the ropes. Her eyes flicked, over and over again, to the window.

The ropes started to give way.

Thread by thread.

Fiber by fiber.

Her skin started to give way, too.

Was that a sound? Her head shot up.

No.

She sawed faster, her breath firing in and out of her lungs.

Molly froze.

She definitely heard a sound that time.

Someone was coming!

She started to cry and sawed faster.

Faster.

Faster.

The door opened.

Molly looked up in time to see him barreling toward her.

NOW

I haven't slept in two days.

Not that I was sleeping much before, but ever since the reporter announced that Molly ran away, I can't tear myself away from my phone. I scroll through pages and pages covering Molly's disappearance and the letter, but the information is all the same, and the links are slow to load because my phone is crap. Briefly, I allow myself to think of all the things I could have bought if I'd kept my job at Steel. I had my eye on a new phone, for one, and on a necklace for Molly, and on a car because her mom's wasn't reliable.

I'd allowed my mind to wander on slow days at the gym. Maybe I didn't want to own an art gallery after all. I mean, what the hell did I know about crap like that? This, however, I knew.

I knew persistence.

So why couldn't I become a shift manager like Chad, who was a complete tool? Why couldn't I be like Pam, who opened a second location of Steel and ran it like it was her own place?

I could have gotten an apartment with that kind of money.

I could have had a life of opportunity like my brother does.

Could have.

It had been more important to help Molly. But now she's free as a sparrow, and she flew far away from me with newfound wings. I know she misses me. She must. So I will find her and make her explain.

Why, Molly?

My brother comes into the room, takes one look at me, and stops. "Shit, man. Have you slept at all?"

I shake my head.

He sits down on the couch. "Talk to me."

I lower my phone. "I just can't wrap my mind around why she left without saying goodbye. Her mom, I get. But we... I don't know."

Holt leans back. "You feel like something happened to her?"

I glance at him. "She mailed that note."

"Her mom *said* she mailed a note."

"You think something else is going on?"

Holt gives me a sad smile. "No, but I think you do."

I hang my head. "It just doesn't add up. Something is missing. I know it."

"Well, the cops have stopped looking for other causes. You know they have."

"It's not like I *want* something bad to have happened," I say.

"But maybe you do, just a little bit. Because then you can play the part of the hero, versus the fool."

"Fuck you, man," I say, but I'm not sure if he deserves that.

Holt holds his hands open but doesn't apologize.

"Don't you have class?" I snap.

"It's our first week back. There's not much going on. Besides, I thought you might need me here."

"I don't."

Holt starts to get up, but I reach out and grab his arm. It

feels strange to touch him, and I find myself dropping my hand. "Sorry. I'm just…"

"Look, I want Molly back in your life, too. You were better with her. I know everyone says you've got to be happy on your own, but you haven't been good on your own in a long time. So, yeah, I think it's cool that you found someone to lift you up. You needed it."

"So what do I do?" I ask.

Holt shrugs. "Let's find her."

I nod too quickly. "Yeah, okay."

"You have any ideas where she might be?"

I think of the notebook in my room. "Yeah, I've got some ideas." I hesitate, then add, "There's this Nixon guy."

I think back to the number of times Nixon tried to join Molly and me on what should have been private dates. I recall the note from him I once found in her pocket, asking if she understood the homework, and could they work on it together if she did? I didn't think much about it then.

I do now.

"He always had a thing for her," I add.

Holt grabs his jacket from the kitchen counter. "You think he took off with her?"

"No." I head toward my room, saying over my shoulder, "But maybe…I don't know…"

"Yeah," Holt says as I jog to my bed and slip on my jacket.

I come back out and try to read his face. I can't tell if he's doing this because he believes something bad might have happened to Molly, or if he just wants to help me let her go. Doesn't matter. I'm happy for the company.

We jump in Holt's F-150 and drive to Nixon's house, a place I've been only once. It takes me a while to find it, and twice I have to make Holt turn around. When I see the blue siding and black shutters, I tell Holt to pull over. We watch the house. I don't know what I'm waiting for, but it's Saturday, so I know Nixon will be dragging his rear somewhere today. And when he does, maybe we'll follow him. Or better yet, maybe I'll slip into his room. Look for anything that tells me he knows where Molly is.

Holt crosses an arm in front of his chest, stretching.

"What, you been working out?" I ask.

Holt makes a sound that tells me that's the last thing he'd be doing. "Just slept wrong," he says.

We wait in silence for a few minutes before Holt says, as if the thought just popped into his head, "What happened the last time you saw Molly? Maybe it'd help if we went through that."

I glance at him. I can't tell him that. It'll come out wrong.

"We just went out to eat," I mutter instead.

"Oh, yeah? Where?"

"I don't know. Lending's Deli."

"Did she seem okay to you then?" he asks.

"How do you mean?"

He bobs his head side to side. "I don't know. Did you guys get along or whatever?"

"Did we fight? Is that what you're asking?"

"Nah. I'm just wondering—"

"I know what you're wondering. Leave it alone. You're looking in the wrong place."

But my brother knows me better than I know myself, and if he's wondering what *exactly* happened to Molly, and whether I had anything to do with it, then the situation can't look good, despite the letter.

He sighs. "Cobain, I'm your brother. If you can't trust me, who can you trust?"

"There's nothing to say. She mailed a letter," I remind him. "She's probably in California by now. Or wherever."

"Maybe," he says. "What did she mean by 'My compass is broken'?"

I press my lips together and pretend it's not all I've thought about since I heard those words. Then, because I really don't know, I shrug.

Neither one of us says anything for a long time as we watch the house. Finally, I lean over and punch him in the shoulder, harder than I should. "I've got a little cash. Let's grab something to eat. Want to hit Dino's?"

He raises his eyebrows. Lowers them. "I'd rather do drive-through. How about Micky D's?"

"Done."

Holt pulls onto the road and drives away, but not before I spot Nixon coming out of his house. He's carrying a large duffel bag and glancing around as if he's looking for someone. He doesn't see Holt's truck.

But I see him.

He throws the bag in the trunk of his car. Runs a hand through his hair like he's nervous.

"What are you looking at?" Holt asks.

"Nixon," I say, craning my neck. "He just came out."

Holt hits the brakes. "Want me to go back?"

"Nah," I say. "Keep driving. This is a waste of time."

Maybe I say it just to see how Holt will respond. To see whether he really believed that anyone else might be responsible for Molly's sudden departure. When he keeps driving, I decide I have my answer. I *can* trust my brother. He has my back in all things. But I realize something, then, that rattles me to my core.

My brother doesn't trust *me*.

Which is why I don't tell him that I'll be returning to Nixon's house alone.

THEN

I'd never been this nervous, this vulnerable.

I'd walked past this gym a thousand times on my way to school, but never had I been this close, more hope in my chest than seemed possible.

You reached over and squeezed my knee. "Why don't we forget this? Let's go to the mall and walk around. Make fun of small children and old people."

"You love small children and old people."

"So true. It's everyone in the middle I don't trust."

I bit the inside of my cheek. "I want to do this."

"As long as you're doing it for yourself."

"It was my idea," I said, looking at you.

"Yeah, but—"

I put a finger to your lips. You grabbed my hand and took my finger into your mouth, and I just about lost my shit right there in the parking lot. You must have known why I wanted that job. I wanted to take you out for a proper dinner. Wanted to buy you the velvet choker you saw at Sabrina. Wanted to buy a car of my own so I could stop begging my dad anytime

I wanted to be alone with you.

Today, you'd picked me up in your mom's car. You let me drive, and I wanted to thank you for that. Wanted to, but didn't.

"I'll be back in a few minutes," I said.

"I'll be here."

You leaned over and kissed me. I had to pull away quickly so I didn't march into the guy's office with a hard-on.

The gym was nicer than the pictures I'd seen online, with sparkling locker rooms, an indoor pool, a sauna, basketball courts, racquetball courts, a smoothie bar, and rows upon rows of glittering barbells.

If the gym at my high school was kindergarten, then this was college. And I wanted in so badly my bones ached.

"Cobain?" someone said.

I glanced at the man behind the counter, and he held out his hand. "Chad."

"Yeah, I'm, uh…"

"Here for an interview, right. Duane will watch the counter while we go in the back."

"The back" was a white room with a cluttered desk—brochures, photocopies of membership plans, scattered pens, and a laptop. Like a doctor's office, it was impersonal, the overhead lights too bright. But that didn't stop Chad from situating himself on the other side of the desk like he was sitting on a throne instead of a creaking chair.

"So, tell me why I should hire you," he said.

And I froze. I fucking *froze*.

Chad waited a few seconds, then said, "I'm just kidding, man. Relax. Though, I would have been impressed if you'd at least tried to answer the question. Would this be your first job?"

"Yes. Yes, sir."

"So, no resume."

"Uh, no. Sorry." I shift in my chair, my palms sweating.

"Your application says you can work nights and weekends."

"Yes."

"You'll have to sell memberships. That's your main job here. Think you can do that?"

"I think so."

Chad leans forward. "You think so, or you know so?"

"I know so."

"You old enough to work?"

"I'm eighteen."

"Good."

Chad looked to be only a few years older than me, but he was enjoying flaunting his seniority. I tried to think how Molly would handle this. She'd look for what this guy was most proud of, or most afraid of, and zone in on that.

Chad was about to open his mouth to fire another question at me, but I cut him off.

"Can I ask you a question?"

He raised his eyebrows. "Shoot."

"How, uh… How does someone like me get to your level? I mean, if I worked really hard here, is there a chance I could move up one day?"

"You looking for a long-term opportunity?"

"I just want to be in a respectable position one day. I know it'd probably take a really long time to get to where you are, but even if I could get close, you know?" I paused for authenticity, and also because I was sweating. I didn't know. "Is that stupid, what I asked?"

Chad smiled. "I like you. You're ambitious, but not annoyingly so. Let's see what you can do on the floor."

He rounded the desk, opened the door, and waved toward the counter. "I'll have you watch Duane talk to a new member. We have someone coming in now. I always schedule interviews and new membership sign-ups together."

"That's smart," I said, with as much enthusiasm as I could muster.

Chad gave an arrogant shrug.

I watched Duane give his pitch to another dude. He talked about the plans, what they included, and how much sign-up fees were. He knew so much and rattled it off like it was nothing. I thought he had probably memorized a script, and I knew I could never do the same. I could hardly remember to bring my books home to do homework. And how, exactly, was I planning on going from someone who rarely spoke to anyone, to someone who made small talk with every person who walked through the door?

It made me sick to think about it.

The guy Duane was talking to chose a month-to-month plan, handed over his card, signed a digital form, and said he'd be back tomorrow.

"All right," Chad said. "So, we'll probably have you come in again to try signing up members. If that goes well—"

The door chimed, and you strolled in.

"Hi," Chad said, plastering on a false smile.

"You have your key card?" Duane asked when you didn't move.

"No, I...uh," you faltered.

I'd never seen you stumble before. It was fucking adorable. Your eyes connected with mine, and I could tell you regretted coming in. You probably thought I needed saving. You were like that, Molly. You used your knowledge of people to get what you wanted, but you also used it to save people.

Remember when you helped Rhana get out of detention?

Remember when you talked down the mechanic working on Nixon's car?

Remember when you stopped to talk to that homeless dude? You asked him two questions and said something that made him smile in a way I bet he hadn't in a long time. Then you gave him the cash you had in your purse. Cash you could have spent on wristbands at the fair, but you didn't want to embarrass me by paying for them yourself.

You were an enigma.

"I'm just here to pick up my friend," you finally managed.

"You don't work out?" I said, finding my voice. Because seeing you unsure summoned my courage.

You shrugged one slender shoulder. Scrunched your nose. "Not really my thing."

"Well, we have a package that—" Duane started.

"Why not?" I interrupted, not taking my eyes off you.

"Why bother?" you answered. "What? Am I going to get ripped? I don't have the body for it."

"It's as much about the mind as it is the body."

Chad looked at me, and I could tell he thought I'd said the wrong thing.

I didn't care. I liked the way you smiled at me, so relieved I wasn't mad at you for coming inside.

You folded your arms and smirked. "I'm in college. Hotel management. I don't have time to get to the gym."

"Hotel management?" I asked, surprised, and also wondering if you were actually interested in that. "Bet that does take a lot of studying. I can see how you wouldn't have time for running on a treadmill." I walked toward you. Leaned across the counter on my forearms.

"Right." You lifted your chin, then your eyebrow, like you'd won, but I could tell you were also wondering if you'd worked me into a corner.

"Except that cardiovascular exercise creates new brain cells, reduces stress, sharpens memory, and leads to higher productivity." I wave all that away. "But you don't need any of those things."

You laughed, and it shot a hole through my heart. I mean really, Molly, there I was, bleeding internally, and you were smiling and shaking your head.

"All right, what do these things cost, then?" you asked.

Duane started to step forward, but you held up your hand. "Just give me a sheet or something. I'll look at it in the car."

Duane handed you a pamphlet, and you shoved it into your back pocket.

"Can I call you to follow up?" I asked.

You pursed your lips like you were debating this.

"Just if we have any specials going on," I added.

"All right." You nodded, and Duane asked you to fill something out.

"I'm going to my car now," you said, and pointed outside.

"Thanks for coming in," Chad said, too loudly.

As soon as you swung through the door, Chad slapped me on the back, too hard.

"Look at you, you little prodigy," Chad said, and waggled his eyebrows at Duane. "If that girl signs up, she won't work out past a week. Best kind of members. Only half our members come on a regular basis, and that's the way we need it."

The phone rang as Chad talked, and Duane told him it was Rachel.

"Be right back," Chad said, and marched toward his office.

Duane pulled out a bottle of orange liquid and sprayed down the counter. "Guess you'll be working here. Kiss your social life goodbye. I always thought I'd meet so many chicks, but once you're wearing this stupid-ass polo, they don't even look at you."

I glanced out the door, trying to see where you went, wondering if you were in your car or standing just outside.

"Did you see that chick, though?" Duane asked. "I would wreck her, man."

Squirt, squirt.

Wipe, wipe.

My eyes flicked toward Duane, a part of my brain waking up that I didn't know existed.

"I usually like fit girls, you know? But I'd be willing to make an exception."

You don't know Molly, I thought. *You don't know shit.*

"Hey, dude, let me call to follow up," Duane said, and I started breathing faster. "I bet I could close that shit."

Squirt, squirt.

Duane bumped me with his elbow, and my fists clenched into tight balls.

I closed my eyes. He had to stop talking about you, Molly. I didn't know what I'd do if he didn't—

"Oh, man. I think she's still out there." Duane grabbed something. I couldn't see what because I still had my back to him. I couldn't turn around or he'd know I was about to blow.

"I'm gonna go out there and clean the windows," he said. "Then you bet your ass I'm gonna ask her out. Chad doesn't like it when we hit on members, but hey, she ain't a member yet."

He came to stand beside me, leaned over the counter. "That's her next to the car right there," he said, his breath smelling like stale coffee. "Can you tell how big her titties are? I can't really—"

I spun around, my shoulder slamming into Duane's with enough force to take him off his feet. He flew backward and landed on his rear, the orange bottle rolling away from him.

"The fuck, dude?" he yelled.

"My bad." I almost reached down to offer him a hand up, but I couldn't bring myself to do it. "I, uh…I thought Chad was calling me."

As Duane was climbing to his feet, Chad appeared.

"I moved too quick," I continued. "Sorry, man."

Duane brushed himself off, still wearing a frown. "It's cool."

Chad roared with laughter. "This kid nearly sold a girl who doesn't work out a gym membership, *and* he laid you out during his interview? Talk about a solid hire."

I shoved my hands into my pockets. "Does that mean I have a job?"

"Yeah, yeah. You start Monday. Bring your social security card and driver's license."

I rushed out before Chad could change his mind, and found you leaning against the back of your car. My heart was pounding, and my blood was pumping, and I wanted you, right there, right then, pushed back on the rusted steel, the sun shining a spotlight on our bodies.

You curled your finger, beckoning me closer, that one motion my undoing.

"I'm sorry," you whispered as I wrapped my arms around your waist and spun you in a circle.

"Stop," I said.

"I shouldn't have—"

I kissed you.

I kissed you, and you held me tighter than you ever had.

Almost as if you were afraid to lose me.

Imagine that—

Molly Bates, afraid.

HER MOM

RHANA

NIXON

JET

DUANE

MOLLY
RAN AWAY?

MOLLY

When Molly awoke the second time, her head was clear. He'd drugged her again, but she'd expected it. And so when her eyes fluttered open, she'd stared at the ceiling and allowed her mind time to sharpen. She knew he was outside the door, could feel the shadow of him pacing back and forth like an animal awaiting its meal.

"I hear you," she said, emboldened.

The shuffling of his feet stopped.

"I don't know who you are," she said. "I didn't see your face."

She sat up, and though her body buzzed with terror, she plucked each word carefully. Reminded herself that fear was the enemy. People lowered their guard in the face of confidence.

If he was hiding his appearance, Molly reasoned, then he wasn't certain if he would murder her. If he *had* planned to kill her, he wouldn't care whether she could identify him.

Her eyes darted to where the vase once stood. The flowers hadn't been replaced. He'd be upset about that because the flowers were a gift. That much was clear.

The guy behind the door moved. Closer or farther away,

she wasn't sure. She had to say something else before he left. Because the only thing more petrifying than being locked in this room was being left alone in it. With him here, she could strategize. With him here, she needn't worry what he was doing, or planning, while alone.

Molly would not be a passive victim. If this was a game, and everything was, then she had to make her next move swiftly. Her first had been a mistake, but she didn't fault herself for acting as anyone would in the same situation.

The guy moved again.

He was walking away!

"Wait," she called out.

He stopped.

"Could I…? Could I have a glass of water? I'm so thirsty." She bit her lip and then added, "I won't break the glass. I promise."

He left quickly, and Molly pulled her legs over the side of the bed and shook with anxiety. Her mind went to *him*. Not the person walking up a flight of stairs, but the person she left behind. She touched a hand to her lips and clenched her eyes shut. If he were here, he'd tear down that door with his bare hands. He'd dismember this person who thought he could touch his girl.

But she'd left her wolf behind, hadn't she? And so she had to become a wolf herself. Or rather, a fox.

Cobain, she thought.

Her heart of stone cracked and bled when she pictured his face. His hands. The way he tilted his head and looked at her with narrowed eyes. Eyes that opened her rib cage and exposed what lay inside.

Cobain.

She dashed to the bathroom, relieved herself, and stood before the sink. The bonds on her wrists prevented her from reaching the window, but she wasn't concerned about that. Not yet.

Molly turned on the water and splashed it on her face. It was shockingly cold, but good. It reminded her that some things never changed, regardless of where you were. Sometimes, when things got really bad at home, she'd play a game—take a situation and make it worse in her mind so her present situation paled in comparison.

She did that now. Asked herself, *What if I didn't even have a toilet? What if I didn't have a bed? A window? Water?*

Water.

She already had water.

Idiot! She'd been stupid. She should have asked for something to eat instead. Given him a reason to be kind to her. Her request had been a test, of course. If he obliged, she'd know not all was lost. It would connect the two of them, however subtly.

Another lesson from her father.

Ask for things. Small at first, and then larger. Return the favor. This, and face time, are what connect humans more than anything else.

She shook her head, harder and harder, tears stinging her eyes. Even here, even in this situation, her daddy could still make her cry.

She wet her hands in the sink and scrubbed her face. Cleaned around her eyes, her nose, her ears. She released her hair from its rubber band and ran her hands through it, working out the tangles until it fell uninterrupted down her shoulders like sheets of virgin sand.

A virgin.

Could that be the part she played?

Or perhaps the vixen.

Or the playful free spirit.

There was a solution here, and it came in the form of a character. Who would she become to save her own life?

Molly heard him coming and ran from the bathroom. She leaped onto the bed and hugged her legs to her chest. Then she reminded herself to not take the appearance of a victim and uncurled her legs and hung them off the side of the bed. *No, too casual.* She folded them beneath herself with only a moment to spare.

Her abductor lifted a heavy, squeaking flap over a slot near the top of the door and held out a glass of water.

It was in a plastic cup.

She walked toward it slowly, nervous he might have put something in it. She reached out a shaking hand and took it. Tried to tell herself to not lurch backward but did anyway.

She looked down at the water, hesitated a beat, and then raised the glass.

It tasted of rusted metal, as if the water had sat too long in unused pipes.

"Thank you," she whispered.

Deep down, she felt as if she'd won a battle.

The guy moved closer to the door and leaned his head toward her. His face was cast in shadows, but she could see that he still wore the same mask—white plastic, with a pair of black eyes and a red, red mouth drawn across the front. A white band wrapped around the back of his head.

She inched closer, trying to gauge the size of him. Was he big, like Cobain? Or smaller, like her friend Nixon?

She leaned closer, narrowing her eyes, trying to get a better look.

He lifted a black device and held it to his mouth.

"You will call me Blue," he said.

Molly's heart jerked in her chest. His voice was deep and robotic and disguised by the contraption he held. It should make her feel better, should lend itself to the idea that he would eventually release her.

But instead, it sent chills over every inch of her body.

She lifted her chin, bit down to keep it from quivering. "Blue?"

He nodded, partially obscured by the door. More words through the device. "You will be quiet. You will obey."

She licked her lips. Pulled in a deep breath. "And what will *you* do?"

He cocked his head, examined her. "Whatever I want."

She scooted backward, needing distance. As the back of her knees hit the mattress and she sat, he took a step closer. Pressed his face to the door slot and leaned his head to the side until one black painted eye filled the space.

"You will wash yourself," he said, and pushed through a piece of cloth. Something else followed the rag—a fluttering of paper and the pop of a ballpoint pen hitting the floor. "And then you will write."

NOW

$\mathcal{S}$chool is my own personal prison.

The eyes of wardens are everywhere, watching my every move. Judging me. Questioning me. Haunting me. But no one watches me as closely as Nixon.

I study him as he eats lunch, in the rare moments when he isn't looking my way. I don't like the way he devours his food, as if he's unable to be satisfied. He waggles his fork between each bite. Waggles a foot that's lying over his knee.

There hadn't been a single shred of evidence in Nixon's room that told me that he'd been seeing Molly. The whole thing had me twisted up inside. If I'd been able to find something, anything, I could fix all of this. Find Molly and bring her home. Run away with her the *right* way. But finding something would have also meant taking down the only guy who'd ever been nice to me.

I watch Nixon as he rises from his seat. He's built like me, sort of. But I'm bigger.

I'm bigger.

Nixon dumps his tray in the trash and heads down the east hallway. He has a way of walking on the balls of his feet. He hops when he walks. Like a rabbit. Or a coyote.

I follow after him. I'm not certain what I'm doing, but I need to be 100 percent sure he had nothing to do with Molly's disappearance before I cross his name off my list.

I jog down the hallway, keeping far enough back so that he doesn't spot me, and push through the heavy door that leads to the locker room. It smells of sweat and mold and desperation. I walk past the rows of blue lockers, searching for him. Listening for the sound of him moving, though I don't hear anything besides the dripping of the showers.

"I knew you'd follow me."

I spin around and find Nixon sitting on a bench. He's looking at me hard. The sympathy, the *kindness*, he radiated in the weight room has evaporated.

He stands up. "Wanna tell me why?"

"Why what?" I ask.

He walks toward me with the confidence of a guy who's never been bullied. "Why the hell were you in my room?"

My face opens with surprise.

"That's right," he says, his lip curling upward. "I know you went in there. I saw you watching me in your truck. I almost called the cops, you know that? *That* was enough for me to report you. But I thought, 'Hey, maybe he was lonely or some crap, and he lost his nerve to come in when he saw me.' I didn't want to embarrass you, so I didn't say shit."

My heart hammers, and my hands start to sweat. This isn't how this was supposed to go. I was just supposed to follow him for a bit, make sure I wasn't missing anything.

"But I forgot my phone and had to swing back by, and guess who I saw coming out my own front door?" Nixon steps closer. "Want to take a stab?"

"I had to know." I hear how it sounds as those words leave my lips.

Nixon shoves me, and I let it go. I let it go once, but I may not a second time.

"Had to know what, man? If I knew where she went?"

I gnaw the inside of my cheek. "If you did something to her."

"If I…what?"

"You liked her," I say, as if that answers everything.

"Yeah, we all did. But she took off. She sent a fucking *letter,* in case you didn't catch that. There's no conspiracy here. And honestly, who cares?"

I rub the back of my neck. "No, I mean, you *liked* her. Maybe you even…"

Nixon's face relaxes with understanding. "Did I love her? No." He shakes his head but then looks at me like, *Why hide it?* "Yeah, all right, I liked her more than a friend. She was a weird girl, and I thought I'd add more balance to her life than you would. I needed a little weirdness, and she needed some normalcy. But she chose you instead." He shrugs. "It's whatever. I'm dating Sydney now."

I know all about him seeing Sydney because I went through that phone he'd forgotten. Saw their nauseating messages. Seems they've been seeing each other for a while, and that he likes her a lot if the lovesick texts are any indication.

And Nixon—because he's a good guy, even after someone creeps into his house—laughs and shakes his head. "Looks like you already knew that. We're keeping it quiet right now because her ex is a psychopath. Kind of like someone I know."

Now it's my turn to smile.

He shoves me a second time, but with less force. "Look, you and I aren't going to be friends anymore. We both know that. But I do feel bad for you. Molly was like… I don't know, she was like your tether to other people at this school, and now that she's gone, you're alone again. I know that's got to suck, but also…you're fucking weird, dude. You do it to yourself. I mean, you broke into my house. Do you know how utterly messed up that is?"

"I know," I say.

"Do you? Because normal people wouldn't do that."

Then normal people don't love hard enough, is what I think.

But what I say is exactly nothing.

"Look, I'm not going to tell anyone, because as strange as you are, I don't think you'd hurt anyone. And you're going to leave me the hell alone, right?"

"Yeah," I say, shoving my hands into my pockets.

Nixon leans his head back and inspects me as if he's considering telling me something. "You should forget about her."

"I can't," I admit in a rare moment of honesty.

Nixon fidgets, and my first thought is, *He's going to tell me they hooked up. He's going to tell me that, I'm going to break his nose.*

Instead, he says only, "Cobain, I think you deserve to know... The thing you had with Molly—"

Coach Miller bursts through his office door and takes three long steps into the locker room, a half-eaten sandwich in his left hand. "What the hell are you two doing in here?"

"About to rob you of a sandwich," Nixon fires back.

Coach laughs. Says with his mouth full, "I'd like to see you two dipsticks try."

Nixon follows Coach with his eyes as he powers across the locker room and pushes through the door that leads to the hallway. Nixon's eyes glide back toward mine. "Maybe, uh... maybe you should talk to him about things."

"What do you mean?" I ask.

Nixon shrugs. "I don't know. Forget it."

"Forget nothing. What are you saying?" I grab his arm. "And what do I deserve to know?"

"Let go of me," Nixon says, sounding more dangerous than I'd given him credit for.

"Just tell me!"

Nixon yanks away from me and moves toward the door. He stops just shy of it and says without turning around, "If you come near me, or my house, again, I'll call the cops and tell them what happened at the party."

Confusion pulls my brows together. "What?"

Nixon drops his head, shakes it. "The fight, dude. The way you were *shaking* her."

I step back as if struck. "That's not what happened."

"I know what I saw."

He pushes through the door as ice crawls through my veins, as it spirals from my fingertips, covering the entire room in sheets of permafrost. The party. That was the night Molly disappeared. We'd gotten into a fight, but I hadn't *hurt* her.

My heart explodes in a blizzard of fear, and I remind myself, though I shouldn't have to, that I did nothing to Molly.

I did *nothing*.

NOW

*W*hen I spot Holt's truck outside the house, I almost
turn around.

I really don't want to see him right now. He's supposed
to be on my side, but I'm starting to feel more suspicion from
him than support.

I walk through the front door without a sound, as if I'm an
intruder here the same way I was at Nixon's house.

When I don't find Holt in the living room, I head down
the hallway toward the bedrooms. I check his room first, but
it looks exactly like it always has. A full-size bed neatly made,
a poster of Nolan Ryan stuck to the wall, and rows of worn
Western paperbacks on a secondhand bookshelf. His clothes
are missing from his dresser, but a photo of us fishing as kids
still sits on top. Even the plastic basketball hoop still hangs on
the back of his door. How many games have we played with
that stupid plastic ball?

The only thing I ever destroyed him at.

As dated as all this stuff is, my room isn't much better.
Redecorating isn't exactly a priority when your parents can't

even afford health insurance.

I push open the door to my room and find Holt facing away from me, hunched over something.

"What are you doing?" I ask.

Holt jerks with surprise and whips around. He's holding something in his hands. He's holding *my notebook* in his hands.

He holds it up. "What is this, Cobain?"

I cross the room and tear it away from him. "That's mine, is what it is."

The look that crosses Holt's face breaks my spirit, makes me question if I have a heart at all. Or if, like that tin man from *The Wizard of Oz*, I'm made of only steel and bolts, a hatchet in my unfeeling hands.

"You knew I wasn't convinced that Molly ran away," I say.

He nods. "And I was okay with helping you work through that."

Work through that sounds a lot like *humoring you.*

"But Cobain." He gestures to the notebook. "The names in that thing. You have a list of, what, suspects? How are you crossing them off? What are you doing? If the police found out you're messing with—"

"They won't find out." I shake my head. "What am I supposed to do? Sit around? Hope the police know what they're doing? If you cared about me, you'd want me to find her."

"I want the *police* to find her, and they will. I want you to stop…"

I look down my nose at my older brother. "Stop what?"

He sighs. "Stop obsessing."

I'm not sure why that cuts me the wrong way, but it does. "I'm not obsessed. I'm in love. Maybe you're just jealous because you've never experienced that."

Holt frowns. "Cobain."

I know I'm taking my frustration out on him, but I can't

stop myself. "You were always better at everything. You were smarter. More popular. More athletic, even though I was always bigger than you."

Holt scoffs at the last part.

"Mom and Dad always liked you best," I continue. "And you had all these friends because where *you* went to school, the kids weren't sadists."

Holt holds his hands up. "I only went to that school—"

"Yeah, yeah. I know why Mom and Dad got you in there. Because you were *gifted*. Because you showed so much *promise*. They would never have even sent in an application for me."

My gaze locks on him. "You were the best at everything. But I was the best at loving Molly."

I struggle to control my emotions at the end, and Holt must hear it because he crosses the room in an instant and hugs me tight. Slaps me on the back and squeezes me again before releasing me. He takes my face in his hands. Gives my head a rattle.

"I am your brother, Cobain. I love you. All right? I'll always be here."

"Sometimes when I don't want you to be," I mutter.

Holt throws his head back and roars with laughter, and I find myself smiling, too.

"Seriously? Are you going to get kicked out of school?" I ask. "You barely even come home for holidays anymore, and now I see you almost every day."

He shakes his head. "I'm sorry I haven't been around as much as I should've been. College girls are pretty hot."

I try to laugh but can't manage it.

"Hey," he says, and grabs the back of my neck. Taps our foreheads together quickly. "I'm here now, fucker."

He releases me, smiles, and turns to walk out of the room. I'm still gripping the notebook between my hands as he goes.

MOLLY

*H*e came back for her, just as he said he would.

But first, he left the dress.

It was lying on her bed when Molly woke in the morning, the sun from the window casting an ethereal glow against the folds of white. It was vintage, yellowing along the lace sleeves and neckline. Along the lace-hemmed bottom and lace back.

After seeing the dress, she realized two new things:

The door to the restroom was closed.

The restraints on her wrists had been removed.

She knew she was being idiotic, but she still rushed toward the bathroom door. Ripped at the handle until her hands ached. It was locked, the keyhole mocking her with its gaping golden mouth. She tried to jam her finger in the hole, then ripped the shoelace from her shoe and attempted to stick the plastic end inside. Nothing worked to move the lock out of place. In a final, desperate act, she kicked the door—once, twice, twelve times—but she couldn't form even the smallest dent in the heavy wood.

She leaned against the door and caught her breath, closed her eyes, and pictured the window on the other side. So close.

It gave her hope that, soon, she'd find a way through it.

Is that why he left it uncovered?

To give her a sense that escape was possible?

Molly thought again of the letter he forced her to write. He wanted everyone to think she'd run away, and she had been doing just that before he took her, hadn't she?

She'd included a line that he jabbed his thumb at. He didn't understand it, didn't like it, but she hoped the boy she left behind would. And so she pacified her abductor by saying it was something between her mother and herself. A language only the two of them spoke. When he'd shaken his head, adamant that she write another letter without it, she turned her face away and allowed her bottom lip to tremble just so. "I only wanted her to know it was me. So she wouldn't worry."

She'd squeezed her eyes closed as if fighting back tears. Or maybe she wasn't pretending. Either way, he relented. He marched up the stairs with that letter in his hand, slamming the door behind him.

Her eyes fell on the dress, and she walked toward it. She held it up to her small frame. It would be too big, but she would wear it. Of course she would. He was treating her as if she were sacred, and that was something she didn't dare challenge. What was the alternative? Submitting in this way was a form of fighting. And Molly was a born fighter. Came from a long line of warriors dressed in human flesh.

So she pulled her dirtied sweater over her head and slipped her jeans off, slowly, one leg at a time, pointing her toes, arching her back…just in case he was watching. Yes, she would be beautiful. And sacred. But she would find out what he *really* wanted.

That, he would try to hide.

But she would figure it out.

Of course she would.

She thought of Cobain as she dressed. Remembered the day he'd taken her on a proper date. How nervous he'd been. And how proud. He'd spent nearly every cent of his first paycheck buying her a strawberry salad with a strip of flaky pink salmon on top. She'd ordered the cheapest meal she could find on the menu because she didn't want him doing this for her. She'd have rather he spent his money on himself, or at least saved it. Yes, that's what she really wanted—for that money to be secreted away for use at a later time. For it to be…available.

But she saw how happy it made him to do something for her, and so she'd eaten her salad, and she'd groaned with pleasure after every bite, though she despised fish. She'd watched him that night, the way he held his shoulders back. The way he fidgeted in his father's charcoal-colored suit jacket, much too small for him. The way he'd flicked his eyes to those around him, picking up subtle clues on how to eat correctly in a place like that.

Molly could have recited every last etiquette rule even if she were fast asleep. But she was too busy feeling guilty. Guilty for what she would do to this boy she was quickly falling for. Try as she might to hold on to that ledge, fingernails digging into the brick-and-mortar, she would lose her grip eventually to Cobain. And she'd tumble headfirst into his arms and forget all about what she had to accomplish.

Survival.

Or love.

Did he realize that's what he was forcing her to choose between?

That was never part of the plan.

After dinner, but before dessert, he'd complimented her on her dress. As if he was just now remembering this was important. His face scrunched, and he said, "You look amazing in that dress. Sorry, I should have… White looks good on you." He swallowed. "I like the lace."

Molly slipped her arms into the dress she held now. Different, but similar. She pulled the body down over her torso and wiggled her hips until it fell to her ankles. In a moment of clarity, or perhaps empowerment, she slipped off her tennis shoes and socks. Stood in bare feet on the cold concrete floor.

She tucked her shoes, socks, and the clothing she'd removed under her bed and stood facing the door. She knew he'd come. He said he would. She was thankful the dress was long enough to hide how her legs shook. She was thankful for the length of the sleeves so he wouldn't see how goose bumps rose along her arms. She must remember, above all else, that if she appeared to be prey, he would become a hunter.

It was simple biology.

When he came for her, her goal would be to get answers to as many questions as possible. But she'd start with these:

What did he want from her?

Did she know him?

It was too soon to question why he'd taken her, of all people. Besides, humans always thought things were about *them*. So they looked internally. Even when involved with another person, they still looked inward, but dismissed the fact that the other person was doing the same.

This kidnapping. It wasn't about *her*.

It was about *him*.

She had to remember that. Daddy would tell her she had to remember that.

Molly paced the floor for fifteen, maybe twenty minutes before she heard the sound of him. Footsteps on stairs. It confirmed what she already knew from the position of the window. She was being held below ground.

The slot in the door opened.

"You will come with me now," he said, still using that strange voice changer.

A chill rushed down her back. She thought of Cobain again. Wished with every fiber of her being that she hadn't betrayed him. Wished, wished, because then he would be with her, and this wouldn't be happening.

The door opened, and even as she raised her head and bit down to keep her chin from quivering, a single tear raced down her cheek.

The guy—Blue, he said to call him—stopped in the doorway and studied her.

She said to herself, *I am not afraid of you.* And she forced a smile onto her face. A small one, so as not to overdo it.

"I was afraid you wouldn't come," she said.

He'd started to move toward her but stopped when she said this. He tilted his head in a question, and those painted eyes with the mesh covering peered beneath her skin and muscle and bones to the heart that jackhammered in her chest.

She caught the unbelievable nature of what she'd said, and added, "I thought you might leave me down here forever."

He seemed to accept this as reasonable and grabbed her arm.

His gloved hand was large, his fingers digging into her body. She tried to get a glimpse of what lay behind the mask, but he forced her to walk ahead of him.

Molly climbed the stairs slowly, feeling the size of him behind her. He wasn't small, but since he wore a heavy black winter coat, she couldn't tell just how big. Instead, she focused her gaze on what lay ahead—a second door, closed, with a sliver of light beneath it. An uncovered bulb shone over their heads, thick with dust. The steps creaked beneath their feet, and she found herself thinking that what lay behind that second door could be far worse than being trapped below ground.

She wanted to go back. She wanted to run. She wanted to turn and shove this guy down the stairs because she was not

an item to be possessed. She was a human being. She didn't
deserve this.

Or did she?

"Keep walking," he said, shoving her just hard enough in
the spine that she had to move or risk falling forward.

She reached the top, and Blue pulled a key from his pocket,
unlocked the door, and pushed it open. The twosome came into
a short hallway, and he motioned to the right. Molly walked
ahead of him, her pulse racing, nails cutting into her palms.

She entered a small dining nook that flickered with light
from a stone fireplace. There was a single window in the kitchen
beyond the table, but it was boarded over. Were the other
windows in the place boarded up, too?

He doesn't live here, she realized. *This is just a place he
found.*

She wanted to search every inch of the house, but her
stomach growled when her eyes landed on the food. Oh God,
food. A bowl of something thick and creamy wafted heat as
if freshly poured. A tin mug of milk sat beside it, along with
a wedge of crusty bread. Molly locked her eyes on the silver
spoon sitting forlorn next to the bowl, and her mouth watered.

He waved his hand toward the food, and she rushed toward
the table. Threw herself into the chair. She had the soup into
her mouth before he could change his mind. And it was good.
Wonderfully, body-shakingly *good*. It could be poisoned, she
realized, but she didn't think he would bring her all the way
here just to end things in that way.

Before she could stop herself, a sigh of contentment
escaped her. She covered her mouth and looked at him. Then
she ate another bite, licked her lips, and decided to take a
chance.

"It's good," she said.

He didn't move, only leaned against the wall, watching her.

She studied him swiftly, ran her eyes from his head to his toes. He *was* big, wasn't he? Or was it just the light that—

He moved quickly, snatched something off the counter, and swept toward her as if he knew what she was doing.

His hand came down on her wrist, stopping her from taking another bite. She dropped the spoon and cried out. Clenched her eyes shut and waited for the blow to come.

She could feel him coming closer. Lowering his head until it was…where? Next to her? Behind her?

She had to look.

She opened her eyes and saw the side of his head next to hers, as if they were hand-in-hand at an art gallery, admiring the same painting. He tilted his head until his mouth was next to her ear. Though she fought the reaction, her entire body shook.

Slowly, he lifted that black contraption until it brushed her ear.

"Say my name," he said into the device, his voice a robotic current that sent shivers down her back.

He gripped her wrist firmer. It didn't hurt, but it seemed a promise that things could worsen if she didn't listen.

"Say my name," he repeated in a growl.

"B-blue," she said, her voice quivering.

He lowered the device and cocked his head a little more as if *she* were the art he was most interested in seeing—*Molly Beneath a Microscope.*

She swallowed her fear, heard her father speaking in her opposite ear, reminding her to regain control of the situation. She turned to meet his gaze so that their eyes and nose and lips were a fraction apart, then lifted her chin as if accepting a challenge.

He startled but didn't move.

He stared at her.

And she stared right back.

"Blue," she said again, and her voice held not a single note of fear.

He bolted upright and stumbled away from her. Turned to face the way they'd come in, and didn't utter another word.

Molly watched him for a moment, and then picked her utensil back up. Dipped it into the bowl. Lifted the soup to her mouth. And then she smiled—just a bit, just to herself—behind the spoon.

THEN

*Y*ou looked like a beautiful nightmare that stepped, long-
legged, from the recesses of my brain.

That's what I thought when I saw you that night, dressed
in a short white dress, your hair hanging over your breasts,
your nails and lips painted ruby red. You looked like a girl
who should never be trusted, and yet that's what people did.
They trusted you.

I had a pocket full of cash and good intentions. But those
intentions vanished the moment I saw you in that dress. Then
I thought—*bare flesh, my hands on your body, your mouth on
my neck.*

"Are you sure you want to go here?" you asked.

And I responded, "You said it was your favorite."

"I didn't mean for you to—"

I stopped you with a kiss. Call me weird, but I wanted
your lipstick on my skin. Wanted people to see us together,
spot the red smears on my mouth, and envy me. No one had
ever envied me.

A guy in a suit took us to a table. I wasn't sure if he was a waiter or something else. I'd never been to a restaurant this nice. I didn't know what to do with myself, and I was nervous as hell. The guy started to pull out your chair for you, but I cut him off, pulled the chair from his hands, and gave him a look like *I got it.*

"Thank you, sir," he said, and then I felt like an asshole.

They put down two menus in front of us with black leather covers. I was terrified of what waited inside. Dishes I couldn't pronounce. Prices too high for three weeks of part-time work at Steel.

You must have noticed how nervous I was, because you leaned across the table once the guy had left and said, "This place is really nice. I only came here once with my mom and felt like a poser the whole time."

I laughed, feeling relieved. Remembering the state of your house. Knowing you were no more accustomed to this than I was. But also knowing you'd somehow have the waiter forgetting his other tables by the time the meal was over.

You reached under the table and grabbed my hand, leaned that red mouth toward my ear, and said, "We should pretend to be different people tonight. My name is Roxanne, and I am new money. My father is considering buying this place, and I'm here to see if it's worthy."

I laughed. "I'm old money. My mom is interested in buying this place, too. We are rivals."

You kissed my ear, quick. "I'll have your head."

I grabbed your cheeks and pulled you back in. Said against your mouth, "I'll have all of you."

Our waiter appeared. "Hello, my name is Tim, and I'll be serving you tonight. What can I get you to drink this evening?"

He shook out our napkins and laid them over our laps. You leaned back instinctually, but I was less graceful, watching his hand as it came close to my junk. Tensing.

"I should tell you I'm Arturo's daughter," you said suddenly.

The waiter looked at you with a blank face, and you smiled.

"You'll want to find out who that is," you said sweetly. "We'll have red tonight. A Malbec."

"And an appetizer," I added, fumbling for the menu. Jabbing my finger at the first one I saw. "This one."

The waiter looked back at you.

"That one," you confirmed before setting your gaze on me and starting to talk about your day.

"Certainly," the waiter said, and dashed away.

I watched him go and then laughed. "He'll think you're a mobster's daughter."

You giggled. "Hopefully."

You watched the waiter disappear with regret. That look always came across your face when you'd manipulated someone. There were two parts of you, Molly. Have I told you that before? I'm sure I have. There was the part that celebrated getting what you wanted, however you had to. And then there was the human part, the part that hated being what you were.

As for me, I like the first part of you best.

The ruthlessness.

The meal was the best I've ever had. I ordered the strip steak with mashed potatoes, and you ordered the salmon salad. We drank the wine the waiter brought us—two glasses and no more because surely he knew we were underage—and we finished the meal with a chocolate-raspberry torte and a cup of espresso because I saw other guests doing the same.

When the waiter came along to drop the check, you dabbed at your mouth with the linen napkin and said, "You can tell the chef they can come over now."

The waiter's eyes popped, but he recovered quickly. Grinned from ear to ear and said, "Of course, ma'am. Right away."

I bit back a smile as you waited. Hands in your lap. Back straight as a stretch of highway.

The chef came out of the back, wiping her hands on a rag. She handed it to the waiter before offering her palm to you. You shook it firmly.

"I'm so glad you could join us," the chef said with an uncertain smile.

"As am I," you said. "You can rest assured it'll be a positive note I send my father. The tuna tartare was divine, and your staff"—you referenced the waiter, who squared his shoulders—"was most gracious and intuitive. This man alone is worth my father's attention."

The waiter beamed, and the chef laid a hand on his shoulder. "I have a great team. I'm so pleased to hear you enjoyed yourself."

The chef excused herself, but not without glancing back over her shoulder.

I handed my money to the waiter in a black folder, and after he took it, I looked at you.

"You are absolutely wild," I said.

You seemed as if you were about to say something but then stopped. Your entire face changed in that moment. I turned to see what you were looking at, and you said, "Cobain."

I saw him.

He held a phone before him, clasped between two eager hands, the camera lens turned directly onto us. He had thick graying hair, sharp blue eyes, and a mole just to the right of his nose.

"Who is that?" I asked.

But when I turned back around, you were frozen, your eyes twice the size they normally were.

"Molly, do you know that guy?"

You shook your head, and the look on your face said you

were telling the truth. But you still seemed absolutely *terrified*. You shot up from your chair. Reached into your purse and produced a wad of cash, threw it on the table, and ran.

I glanced down at the money for only a second before racing after you, leaving the waiter with an enormous tip.

"Molly," I yelled when we spilled out onto the sidewalk. You powered forward, not looking back. Not remembering that our car was in the other direction. "Molly, *wait!*"

I reached for your hand, but you ripped it from my grasp. Spun around and glanced over my shoulder, searching for someone. "What do you want from me?" you snapped.

It was the first time I'd ever seen you truly angry. Your body was a ball of smoldering black coal. I wanted to hold you in my hands and see how long I could stand the pain.

"What do you mean?" I asked.

You jabbed a finger into your chest. "What do you want from me?"

"Nothing." I shook my head. "Everything."

You winced and looked down at your feet. "People only love me because I fill a hole in their life. I'm…useful."

I grabbed your hands again, and this time I held on too tight for you to pull away. "I am *not* your mother, Molly."

"What about my father?" you said so quietly I almost didn't catch it.

Surprise shook me, because you never talked about him. It had been an unspoken rule. *Don't ask.* And so I didn't. But now…

"I don't know your dad," I said. "So I don't know whether I'm like him or not."

"What about me?" you said, speaking to yourself but raising your eyes to mine. "Am I like him?"

I shook my head. "I don't know that, either."

Tears threatened to spill down your face, and I took a step

back, aghast. Seeing you cry was like watching a statue weep blood. It was unnatural. Bone-shaking.

I wanted to tell you that you were nothing like your father. That you were most likely born from Immaculate Conception. But one look in your face said you already knew the answer to your question. *This* was the reason there were two halves to my girl.

"You should break up with me," you said.

"You'd have to try and kill me first," I said.

"I might." You laughed, just a little. Then the smile fell from your face. "You can't like me as much as you think you do. It's just that I'm the first person your age who's paid attention to you in a long time."

Your words stung, but I knew you were only testing me. Trying to get me to admit that I didn't really want you.

"Molly, I could name a hundred reasons why—"

Your eyes lit up, and you grabbed my other hand. Pulled me against the side of the restaurant, several steps into a shadowy alleyway. You'd seen him again, that same man who was snapping pictures of us in the restaurant.

"I want to get away, don't you?" you asked me suddenly, manically. Your eyes darted across my face, and you looked certain but afraid. Like you were admitting something you weren't prepared to share yet. "I just…I just want to escape."

I interlocked my fingers with yours. Glanced to the side, looking for the man. "Molly, who is that guy? Why was he watching us?"

Your chin quivered, and my bones stretched and cracked with the need to repair you. To murder and maim if that's what it took to see you smile again.

"Cobain," you said, your voice soft enough to split me in half. "Take me away from here."

"Okay." I buried my head in your neck. Without you, what

did I have? A father who gazed at me with a hopeful, never-ending smile? A mother who said she loved me, but couldn't stay in the same room with me for more than ten minutes? A brother who was never around? "Okay."

NOW

*N*othing is as unsettling as the smell of disinfectant.
My nose stings and my head swims from the chemicals, but the police officer sitting in front of me doesn't seem to notice.

"How have you been, Cobain?" Detective Hernandez asks.

I shrug.

"I've been thinking about you," she says. "I know it probably wasn't easy learning that your girlfriend ran away."

"Better to learn she ran than to be suspected of doing something to her," I clip. "Why am I here? I figured you wouldn't be looking for her anymore."

The detective frowns her bulldog frown. "Do you want us to be done looking for her?"

Anger fires through my body. I lay my forearms on the table, grip my hands together until I'm afraid my fingers will break. "No. It'd be nice if someone besides me believed there's more to the story than her needing some *time away*."

Detective Hernandez nods, looking at me in a way she hadn't the last time I was here. I move my hands to my lap, uneasiness swimming through my gut. I wasn't surprised when the cops showed up as I was walking home from school. I figured I'd pissed Nixon off enough to tell them I'd snuck into his house. I *hoped* they'd found Molly and wanted to let me know. But as I sat across the table from Detective Hernandez, I knew this was something more.

"As I said before," Detective Hernandez begins, "I want to bring Molly home. She's a minor. And I don't want something bad to happen to her while she's out there, alone. If she is alone."

If she's alone?

Who the hell would she be with if not me?

"Is there anything else, anything at all, you'd like to tell me?" she asks.

It's the way she's looking at me, studying my face closer than she has in the past. It makes me squirm in my seat, even though I should be giving her the same look. Demanding to know what they're doing to bring Molly home. Showing *my* frustration.

"I think maybe someone did take her," I say, if only to get her to stop looking at me that way.

Detective Hernandez raises her eyebrow.

I wonder if I've made a mistake, but it's too late now.

"Why would you think that?" she asks.

I glance around the room. Run my chewed-off fingernails over my knees. "Where is the other one? Detective umm?"

"Tehrani," she supplies, and smiles like she knows I remember his name. "He's working another case right now."

The tension in my body eases. If they really believed, without a shadow of a doubt, that something bad happened to Molly, they'd have more than one head on the case.

"There's this kid at school. He told me to talk to Coach Miller about Molly."

Detective Hernandez's brow furrows, but she's quick to

jot down the name.

"Who was this that told you to talk to him?" she asks.

I bite my lip. There's no way I'd mention Nixon. The last thing I need is for them to bring him back in for questioning.

"That's okay," she says. "Let's talk about Coach Miller. Has he ever—"

"There's this girl Molly used to hang out with, too. Rhana. She was always jealous of her. And this guy, Jet, he didn't like her. I know that for sure."

I don't mention that I saw a picture of Jet with Destiny posted online from the night of the party, the night Molly vanished. Jet's been into that girl since middle school, everyone knew it, and no way would he risk that relationship to screw with Molly or me.

I just keep grasping anyway.

Detective Hernandez nods. Makes another note. "Okay. Between those three people, who would—?"

"And there's a guy I used to work with at this gym. Duane. He made comments about her one time. And every time after that he'd always look at her in this way, you know? Just like… ogle her. I shoved him once."

Detective Hernandez leans back. Tilts her head.

"And have you talked to Molly's mom? Like, *really* talked to her? She's a nutcase. I wouldn't be surprised if she kidnapped her own daughter. Or did something to her so terrible that Molly didn't have a choice but to run away."

"We went by—"

"There's one other thing," I say, my voice low. My eyes lock on her so she knows how serious this is. "There was someone watching Molly. A man. He was at this restaurant I took her to, and he started taking pictures of us on his phone. She wouldn't say who it was."

Detective Hernandez stares at me for a long, hard moment.

"Your girlfriend has been gone for almost two weeks, and you failed to mention that someone was *watching* her, or that you suspected any of these other people"—she nudged her notebook—"until I brought you in for questioning a second time?"

"I'm telling you now," I shoot back.

She sighs and glances down at her notes. "Okay, well, better now than never."

My body relaxes, imagining her looking into these leads. And finally, with my help, figuring out what happened to Molly.

Detective Hernandez is quiet too long.

"Did you need last names?" I ask. "Or addresses? I think I know Rhana's—"

"Just one more question, Cobain, and we'll get you out of here." She flips a page. Another one. "You said you and Molly skipped school on October eleventh, correct? Shortly after you met her?"

"Yeah."

She smiles, but I see the cracks in the gesture. "Just a little thing. When I called the school, they actually told me you guys were absent a second time. Eight days before Molly disappeared, to be exact. Why didn't you tell me you two cut class more than once?"

A jolt shoots through my body, because if she knows we skipped that day, she may also know about our…disagreement. But that's all it was. One little disagreement, which is perfectly normal in relationships, but I didn't want to mention it because she'd have turned it into something it wasn't.

I shrug. "I forgot about it. It was just for a few hours."

"What'd you guys do?"

"I don't really remember," I lie, because I'll never forget what we did. "Maybe went to see a movie."

"What movie?"

Now it's my turn to go on the offensive, because I didn't do anything. And as she has reminded me time and again, I don't have to *be* here.

I stand up.

"I don't have to answer that," I say. "I don't have to answer any of your questions, because you know what? They aren't doing anything to bring my girlfriend home. You're looking in the wrong place."

"I was just asking a question, Cobain." She flaps her notebook closed. "We're done anyway. You've been very helpful, once again."

She stands and offers her hand.

I consider not shaking it, but in the end, I do.

She holds on a bit too tight, looks in my eyes a beat too long, and so it's me who ends up pulling away. I back up a step and stare at her, my heart beating in a strange new way. I look down, then turn and walk away, feeling sick in a way I can't fully explain. I don't like the way she looked at me just now. The detectives were covering their bases when they brought me in the first time, but this felt like…this felt like *suspicion*.

As I push through the glass door, I find myself thinking of the way my brother looked at me with that same level of uncertainty. I think of the way Nixon looked at me when he said, *The way you were shaking her.* I think of the way the kids look at me at school every day.

Their faces, their words—it makes me squirm. Makes me uneasy. But I have no idea why.

Because I have nothing to hide.

MOLLY

*M*olly discovered Blue's weakness—his desire to feel *needed*—and she nursed it every chance she got.

How long had she been there? Four days? Five? Long enough for him to bring more dresses. More flowers. Food, sometimes ripe, sometimes half rotten.

She thanked him for it all.

And she took an interest in him.

She was careful with her requests because she knew she could only make so many. He wanted to feel needed, yes, but also sought control. So first, she'd asked for the water. The next time, she asked for him to visit her at night.

He'd made a strange sound when she'd asked this, but she was quick to clarify that she just wanted someone to talk to.

"I'll go crazy if you leave me alone," she'd said when he didn't come for two days after their night in the kitchen. "Please don't leave me alone."

In truth, Molly wanted to be as far away from him as possible. But she was afraid he'd panic and leave her down there to die. He may not have wanted to kill her, or even hurt her, but maybe he could convince himself to simply walk away. It'd be easy, she knew.

If she was to gain his trust, she had to keep them interacting. So she asked for him to visit. And he had. This was the third night he'd come, and so she sat on her bed, cross-legged and ready.

She wore another oversize dress—this one a short sundress she shivered in—but she'd let him see all of her in it. When she heard him descending the stairs, she slipped a strap off her shoulder. Flipped her hair over the other. Bit her lips to bring color to them.

Molly knew what she was risking by drawing him to her, but if he wanted to do *that* to her, he would do it regardless of what she did. *Go ahead*, she thought to herself. *Come close. Unbutton your pants. Lower your guard, Blue.*

I'll destroy you in the end.

"I hear you," she said.

Blue made a sound, and Molly imagined him sitting on the bottom step. It's what he'd done the last two nights. He didn't show himself to her often. She figured it was because she knew him. But maybe it really was that he didn't want to get caught should he ever decide to let her go.

"This dress is getting dirty," she said. "I'd like to change."

It was the only time he removed her wrist restraints. He'd stand inside the bathroom and wait, not looking out even once. She'd have to yell that she was done in order for him to come out again.

Once, while she changed, she'd studied his turned back. He was broad in his winter jacket. Much taller than she was, with large hands. Yes, she'd seen his hands ungloved. Seen his dirtied fingernails. Did she recognize them? She wasn't sure. But she knew if she got out of here, she'd memorize every part of every person who ever crossed her path again.

When she got out of here.

Not *if.*

When Blue didn't respond, she swallowed and said, "I'd like to sing a song."

She could almost hear him sit up straighter.

"It's called *Alice Blue Gown.* Have you heard it?"

He didn't respond.

"If you don't want me to sing—"

He hit the door.

She smiled triumphantly. "Okay, then."

Molly planted her feet firmly on the floor and stood. She faced the window in the bathroom, opened her mouth, and began to sing the lyrics.

I once had a gown, it was almost new,
Oh, the daintiest thing, it was sweet Alice blue,
With little forget-me-nots placed here and there,
When I had it on, oh, I walked on the air!
And it wore, and it wore, and it wore,
'Til it went, and it wasn't no more.

She sang on, repeating the words to the old songs her mom used to play, back when they were a different family. When people said, "Yes, ma'am," and, "Right away, ma'am." Now, they said, "When will you pay us? Where is our money?" and "Who do you think you are?"

Molly lost herself to the lyrics. No, she *pretended* to lose herself to the lyrics. She raised her head and sent her words dancing in the moonlight, and when she heard him rise from the floor and peek through the door, she forced two tears to squeeze from her eyes and spill down her cheeks.

He watched her.

And she became someone worth watching because his eyes were on her.

When she finished, she turned toward the door. He dashed

out of sight, and she heard the sound of stairs as he started to take them.

"I miss the sun," she said, quickly. "I miss the warmth."

He didn't respond, but she knew that he'd stopped.

Her eyes darted to the window, and because she didn't want him to simply open it for an hour or two, she said, "I want to feel it on my skin."

When he still didn't reply, Molly added, "I feel alone with the door between us."

He didn't move, but she knew he was contemplating what she'd said. She knew because she was her father's daughter.

People don't enjoy being asked to do things, Mockingbird, he'd said. *But if you tell them what you want and allow them the pleasure of making you happy... Well, therein lies the easiest path to getting your way.*

Molly could have said, *Would you please open the door?*

But she didn't. And so, after several strained moments, she heard the sound of the key slipping into the lock.

Blue pushed the door open and stood staring at her. Molly strained to make out the color of his hair, to see *anything*, but the mask wrapped entirely around his head.

"You know I'm afraid of you," Molly said, sitting on the floor. "But I'm more afraid of being alone."

It was an invitation. One she desperately needed him to accept.

The more time someone spends with you, the more unlikely they are to do you harm. Her father's words in her head. How she hated them. And yet... *Imagine holding a gun to a stranger's head. Now imagine doing the same to your neighbor.*

Blue took a small step backward so that his mask and body were shrouded in shadows. And then he sat.

Molly smiled and sighed with relief. "Thank you."

Blue nodded.

Molly thought about what to ask him. But no matter what popped into her head, she knew it would lead to his discomfort. It would feel forced. If she were to escape, she needed to gain his trust. And his affection. But how could she grow close to him when even his voice wasn't his own?

It hit her.

"Let's play a game!"

He cocked his head.

She looked around the room, searching for an easy one. Then she laid her hand in her lap. Made a fist with it, and put an open palm beneath it.

"Rock, paper, scissors," she said.

He stared at her.

"Best three out of five," she went on. "If you win, I'll make dinner tomorrow night. If I win, you let me go outside for ten minutes."

Blue stared at her.

Unmoving.

Then he bolted to his feet. Turned to power toward the door.

"No," Molly yelled. "Wait. Please!"

She hesitated only a second before jumping up and throwing herself at him. Even with her restraints, she was able to reach him. She grabbed his arm. She *touched* him!

He tore around, his concealed eyes landing on her hand.

She gripped him hard.

Her breathing scarcely left her lungs.

He shook his arm. *Let go,* the movement said, *or else.*

As a terrified sound escaped her, she threw her arms around him.

It was the opposite of what she wanted to do.

It was exactly what she needed to do.

She hoped, hoped, hoped.

She held him close. Heaved for oxygen. Her eyes were

wide, wide as she listened to his heart beating. Her head fit snugly against his chest made wider inside a thick winter jacket. His chin was more than a few inches above her head. Did she recognize his height, his build, his smell?

She breathed in and caught only the scent of soap, as if he'd just showered.

He didn't touch her.

His arms hung stiff at his sides.

But, was it her imagination, or did he lower his head to lie on top of hers?

Molly thought of hitting him. Of tearing the mask from his face and screaming, *I will kill you. I will burn you alive!*

If she'd had an ax, she'd have buried it in his back. But she only had this. She only had her mind and two arms gripping his back.

She raised her mouth to his ear.

Said, "I know you aren't bad."

He grabbed her arms and shoved her backward. Not hard enough for her to fall, but hard enough so that he could get to the door. Could lock it behind him and march up the stairs, leaving her alone with the spiders.

Leaving her alone with the aching familiarity of that hug.

Or was it that she hoped it was familiar?

THEN

I saw you before you saw me.

I loved it when that happened. When I had a rare moment of seeing you in your natural state, before you became the girl who slipped into roles like an actress beneath stage lights.

You were different with me than you were with everyone else, but I often wondered—which was the real Molly?

Would the real Molly Bates please stand up?

You spotted me through the car windshield and raised your middle finger. I raised mine back and yelled to Duane that I was out. Took my name tag off and tossed it in the drawer.

Duane leaned across the counter and looked at you, too. I rounded the counter and slammed my hand down in front of him, hard enough to get him to take his fucking eyes off of you.

"See you Sunday," I said.

"Cool," Duane replied, already turning around.

I kissed you when I got in the car, and you arched your back. I wondered if I was kissing you more because I wanted to, or in case Duane was watching. I worried about losing you in those days. Every hour I spent with you pushed me a little further into an ocean of *us*. I was drowning in me with you, you with me. And I didn't want saving. But I worried, incessantly, that someone would save *you* and leave me to disappear beneath that black tide.

I didn't want to drown without you, Molly.

"I have a surprise," you said.

"Okay," I answered, and eyed your legs in those navy tights with white cat faces on the knees.

"Stop looking at my legs," you said.

I smiled and said, "I will not."

But I did.

Sort of.

*Y*ou took me to the woods, where gnarled trees stretched toward the sky. They arched over us as we left your mom's car behind, getting lost in the shadows.

The snow was falling, but you were bundled against the cold. Is it bad that I wanted you to be a bit colder than you were? I wanted to be the thing to give you warmth, Molly. I wanted to be the thing that gave you everything you needed.

We spilled into a clearing, and I decided you must have been here before. I wondered if you'd ever brought another guy here. *No,* I decided. You hadn't lived here that long. You'd just moved here from California. Or was it Colorado?

I think you'd told me both.

You held more lies than you did truths, you wicked girl, but I knew you wanted me. And, well, my intentions for you weren't completely pure.

So maybe I was wicked, too.

There was a rotted log, but you chose to sit on the ground.

The snow seemed to pull back to make space for you. I sat next to you and put my forearms on my knees.

"This place is cool," I said. "I've never been here."

"Me, either," you said, but we both knew it was another lie.

You picked at the hem of your jacket. "I thought I should tell you about my dad."

The way you said it, sadly, I knew you were going to tell the real story, and I found myself leaning closer.

"He was a preacher," you started, just like that. Because when you were intent on doing something, you dove in. "And he wanted Mom and me to be just like him, perfect in our faith. Perfect in our walk with Christ."

I studied your face as you spoke. Your lips were red like they always were, but the rest of you was white as the snow falling over your shoulders. Your hair, your skin, even your light green eyes—they were like camouflage in this forest. But you wouldn't have been the prey out here. You were the girl so strange that snakes slithered backward when they saw you walk by.

"I tried everything I could to make Daddy happy. But I—" You pointed to your chest. "I wasn't enough. So I became someone else. I learned to do what I needed to do so that he could stand at that podium and be so damn proud of his pure family."

You shook your head. "He left us anyway. Isn't that funny? After I'd learned to be a chameleon. After I'd learned how to be exactly what he and everyone else needed, he took off with some woman he met on a retreat, and they had a kid together."

I put my hand on your knee.

"He still writes to us, and I see him once or twice a year. But that's it. He's happier with his new family, and Mom is... Well, she's the way she is."

"And what about you?" I asked.

You shrugged and gave a halfhearted smile. "I have you."

I nodded. "Yeah, you do."

You started to lean toward me, and I wanted nothing more than to lean, too. But I stopped myself to ask a question I'd harbored since that night in the alleyway. "Molly, was that guy in the restaurant your dad?"

You flinched then forced yourself to nod. "Yeah. I think…I think he's finally going to ask for partial custody. Out of guilt, maybe."

I could hear the lie on your lips. Knew you didn't believe what you'd said any more than I did. Your father had left you and never looked back. But what was I supposed to do, Molly? What could I do besides pull you to me, palm the back of your head, and keep it against my chest?

I held you there for a long time. Finally, slowly, you leaned back until you were flat on your back, tugging me along with you. You guided my hips until I was almost on top of you, one of my legs between yours.

You put your hands on either side of my face, your hair white against the ground. Whiter than the snow. Whiter than the explosion that made you and me and this entire universe.

"I can't go back to living with him," you said.

I shook my head. "You won't."

"I have to get out of here."

"I'm working on that."

The truth was, I hadn't been certain you were serious. Not before. But right then, as I looked into your green eyes, so wide I thought I might fall inside of them…right then I knew this was one thing you *meant*.

I wondered how long it would take me to save enough money to get us far away from here.

I wondered what would happen if I just *took* it.

You seemed to read my thoughts. Seemed to measure just

how committed I was to getting you anywhere you wanted to be.

"Touch me, Cobain," you whispered.

I studied your face for only a moment, and then lowered my mouth to yours. I kissed you, my tongue slowly tracing the softness of you. My hand slid up the side of your body until I reached your jacket, your sweater, your T-shirt. I moved my fingers beneath it all and kissed the gasp that rushed from your mouth.

My hand must have been cold, but your skin was warm, and I felt myself react as I inched farther upward. I touched the lace edge of your bra, and I pulled my head back, watched as your breathing quickened. Slowly, I ran my thumb beneath that lace, feeling the slight rise of your breast. I pushed my thumb higher, and when you closed your eyes, I slipped my entire hand beneath the fabric, drawing soft circles over your nipple.

I felt myself throb inside my jeans, and before I could stop myself, I pushed your clothing up and put my mouth where my hand had been. You gasped, and I thought my body would explode if I didn't get inside of you. If I didn't have every last inch of you.

Over our heads, the birds called to one another. And the snow continued to fall over us, but neither of us shook from the cold. I buried my face in your neck and pulled your sweater down.

But I wasn't done with you yet.

I leaned back and looked into your face once more. You were so vulnerable. And powerful. You seemed afraid of how much you wanted this, of how much you wanted me, and yet you had the ability to crush my entire world inside a closed fist.

I slipped my hand beneath your jeans. Just the tips of my fingers, but you lifted your lips toward me. Closed your eyes because you knew what I would do to you. I hooked my arm beneath your knee and pulled your leg open wider, then crawled my fingers back to where I'd been. I drew slow circles beneath your waistband and kissed you until I couldn't wait any longer.

I unbuttoned your jeans. Pulled down the zipper. Bit the soft skin on your neck and moved my hand beneath your underwear. Found that part of you ready for me. You moaned in anticipation, and I was there to meet that need.

I sank my finger inside you and stroked the outside of you, too.

You arched your back, closed your eyes, and said my name.

I moved faster, pressed harder, and when I felt your hand moving toward my jeans, I pulled your head into my neck. Your hand worked faster than mine. Gripping me. Moving with me.

I hadn't been touched like this before, let alone by someone I cared about. With someone I wanted so badly that hell itself could swallow us whole, and as long as we stayed this way, I wouldn't have minded the heat.

We stayed like that, on the ground, in the snow—heavy breaths, rocking bodies, gripping flesh—until release washed over us both.

As you gripped my jacket, as the cold slammed into us and we both said—*We should leave, we should leave*—the words were on the tip of my tongue.

I wanted to tell you then. Had it been long enough?

It was only December. Only the first frost, and I knew winter would get much colder. *Maybe I should wait*, I told myself.

I should wait.

So I didn't tell you then how much I cared. How I'd never survive the loss of you. I shouldn't fall this fast for a girl. It'd only been a month and a half of stolen moments. Of peach jam on the corner of your lip, and me singing the lyrics wrong, and you taking your shoes off because you wanted to feel the water, and us sneaking into the movies and then buying tickets for strangers in line, and you kissing me and me kissing you and you caring about me and you caring about me and you caring about me.

I didn't tell you what I was feeling because I couldn't have handled it if you didn't say it back. I rolled away from you, and my eyes fell on the sky. And then, in an instant—a change.

Blue sky *gone*.

Trees—different trees—suffocating the once empty space.

A dog, barking.

I clenched my eyes shut, reopened them.

The sky was back.

I bolted upright, looked around, fear seizing me by the throat.

"You okay?" you asked, sitting up beside me.

I didn't know what had happened. Didn't know exactly what I'd seen.

But I knew *why*.

The more I fell for you, Molly, the more I felt something else pressing on me. Something I needed to remember.

When you get too emotionally charged, the therapist had said, *that's when you lose yourself. So we need to keep you stable. You have to keep* yourself *stable*.

But I didn't want stable.

I wanted to feel alive.

I wanted to feel *you*.

But I could tell that I was slipping.

Could you?

NOW

When I get home from school, my dad is waiting for me on the couch. He's strangely silent while I drop my bag on the kitchen table, and then he asks—no nonsense—if the police brought me in for questioning again. I hesitate only a beat before nodding, because I can tell he already knows.

My father is quiet for a long moment and then stands up, sighs, and insists we go for pizza. I don't want to go and nearly refuse, but he's wearing that expression that says he won't take no for an answer.

He puts a hand on my back as we walk toward his car, and it should be comforting. It should, but it doesn't feel that way. He opens my door, and I climb in. I'm suddenly worried that I finally screwed up enough for my father to scream at me. For him to grab me by the shirt and shake me and ask, *What's wrong with you?* Instead, he drops down into his own seat, closes his door, and pulls in a long breath.

He looks at me. "Are you okay?"

I'm not sure why, but his loving words feel like a dagger to the chest. But why?

I nod.

"That was the second time they questioned you, right? Or have there been other times?"

"No, only those two."

He runs a hand over his jawline, thinking. "Listen, next time they ask to speak with you, you tell them no. You tell them to come talk to me or your mom."

"Because she's always available," I mutter.

My dad drops his head to the side, looks at me with sympathy that sends needles beneath my skin. "You know your mother loves you. She loves both of us. But she cares about other people, too. The world would be a better place if more people were like her."

Shame floods my face, and I try to see my mom the way others do. With relief. With gratitude.

I just miss her, that's all.

"What did they ask you about in there?" my dad asks. "Molly?"

"Yeah," I clip. "I gave them some people to look into."

He sighs and scratches at his beard. As he stares ahead, the vehicle still cold beneath his hands, I study my father. See the way his shoulders stoop in his faded flannel shirt. He's thin from long nights at work. From drive-through value meals instead of the ones my mom made when I was younger—apricot chicken and mashed potatoes and southern biscuits. At least, I think I remember meals like that.

And then suddenly, I'm remembering more.

A time when my dad sat at the table, chuckling at something my brother said. When my mom refilled my glass and ruffled my hair and Holt kicked me under the table because he made Mom repeat a word that we both knew was slang for masturbation, but she certainly didn't.

Dishes clanging.

Demands to finish soggy salads.

Giggles when Holt farts at the table, because good God, nothing pissed off Mom more than mysterious, offensive smells.

And something beneath the table, brushing against my knee.

A dog?

Dad starts the car, finally.

"Did we ever have a dog?" I ask.

My dad turns slowly to look at me, and I know this was the wrong thing to bring up after admitting to being questioned by police for a second time, but I don't care.

"A dog," my dad repeats.

"Yeah, did we have one?"

Dad backs out of the driveway and starts down our streets. Pulls onto the business road off our neighborhood and shakes his head. "No, no dog."

I glance out the window, thinking.

"Are you, uh…are you feeling okay?" he ventures.

I nod.

"It's been a long time since I've seen you like this," he adds. His voice is cautious, his tone gentle.

"Like what?"

He bites the inside of his cheek. Shakes his head. "You just seem to be a little confused again lately, that's all. Do you think… Do you think you might want to go back and talk to Dr. Lange? It'd be tougher without insurance, but maybe we could—"

"No," I snap. "And I'm not confused. My girlfriend disappeared. That's enough to make anyone feel a little crazy."

"Okay, well." He hesitates. "So, bad segue here, but I want you to know the police can't access your medical files without your consent or a warrant. And no way are they getting a warrant when there's no proof of a crime." My dad clears his throat. "Your mom and I looked it up, so… If the police ask—"

"Dad, no," I say. They'll never ask because they have no reason to. I did nothing wrong. Now *or* then.

Dad tightens his hands on the wheel, nods like he understands how I'm feeling.

He doesn't, though, because he's never been accused of hurting the girl he loves.

"Your brother has been coming around a lot more often," he says. "Is he helping?"

I shrug.

He opens his mouth once like he wants to say something, and then shuts it. Waits a beat and tries again. "Look, son. You aren't going to like what I'm about to say, but have you ever wondered whether Molly leaving was a good thing? You seemed like you were getting a little…emotional…with her in your life. And you were doing so well before that."

I look at him in disbelief.

He rushes onward. "It's not that I didn't like Molly. It's that your happiness is our first priority. Your mother and I would do just about anything to keep you happy. Someday, when you're a parent, you'll understand—"

"I wasn't happy," I mutter.

"What's that?"

"I wasn't happy. I was the furthest thing from happy. But Molly, she made me feel that way. She gave me something to look forward to every day. She gave me someone to sit next to, to talk to. She believed I could do big things, and she saw me in a way no one else ever has." I sigh. "And she drove me crazy because she was so weird. And sometimes it was too much to handle. But I loved that about her, too."

My dad absorbs everything I say and remains quiet. Finally, he clears his throat and says, "Cobain, I have to ask you this. I wouldn't be a good father if I didn't." He swallows. "Do you know where Molly is?"

My head snaps toward him. "What?"

"If you said something to her, or maybe talked to her before she took off, or if you've had contact with her since she disappeared, you'd tell me, right?"

"Let me out of the car," I say.

"Cobain. Son." He grabs my shoulder. "I know you're a good kid. If you say you didn't play a part in this whole thing—"

"She left a note!" I roar too loudly. Way too loudly.

"Then why are the police still talking to you?" he counters.

"Stop the car, Dad." I don't like the sound of my voice, because the request sounds more like a threat. And this is my *father*.

My dad pulls over. "I'm sorry. I know you didn't do anything. I was just—"

I'm out of the car in a flash, walking, and then jogging, in the opposite direction. I glance back a few times and see my dad sitting in the car, his head hanging. Then he starts the engine and drives away, giving me space to breathe.

There at the end, he said something that twisted my gut into knots.

Your mother and I would do just about anything to keep you happy.

What exactly does that mean?

I can't shake this terrible sensation that everyone, including my own dad, is looking at me and wondering—

Did he hurt her?

Did he take her?

Does he know where she is?

I change course and start jogging toward Molly's house. I want to ask her mom about that letter. I want to see her face when I say her daughter's name. One way or another, I have to uncover the truth about Molly's disappearance. I have to find out what happened to her, even if it breaks the last piece of my blackened, shattered heart.

NOW

I march up the sidewalk to Molly's house, wondering if her mom is even home.

I'm still uneasy about the letter Molly mailed. And I can't get past that line she included—

My compass is broken.

I can't shake the feeling that her mom knows more than she told the police. What if Molly told her our plan? What if her mom did something terrible to Molly when faced with the possibility of losing the only thing left in her life?

Would she allow herself to be abandoned twice?

I raise my hand to knock, turning once to see who might be watching. Realize how shady this makes me look.

First, he took the daughter, they'll think.

Then he went back for the mother.

We always knew he was trouble.

A car catches my eye, parked a little way down the street. There's a man sitting inside.

He's watching me.

And I recognize him.

It's Molly's dad.

Why is he here?

I can't let him get away without finding out.

I turn back to the door. Take two substantial breaths. Close my eyes. Open them.

And start running.

I run toward the car, my muscles firing, my body a machine as I cover ground. The guy sees me hurtling toward him. Fumbles with the keys.

He glances up, his eyes huge.

"Stop," I say, running even faster.

The engine purrs to life, but it's too late. I'm too close. And I'm not letting him get away.

He starts to pull away from the curb.

I land on the hood of his car, my forehead pressed against the glass. The man flattens back against the seat, breathing hard. He's terrified. If he has any idea where Molly is, then he should be.

I tap my finger against the glass, point directly at his face.

"Get out of the car." My growl sounds terrifying, even to my own ears.

He shakes his head, goes to grab the steering wheel.

I leap off the hood of the car and reach through the open window. I grab the wheel and yank it toward the curb. "Just a little gas," I snarl. "*Now.*"

He raises his hands. "Okay, okay."

I stand in the street, blocking his exit, ready to throw myself in front of his vehicle should he try to flee. But he doesn't. He pulls toward the curb.

I'm there to reach inside and yank the keys out of the ignition.

I remember my size then. Remember it's a source of power. Why don't I use it more?

"Get out," I demand.

He opens the door and stands up. Slams it closed. He's wearing a sports coat and slacks. Brown shoes that shine. He's got circles beneath his eyes that I suspect never go away, no matter how much sleep he has. The man looks like a well-dressed cocaine slinger, not at all like the reverend from Molly's story.

I step closer to him, and he raises his hands. "What are you doing here? I know you know Molly's gone."

He shakes his head. "I'm just trying to do my job, man. I was going to talk to Molly's mom for a piece I'm writing, but she kicked me out. So I thought—"

"Your job?" I say. "What the hell are you talking about?"

He lowers his hands. "I'm a journalist from Florida. I'm running a story on the family."

"So…" I swim a hand through my hair. "So you're not her dad? When you were taking pictures of us at the restaurant… Molly said…"

"Her dad?" He releases a nervous laugh. "God, no. Her dad is…" He narrows his eyes at me. "How much do you know about her dad?"

He seems like he's digging for information from me now. "She told me about him."

"Oh, good, good. Hey, uh, think I could take you out for a meal? Or a cup of coffee? Or maybe get you…" He shrugs. Shakes his head. "A beer?"

"Why do you care so much about Molly's dad?" Anger fires through me. "Do you know what happened to Molly? Where she went?"

"As far away as she could get, I'd imagine," he says. "Especially once she saw me. I mean, someone was going to figure out where they went. I just happened to get a lead from a teacher at her new school. We went to college together, and he knew I was—"

"Wait." I hold up my hand to stop him. "What are you talking about? Molly's dad was an asshole that walked out on his family. Why would anyone be interested in that?"

A look of surprise, and then sympathy, washes over the guy's face.

"I'm going to back up," he says, gently. "I'm Nick Parco. I work for the *Miami Herald*. I haven't been there long, and I need to make a good impression, right, because newspapers don't exactly keep journalists around who aren't breaking major stories."

I sigh with impatience, and Nick waves his hands.

"Right, right," he says. "Anyway, I thought maybe I could figure out what happened to the wife and kid of Frank Manning."

"Manning?" I say.

"Yeah." He jabs his thumb toward Molly's house.

I think of how Molly and her mother are going by a different last name now—Bates. I wonder if it's Molly's mother's maiden name or if they changed it for a darker, more sinister reason. My stomach churns. I don't want any more mysteries. I want *answers*.

I don't want to show my ignorance, but I find myself asking, "Who is Frank Manning?"

"He's your…*girlfriend's?*…dad."

I nod to confirm Molly and I were dating. *Are* dating.

"Anyway, Frank Manning is the guy that swindled hundreds of people out of their life savings. You might have read about him?" He raises his eyebrows, but I have no idea what he's talking about.

"Right, kids don't read newspapers," he mutters. "Anyway, this guy who worked for Frank figured out that he was basically running a Ponzi scheme and threatened to tell. Most people would turn themselves in or flee the country. Or, I don't know, pay the guy off or something. But people close to Frank say he could talk someone into doing almost anything. So, basically, instead of quitting while he was ahead, he decided to convince this poor guy that he was depressed. He, like, I don't know, changed the chemistry in his brain. Made him question his marriage. His children. His career. Made him question why he was alive at all.

"So here's Frank playing the part of the helpful friend while this guy is getting closer and closer to taking his own life. And finally, he just does it. At the office. Just stands on his desk and offs himself."

The ground beneath my feet sways.

Molly lied to me.

Molly is not who I thought she was. Or maybe…maybe she's exactly who I suspected she was, and this is the reason why.

"Frank ended up going to prison anyway," he continues. "Someone else ratted him out once the police started sniffing around. He's there for thirty years. Course, that doesn't help any of the people who lost their money."

Nick looks at Molly's house. "These two were basically run out of town. Their possessions were seized, and their accounts were frozen. But people want someone on the outside to blame. And they've got questions. Like, did Frank's wife know how he was making the money? Did she hide any of it? How often does she talk to Frank now?" Nick shakes his head. "I can only imagine what that guy's doing to the other prisoners he's with. Or to the guards. He's probably building an empire on the inside." He shrugs. "He won't talk to me, but I thought maybe his wife would. That'd still be something."

I look at Molly's house, too, and sort through what this means. Do the police know that Molly Bates is really Molly Manning? They must. And what about all those people out there that lost their money, or their homes, or their children's college funds? Would some of them want revenge? How careful was Molly's mother when changing their names and covering their tracks?

My list of suspects just grew to hundreds of strangers. Maybe thousands.

How am I ever going to find her?

"So will you?" Nick asks.

I realize he's been talking, and I haven't heard a word he's said.

"What?" I ask.

"I was wondering if you wouldn't mind answering a few—"

"What do you think happened to her?" I ask suddenly.

"To Molly?" He thinks about this. "Sounds like she just took off. She probably knew someone had figured out where she and her mom were. But seems like some people think someone might have taken her. It's an interesting twist in the story."

I glare at him, and he shifts under my gaze.

"What's she like anyway?" he asks, and I can tell he's slipping into his fact-seeking role even now. "Is she like her dad?"

I pull in a deep breath. Release it. "Yeah," I say. "I think she probably is."

"Shit," he says, and shakes his head. "Well, if someone did take her, and she's anything like him, then I'm more afraid for the kidnapper than I am for her."

PART III

drain you

MOLLY

*H*e visited her three nights in a row.

　　　　Each time, he'd bang once against the door—
Sing.

And she'd stand, her white dress dirtied, and sing until her throat grew raw. Molly wasn't an exceptionally good singer. Quite the opposite, really. But what she lacked in talent, she made up for in emotion. That's who music was truly intended for—the passionate. Those with things to say which couldn't simply be said.

When she grew tired, she'd ask only one thing in return.

"Come again tomorrow?"

Blue would leave, taking the stairs slowly, and then she'd hear the door at the top of the stairs open and close. He was leaving more reluctantly, she noticed. Lingering longer. Watching her closer. She met his enthusiasm with her own. She sang louder, lifted her eyes higher, and once, when desperation struck her, she stretched her arm toward him when she reached a particularly intense part of a song. But it wasn't him she thought about when she sang. It was *him*. It was Cobain.

She'd recall the way he laughed when she told him she hated ketchup. How he brought her an origami book from the library when she'd said she wanted to try it. She remembered his socks, always mismatched, and his strength—something she craved now more than ever. She remembered his fingers inside of her. She remembered the beat of his heart beneath her hand.

Last night, Blue slipped his own gloved hand through the bars.

She crossed the room as she sang, one foot in front of the other, and slowly, slowly, her arm trembling, she lifted her fingers and touched his own. He held his hand there for only a moment before ripping it back. As if *she* were the monster here. As if *he* were the victim.

How close he was to the truth, she thought.

When Molly heard the door each night, she wondered if he would bring her something to eat. Her meals weren't regular, but he kept her fed, opening the slot in the door quickly, sometimes sliding a tray toward her, sometimes tossing a bag of chips or rolls onto the floor before slamming it closed.

She always thanked him for the food.

She always thought of shoving it down his throat and watching him change colors as he gasped for breath.

On the seventh day, he came down the stairs, and Molly whispered a silent prayer. He stopped at the bottom, hesitated, and then opened the door. He was dressed in the same heavy jacket, dark jeans, boots, and gloves. And that godforsaken mask.

Even beneath all that armor, she thought she recognized his mannerisms. Thought she recognized the way he moved. The way he laid his head on hers, however briefly, the night she hugged him.

She often wondered if Blue and the boy she left behind were one and the same. She wondered, too, whether she would want it to be him. If it were him, what did that say about the relationship they'd had? Even still, wouldn't she rather it be him than a stranger?

Blue lifted a package in his hand. It was wrapped in brown shipping paper, but it felt like a gift.

He started to move toward her but stopped halfway and dropped it on the floor. Looked away.

Molly stepped toward him and lowered herself to the ground. She kept her eyes on him, and though he was staring at the wall, she knew he watched her in his peripheral vision.

She took the package and brought it back to the bed. Laid it on her lap.

"May I open it?" she asked.

He huffed as if he were angry, but his body language told a different story. He was *nervous*. Molly felt a victorious thrill course through her. For days she'd endured being down here alone but for the brief moments she'd sung for him. It had felt like an eternity, but she'd taken it without complaint because she was playing the long game. And today, it seemed, her patience would be rewarded.

She slipped her finger beneath the tape and loosened the paper, unfolded it carefully, and exposed what lay inside.

Another dress.

This one in red with sleeves to the elbow.

Though she tried to hide her disappointment, she simply couldn't. Even as she smiled at him, as she thanked him, the tears threatened to spill from her eyes. She fought the reaction, but only because she remembered what her father said—

No one sympathizes with crying. Not really. What they sympathize with is someone trying not *to cry. A mother crying over her sick child isn't nearly as riveting as a father standing at a podium, asking for someone to find his baby girl, with tears in his eyes that he's fighting to hold back. That's what'll be repeated on newsreels. You understand the difference, Mockingbird?*

Blue watched her reaction and then turned sharply away. Stood in front of the wall and pressed his forehead against it. He released a frustrated snarl and then barreled toward her.

Molly dropped the package in fear and raised her hands, terrified he would strike her, or do what she'd been afraid he'd do from the moment he took her.

He grabbed her arm and hauled her toward the door.

"You're hurting me," she complained, but he only gripped her arm tighter and hauled her behind him up the stairs. "Stop! Please stop!"

He pulled her faster, and her feet stumbled on the stairs. Molly became intensely aware that what lay at the top of the stairs this time might not be a warm meal. She found herself fighting against him, convincing herself more and more that he intended to kill her. After all of this. After everything she'd done to try and win his trust, he would simply stab her through with a butcher knife. Or bring her to the top of the stairs only to throw her back down.

Blue dragged her through the door at the ground floor and turned left. She spotted another door. The *front* door. Her heart raced with hope, and she reminded herself to stay calm, though her body ignited with fear.

He pulled keys from his pocket, unlocked the door, and pushed it open.

Then he dragged her outside. Her feet were still bare, and she winced in pain as she stepped across the frosted ground, her steps fumbled because she was still being tugged along. It hit her then, what he would do. He was going to leave her outside. Maybe to die from the cold. Maybe to teach her a lesson that when he gave her a gift, the proper reaction was to rejoice, to sing his praises. Not to fight back tears of disappointment. She shivered from the unbearable cold and from fear.

She spotted a lake in the distance. Or maybe it was a pond.

Blue stopped short of it and all but shoved her ahead of him.

She turned to look at him, rubbing her arm.

He raised his arms to the sky as if to say, *Well?*

She turned her face heavenward and felt the warmth on her skin, cutting through the cold gusts of wind. The sun felt like being wrapped in blankets fresh from the dryer. It felt like the first moments in bed after a long day, your feet rubbing against timeworn sheets. It felt like the tickle of Cobain's jaw against her cheek when he'd forgotten to shave.

Molly turned to Blue.

"Thank you."

He glanced away.

Courage boiled inside her, and she said, firmly, "You hurt me."

It was important that she not tell him what to do. She knew he needed to feel as if he were in control. Before, on the stairs, she'd lost her head to fear, but now she knew better.

He tipped his head, seemed to look at her arm. Then looked down and away.

He understood.

For a fiery moment, Molly considered grabbing the closest stick she could find and seeing how far she could shove it into his throat. She'd delight over the sound of him choking on his own blood.

Revenge would come in time, she reminded herself, and turned her face to the sky once again.

"May I walk for a bit?" she asked.

He seemed to consider her request. Glanced around.

How close were the nearest neighbors?

When he nodded, her heart dropped.

Far, then.

She turned and led the way. As her toes turned blue, she moved closer to the body of water. Evergreen trees brushed her shoulders, and the smell of decay touched her nose. She sensed things she'd normally taken for granted. The tightening of her skin as goose bumps rose along her arms, and the way the very top of her head felt warm while her body continued to shiver. The feel of dirt rubbing between her toes. And the sounds. Oh God, how she loved hearing the sounds of the forest amplified. The nearby whistle of birds she'd only heard through her closed window. The sound of the water gently lapping at the shore. The sound of Blue's footsteps behind her, far enough away to give her space, but not so far that she could possibly escape him if she ran.

Is that why he'd dragged her upstairs before she could put on shoes?

Molly's mind raced as she neared the water. What if this was her only chance to escape? What if her plan to manipulate him into releasing her didn't work? What would she do then? No one would be looking for her after they received her letter. Running would be her only option. The question was when to do it. Now? NOW?!

She felt her blood kicking through her veins as her heart rate spiked. Adrenaline coursed through her body as she flipped back and forth between running, and sticking to the path she'd forged.

A clearing lay before them. She had to make a decision. She wouldn't be able to run once she left the camouflage the trees provided.

What would her mother do?

What would her father do?

Cobain, she thought to herself. *I'm so sorry.*

She ran.

Blue was after her in an instant.

She didn't veer left or right like she'd considered doing. Instead, she ran straight toward the water. It was fifty degrees outside, maybe forty, and it had snowed the night before. But she didn't hesitate. She ran faster, her feet thumping against the ground, her heart firing in her chest as she stretched her arms forward.

When her feet hit the water, it took everything she had not to leap backward. Instead, she rushed onward, head back, arms open—possessed.

When the water reached her waist, the sound of Blue's pursuit stopped. He wouldn't come in, she knew. He wouldn't risk losing his anonymity.

She laughed, manic, and drove her body farther into the water.

The water lapped at her breasts. Her shoulders. Her neck. And finally, it swallowed her head with a satisfied slurp.

She stayed beneath the water for only a moment. But in that moment, she pushed her arms and legs out and floated in the black abyss, a broken butterfly taking flight once more. Then she shot up and sucked in a breath. She filled her lungs until they ached, and then, slowly, she turned her eyes on Blue.

He watched her.

She could see the tension in every muscle in his body. And she knew it was because he wanted her to come back. So she did.

She took one step after another, her toes digging into the mud, the water dripping from her long hair. She held his gaze, firm.

He would be able to see beneath her dress, she knew.

Look at me, she thought. *Look at me, you fuck.*

Blue allowed himself a moment to gaze at every part of her before turning his head a fraction away.

For the first time, Molly was confused. Wasn't this what all men wanted? Wasn't sex what softened them? What made them break their vows and their spines?

When at last she stepped onto the shore, he looked back at her face. Seemed to note the way her teeth chattered.

"I had to feel the water," Molly said, shivering so hard she was afraid her bones might crack. "I haven't had a bath in—"

She stopped when she realized what he was doing.

Molly sucked in a breath as he pulled off his jacket and wrapped it around her shoulders. Gently, he touched her elbow, watched her face. Guided her toward the house with a touch so light that it bordered on an apology.

As they walked back in silence, Molly cast her eyes toward him. He may have confused her when he once again didn't take his chance to ogle her body, but she'd succeeded in her second agenda.

Molly now knew what he looked like beneath that jacket.

NOW

*N*ow that I know the truth about Molly's father, I'm more determined than ever to figure out where she went. And why she lied. Nixon said I should talk to Coach Miller, so that's what I'm going to do.

When Coach sees me standing outside his office, he makes a hard stop, seems to consider turning around.

"I need to talk to you," I say.

He frowns and then says, "All right, kid. Let's go inside."

I take a seat on the other side of his desk, and instead of sitting across from me, he plops down beside me. Removes his baseball cap and runs a hand through his hair. His eyes fall on the mess that clutters his workspace: scattered papers, spilled pens, a Steelers mug, and a photo of him with a toddler I know is his. I look at the kid, at his innocent, smiling face. He's raising one hand and grabbing his father's nose. And his dad, Coach Miller, is holding him with both arms. It'd be impossible for him to fall with so much support.

"You here to talk to me about Molly?" Coach Miller asks.

I narrow my eyes in surprise. And suspicion.

Coach sighs and leans forward, puts his forearms on his thighs. "I'm not judging, okay, kid? I don't know what was going on between the two of you."

He must register the confusion on my face, because he says, "Wait, that's why you came in here, right? The report?"

"What report?" I ask. "Someone told me I should talk to you about Molly."

Coach Miller shakes his head. "Aw, crap, kid. The thing is, there were too many people saying the same thing. I had to turn in what I'd heard. I'm not saying I—"

Unease crawls across my skin. "What were people saying?"

"Look, to me, you and Molly seemed pretty happy. I was glad when you found someone to talk to. To tell the truth, I hoped it might bring you into my office one day, so I could get you on the team." A little smile from him here. It doesn't last long. "Anyway, I started hearing from some of the kids that Molly wasn't entirely…happy, you know?"

"Wasn't happy about what?" I ask.

Coach Miller cocks his head.

"With me?" I ask, stupefied. "With us?"

Coach Miller leans back, and as a look of sympathy crosses his face, pulsing rage fires through me. How can I turn on him this quickly? This man who brought me a scone from his favorite coffee shop when I told him I'd never had one. This man who grabbed me by the shirt and told me, *Come on, kid. I'll drive you home, okay?* when he saw me sitting outside the gym, fuming because someone had taped a photo of a gorilla on my locker.

"Look, I have to ask, Cobain. Are you sure you were both totally in your relationship?"

"Yes." No hesitation.

He frowns. "Well, I think Molly might have been telling a different story to her friends. Some of the guys on my team, I guess she told them or their girlfriends or whatever that you were coming on a little strong."

"A little strong?"

"Like, maybe you were in it more than she was."

"She told people that?" What the hell?

He shrugs. "I think Molly was trying to find a way to break it to you gently."

The breath rips from my lungs. I think about the last time I saw her. Tears on her face. Me gripping her arms. Shaking her.

Did I shake her?

"I know when she talked to you, it hurt. It had to have. Am I right?"

I glance up at him, confused once again.

"Did you know I was married once?" He nods toward the picture of his kid. "He's pretty much the only good thing that came out of it. Anyway, when she told me she was leaving, I hung on too long. I even followed her to her new place one day. So I get it, okay? I get it. But I still had to put pen to paper on what these kids were saying."

"Wait," I say, hardly able to process this. "You're telling me… you're saying that Molly was telling people that she broke up with me and that I was…what…*stalking* her?"

Now it's Coach Miller's turn to look concerned. "Stalking? No. Do you feel like you were stalking her?"

"*No*," I say, too quickly. "No."

Coach Miller looks unconvinced. "I just wrote down what they said. That Molly didn't want to be together, and you were being pretty weird about it. That's all. You have to understand how this school works. If we don't report every single thing someone—"

I push up from my chair. The sound of it scraping against the floor startles us both. He rises to his feet, and now he's staring up at me with this concerned look on his face. But I wish hc wouldn't look at me like that. I wish he'd just hug me or some shit. I wish he'd say, *Hey, I believe you.*

"We were in love," I say.

He opens his mouth to respond, and I yell, "We *are* in love."

I turn around and kick the chair and then barrel through his door and race down the hallway. Toward the double doors. Out into a world that's blanketed in gray. It's always gray. Why isn't the sun ever out? Where did it *go*?

I turn in the direction of my house and start running. I run all the way there. Three point two miles—Coach Miller told me when he dropped me off that day. Three point two miles with sweat dripping down my back and down my face. My backpack slaps against my spine the whole way.

Thwomp, thwomp, thwomp, thwomp.

I run faster when I see Holt's truck in the driveway. I somehow knew he'd be here. It's Friday. He always comes on Fridays, if he comes at all.

I throw my backpack on the couch and power toward his room, shoving the door open. He's standing with his back to me, slipping something inside a shipping envelope. When I realize what it is, my entire body trembles.

He turns around. He's got my notebook safely inside that envelope. He's a few stamps shy of sliding it in a mail drop.

I wince against the knowledge of what this means.

First the police.

Then Nixon.

Then my dad.

Then Coach.

Now my brother.

They all suspect me.

I punch my brother in the stomach, and he doubles over.

"Stand up," I say between clenched teeth.

"I wasn't going to send it," he groans.

I scoff. "Liar. You have it in your hand right now, you asshole. What? Were you going to send it to the police?"

He straightens slowly, one hand over his stomach, the other still clutching the package. He pulls in two steadying breaths and says, "I don't know."

"You don't know," I repeat.

Holt opens his mouth like he's going to add something. Closes it. He hesitates too long.

I shove him, and he falls back onto the bed. He gets to his feet quickly, though. Quicker than I thought he could move.

"Fine. I was thinking about sending it. And you know why? Because it's weird," Holt says. "Your girlfriend takes off, leaves a note, and you keep this notebook with all these suspects."

"I told you why. And you"—I point at him—"you acted like you understood."

"I told you to stop obsessing, that's what I said."

"Why are you always here?" I ask suddenly. "You think I *need* you here?" I study him. "Yeah, you do. You think I need you here. Arrogant prick."

He glares at me. "Yeah, I *do* think you need me, asshole. That's why I'm here instead of having fun with my friends. That's why I'm here instead of going to class like my scholarship *requires* me to. You're my brother. I love you, damn it."

His words gut me. Fill me with guilt. But I'm too angry and too afraid for guilt.

I hit him.

A shot across the jaw that cracks his head backward and sends him flying across the room. He smashes into his old desk and hits his head on the side of his bed. I expect him to stay down. But I'm wrong.

Holt goes for my legs.

He knocks my knees out from under me, and I drop to the floor. Before I can push myself up, Holt gets in one shot. He hits me in the ear, and all around the world, bells toll, sending vibrations through my brain.

I lunge at Holt, and we roll across the ground. He punches me in the shoulder, and I pop him in the nose. Blood drips to the carpet, and I know the stain will never come out.

I hit him again and again and again until I register my mom screaming my name. A light switches on in the recesses of my mind.

"Stop, Cobain," she screams. "Stop!"

She grabs my shoulders and shakes me. Looks down at Holt and reaches for him. And even though I know I'm covered in scratches, too, she only turns her angry glare on me. "What happened here?"

I look at Holt. "Why don't you ask him?"

She glances at Holt and then back at me. "I'm asking you."

"I'm fucking out of here," Holt says, scrambling to his feet and wiping the blood from his face. "Way to be home for the one moment you aren't needed," he snarls at Mom.

"Holt," I yell as he stalks out of my room, because it's starting to hit me what I just did. He's my brother. My *brother*.

Mom ignores him and grabs me. "Why aren't you at school? Why are you fighting your brother? What is *wrong* with you?"

I shake my head. Softly at first, and then harder and harder. "I don't know," I say. "I don't know."

My voice breaks, and I have to stop talking. My mom holds on to my arms for a moment longer as I shake.

Please don't leave me.

Please don't leave me.

Tears slip down my cheeks, and I want to destroy what's left of this room. I hate that I can cry at all. I want to drain every drop of moisture from my body and shrivel to dust just to ensure no one ever sees that I am capable of feeling pain.

My mother looks at me with sympathy so deep I can taste

it in the back of my throat. Then she releases me, shakes her head, and says, "I have to go. I forgot my phone, but they're waiting on me. A new kid came in overnight, and I—

"Mom," I say, my voice barely above a whisper. "Mom, *please*."

She stops and stares at me for a moment that feels like it could change everything. A moment I didn't realize I needed until it stood between the two of us, holding my hand and holding hers. My mom looks at me for a second longer, and then her eyes flick from mine to the bedroom. "Clean this place up, okay? And get back to school. We'll talk about this when I get home."

She stops in the doorway. "Everything will be okay. I don't know what you were fighting about, but you'll work it out." Another pause. "Call me if you need me."

I nod.

I nod because this is what she needs from me.

She points to the room. "Clean. Then school."

"Okay, Mom."

She's gone then.

And Holt is gone.

And Molly is gone.

And I am gone, and I have nothing left to lose, so I might as well drown in this darkness that's right here at my feet, waiting with open arms.

THEN

I took you to my favorite spot.

I figured since you'd done the same for me, it was my turn to return the favor.

I love trains. Did I tell you that? I read a book once about a girl who ran away on one. The cover had purple flowers on the front, and though my brother gave me shit about it, I knew he would read it after I did.

Nerves gnawed at my stomach as we approached the tracks. I searched your face for any sign that you'd laugh at where I'd brought you. But you took my hand when you saw them and said, "This doesn't surprise me."

I was torn then. Happy because you knew me when few people did. Frustrated that I couldn't surprise you.

You seemed to sense this and said, "I wouldn't have taken you for the kind of guy to have a spot, though. You seem more like a weekend drifter."

"You don't know me as well as you think," I said, to complete the circle.

"Have you ever brought anyone else out here?" you asked,

stepping onto the tracks with your arms held out on either side to stay balanced. "Another girl?"

You smiled, but I heard the jealousy in your voice. What's more, your eyes flicked with anger. You, like me, hated experiencing emotions that made you vulnerable.

"Only my brother." I zipped up my leather jacket, something I'd stolen from a thrift store because I thought it made me look even bigger. I'd worn it to school expecting a note of envy in the other students' faces. Instead, a kid everyone called King because he only ever ate Burger King said I looked like a walking garbage bag and threw a paper ball down the back of my shirt.

I found him outside after school that day and beat the shit out of him. He never told anyone it was me that gave him those black eyes. Said he got in a fight and *man, you should see the other guy*. I let him have his lie and stared at the floor when I passed him in the hallway.

"You love your brother, huh?" you said, hopping off the tracks.

I shrugged and took your place between the rails, stepping from one tie to the next.

"You talk about him a lot," you said. "Maybe I should meet him."

"Okay," I said, but I didn't want you to meet him, because everyone preferred my brother over me—my dad, my mom, my teachers. What if you did, too?

"Rhana still won't talk to me," you said. "All I said was that I needed a little space. I mean, she wanted me to spend the night *every* night. Made me claustrophobic."

My heart lurched because I wondered then, *Do I make you claustrophobic?*

"No, you make me happy," you said, because you always knew what was in my brain. I liked it. No, actually, maybe I didn't. No, I did.

"Anyway, now she's pissed that I keep hanging out with Nixon. Guess she thinks I should sulk like she's doing, but whatever." As an afterthought, you said, "Last time I talked to her she wanted to show me her dad's canoe. Like, what are we going to do? Go canoeing? She's starting to make up excuses to be with me."

"Maybe she's in love with you," I said.

You made a face, but when you realized I wasn't joking, you said, "You think?"

You seemed to consider this, and for just a moment, a look of contemplation and a small smile lifted your face. Then you shook your head.

"Nah," you said. "She's just trying to avoid her parents."

"Aren't we all?"

You reached out and took my hand, and we walked like that for several minutes, me stepping over the ties and you stepping through the frozen grass. You had on yellow rain boots. I'll never forget those rain boots as long as I live.

I glanced over at you and saw how your face had fallen. "What is it?"

You shrugged.

"You're thinking about how to get out of here?" I said, because whenever talk of parents arose, you withdrew into yourself. I was reminded of that night beside the restaurant, when I promised you I'd get us out of here. Far, far away from this town and the shackles that bound us.

"I'm still saving money," I said quickly. But it wasn't coming fast enough. Because of school, I could only earn about a hundred and fifty bucks a week. I needed enough for a car. For gas. And we'd need motel money. And money for food and clothing and medicine and all the other crap Mom said we took for granted.

After I graduated I could work more, but could you wait six months, and then even more after that? Could I? If I were being honest, I'd admit that I was afraid you'd change your mind. Pick someone else to run away with you.

You *would* run. There was no doubt about that.

"It's okay," you said, but your voice sounded so broken that I wanted to rip the bones from my body and give them to you for strength. "I've been applying to places."

"Really?" I said, surprised.

"No luck yet, but I'm sure I'll get something soon."

And then what? I thought. Then we'd spend the rest of our lives stuck here, squirreling away what little money we had for a dream we'd never reach. Money would get sucked into places we hadn't anticipated. We'd fight, blame each other, and break up. You'd start dating a mechanic that talked about opening his own shop. I'd run into you, years later, see your swollen stomach and the tiredness on your face, and think, *That could be my child. That could be my tired face I kiss good night. But I was too chickenshit to take her away.*

"Maybe they'll promote you," you said, your spirits lifting. "You're the best employee Steel has. If you became like Duane, you could make more money. He's got that nice car, and he always has cash with him."

Be like Duane? Fucking Duane?

How do you know what his car looks like?

"The cash he leaves the club with?" I ask, unable to hide the venom in my voice. "That's just him making the deposits. Duane is an asshole."

"Is he really that—"

"He's an asshole," I repeat.

I stop walking, and you squeeze my hand. "He is pretty douchey."

I smile. "You have no idea."

Something flashes behind your eyes. I'm trying to figure out what it is when you raise your finger and point in the distance. "A train."

The look on your face is pure euphoria. There's something about seeing you like this—unguarded. Exhilarated. You tried so hard to hide your true self, but I saw you, Molly. If I was sad, then you were lying at the bottom of an ocean. But you smiled when you saw that train. And you smiled every time you saw me. And so I said something I had never said before—

"I love you, Molly."

My eyes enlarged, and my heart enlarged, and I watched, petrified, as you turned to look at me.

You didn't speak. But the train did, releasing a long, mournful wail as it sped closer.

I saw in your eyes what you were going to say before you ever said it, but it still gutted me all the same.

"You don't love me, Cobain," you said with a smile that covered your pain. "Now, get off those tracks and come kiss me."

I released your hand, and concern flashed across your face. "I *do* love you, Molly Bates."

You pursed your lips, glanced at the train that seemed to pick up its pace. "Seriously, get off the tracks."

"Tell me you understand what I'm saying," I insisted.

You shook your head. "What do you want me to say to that? You can't love me. We've known each other for two months."

"I knew from the moment I saw you." I looked at the train. It screamed as it sailed closer and closer. In the distance, I saw the shimmer of water on the tracks—a trick of light and metal.

"Cobain, get off the tracks."

You tried pushing me, but I planted my feet on either side of the rails. It was stupid, but I didn't care. I only cared that you knew how I felt. That you *accepted* that someone could truly love you. "Say you believe me."

Your voice broke. "No. No. Get off the tracks. Cobain, Jesus, please move!"

You were crying, tears spilling down your face. I said, "Is it that hard to believe?"

You shook your head. Looked at the train. Looked back at me and opened your beautiful mouth. "Fine. You love me. Get down!"

The conductor saw me on the tracks and pulled the horn. Once, twice, enough times so that it shook my brain inside my skull.

"Say it like you mean it," I demanded. "I love you. Tell me you understand. Make me *believe* you."

You tried to push me again, and again I stayed rooted in place. Your eyes darted to the train, and you howled and jumped on the tracks beside me, but I pushed you off them so easily.

The train roared toward me.

My heart roared toward you.

And you screamed, finally, with your arms thrown open wide and your face full of fear, "You love me. I believe you, Cobain. You love me!"

I stepped backward off the tracks and stumbled from the force of the train barreling by.

Above the sound of the train rumbling, I heard you shouting my name from the other side of the tracks.

When the last car passed between us, you searched the area until you found me. We stood across from each other. Your chest heaved. Mine did, too.

I took one step toward you.

I took another.

And then I was running. I leaped over the tracks and

grabbed you, but you were there to greet me with a cold slap across my face.

"How dare you?" you screamed.

"How dare I love you?" I said. "Because I do."

"Fuck you," you said, and hit me again. You started to walk away, and I watched you go, realizing I'd pushed you too far. I considered chasing after you. I stood there, wishing I could say something to make you turn around, but words were never my strong suit.

I turned to go, leaving my heart there on the tracks in case you came back for it.

I made it only a few feet before you called my name.

When I turned around, I saw you moving toward me. Slow at first, and then faster. I waited, empty chest aching, as you closed the distance between us. When your body crashed into mine, I grabbed you by the thighs. Hauled you into the air as you threw your legs around my waist. You pressed your lips to mine, and I felt the wetness on your cheeks.

I walked until your back pressed into the trunk of a tree. You grabbed me tighter, kissed me deeper, and I wondered if I'd stepped out of that train's path too late after all. If this were death I'd stepped into instead. If it was, I thought, I'd take it.

I trailed kisses down your neck and lightly bit your shoulder.

"I love you, Molly," I breathed into your hair.

"I know," you said, and kissed each of my eyes in turn, and then my ears, too. There was a difference in the way you touched me that day. Instead of passion and urgency, it was tenderness. And honesty.

"I'm going to get the money to get us away from here," I said. "We'll go to the beach. Or the mountains. Texas or Nevada. Whatever."

You unlocked your legs and slid down my body until those

yellow rain boots touched the ground. Your arms stayed locked around my middle, and you looked up at me with a question in your eyes.

"I'm going to steal it," I said, nodding. "I'm going to steal the money from Duane when he goes to make a deposit."

MOLLY

Blue came for Molly two days after he'd taken her outside. Moonlight invaded her small bathroom, telling her it was story time. Story time happened before bed but after dinner. She would sit at the foot of her bed and recount stories she'd read. She'd change words here and there to make them interesting.

Jack and the Giant Octopus

Cinderella vs. The Stepmother: A Battle of Wits & Magic

Three Sleeping Bears and A Little Girl Devoured by Envy

She wasn't very good at telling stories, but that's why she enjoyed doing it. It passed the time. And the time—those empty hours spent trapped between four barren walls—rattled her more than he did.

She was in the middle of a romance—a story about a prince who stood upon train tracks and declared his love as a dragon barreled toward him—when her door was unlocked.

Blue came toward her, and she noticed he had changed. His jeans were darker, his black boots polished. He wore the same jacket, but beneath it peeked a plum-colored shirt.

He strode toward her with a knife, and her heart lurched, though she should know better by now. Blue cut the restraints around her wrists, and she rubbed the skin there, though it wasn't sore. He was always careful, she noticed, to not secure them too tightly.

He motioned toward the box at the foot of her bed, which still held the red dress he'd brought days earlier.

"Want me to wear it?" she asked.

He stared at her until she pulled the material from the box and went into the bathroom. She hid behind the wall, since there was no door, and slipped the dirtied white dress up over her shoulders. The red one took its place.

When she reappeared, Blue looked at her for longer than he had in the other dresses. Then he flicked his blade toward the stairs. She walked in front of him, ready to slide the next piece of her plan into place. She had shown him that she wasn't going to run away at the first opportunity. She'd shown affection when he expected hostility. Now was the time to reveal the ace she held in her palm.

She came to the top of the stairs, and he reached past her and pointed to the right, toward the kitchen. She allowed her eyes to flick once in the opposite direction where the front door remained locked. Then she forced herself to go to the kitchen table. There lay two plates, two plastic cups, and two polished spoons.

She waited for him to tell her where to sit. He slapped his hand twice against one of the chairs, and she pulled it out, folded the dress beneath her, and sat down. She thought, as he moved toward the kitchen, of Cobain.

If her evenings were for stories and moonlight and the sweet relief of sleep, then the daylight was for thinking of him. Of what she had almost done to him. She remembered his lips on her throat, his gentle hands in her hair.

She remembered his hands losing their gentleness after she told him she didn't love him.

She had to squeeze her eyes shut against the memory. She had to still her heart that beat wildly for him. Once again, Molly found herself watching the way Blue moved. Trying to recall the wonderfully decadent details that made Cobain the first boy she ever truly...

No.

She had to stop, or she'd drown in despair.

Blue positioned himself behind the counter and started slicing carrots with his knife.

Her eyes glued themselves to that blade. She licked her lips. Was there anything she'd ever wanted more than to have that weapon in her hands?

Blue's eyes flicked up at her. Slowly, he retrieved the black device on the counter and raised it to his lips.

"Talk."

She startled at the sound of his distorted voice. It was the first time he'd spoken in days.

Molly glanced around the kitchen, trying to conjure some kind of conversation with her kidnapper. "I like the fireplace," she said. "I've always loved them."

He kept his gaze directed toward the carrots, and the steel pot boiling on the stove. He'd lowered the device, and she knew he wouldn't chance speaking without it, so she tried again.

"My parents took me to this campsite once. We stayed at this cabin that made us feel like pioneers. It was a lot like this. Odd, because it was so different from what I was used to. But charming, too." She smiled at a memory she'd suppressed. She rarely allowed herself to think of the quiet moments with her father. But even though she knew he was a criminal, while she was growing up, he had also been her dad.

"My dad...my dad went down to this stream to try and

fish. He thought just because he bought a pole that he could somehow summon the knowledge to use it. My dad was good at…people," she admitted. "But this was nature, you know? And he didn't have the patience for it."

She giggled, surprising herself.

Even Blue paused, looking up at her cautiously.

"He called me down there to try fishing because he wasn't having any luck. I was younger, probably only twelve or so, and there were all these geese down by the water. They'd been slowly moving closer to where he was. Out of curiosity, maybe, or because there was a nest nearby. I don't know.

"I was afraid to come over because I'd never been that close to geese before." Molly shook her head. "Anyway, my dad finally came up the hill and grabbed my hand and hauled me to where he was. I had to step over these little stones that crossed this stream to get to an island in the water. I went first, and my dad followed after me. This one goose got closer and closer to him, and my dad, trying to show me just how benign these animals were, waved an arm at it and said, 'Get out of here.'"

"When he turned around, the goose bit him right on the ass." She started laughing harder. All the fear she'd held inside these last several days exploded from her chest, and soon she was shaking with laughter. It poured from her body because it was better than crying. "No one made a fool of my father, but that goose sure did. The best part was how *mad* he was. God, if I could have taken that goose home as a pet, it wouldn't have wanted for anything."

Molly laughed again, and she thought she noticed Blue's stomach suck in, as if he was chuckling, too.

The muscles in his stomach relaxed, and she collected herself.

"They sound like good parents, huh?" she said. "But they weren't."

What was wrong with her? Why had she told him that?

Because she wouldn't be here forever, she reasoned. Because if she had anything to do with it, he wouldn't be, either. One of them would leave breathing and forget this ever happened. And the other…

"What are you making?" she asked.

Blue didn't move at first, as if he was contemplating responding at all. Finally, he raised a wooden spoon to show her it was stew.

"It smells good," Molly said.

Blue tossed the carrots into the pot and moved on to an onion, his eyes occasionally darting to an old, yellowing cookbook. Molly watched him with so many questions poised on her tongue. Why did he take her? Was he simply lonely, and would anyone do? Or was the reason more personal? He didn't seem to want to harm her. The dresses, the food, the singing—it seemed he valued her in some way, or was beginning to, at least. That could change, she knew. So as much as she wanted to ask, she silenced those thoughts and instead talked to him about her school and the things she wished she could be better at—dancing, painting…singing.

She thought she noticed Blue laugh at the last one.

She told him she never slept without socks at home (true), and that her favorite memory was one of her and her mom going to see a Broadway show (not true). He glanced up at her occasionally, and the tension began to leave her chest. For now, she was safe. But what would tonight bring? Or tomorrow?

She was telling him about the red piano she had as a child and wondering how she would execute the next part of her plan, when Blue released a garbled sound. He hunched over and hissed.

Molly stood up. "What? What is it?"

Blue slammed into the lower cabinets, stood up, and bent

at the waist again. He was clutching his hand, blood dripping scarlet-bright onto the floor.

"You cut yourself," she said, stupidly.

Blue released his hand, looked at it, and slipped to the floor.

She rounded the counter slowly, her pulse thumping inside her wrists.

He held his opposite hand out to stop her from coming any closer.

But she would not listen.

She took a step closer. Then another. He stood up, still clutching that hand to his stomach, watching her. His shoulders heaved, and blood dampened his shirt.

"It's really bad," she whispered.

She took a step back. Considered running. Running as fast as she could and not looking back. Would he catch her? If he was this injured, could he?

He could.

He kicked the lower cabinets and turned toward her as if reading her thoughts.

Those painted eyes snapped her back to the moment. He *expected* her to run. But Molly had plans for him that were much more sinister than merely escaping. Where would the fun be in that?

She closed the distance between them slowly, one foot in front of the other, and in the same moment, Blue saw what she was eyeing.

He didn't make a move for the knife.

He could catch her if she ran, but he most certainly couldn't get to the blade before she could.

Her hand spidered toward the weapon. She was toying with him, and he knew it. He backed away from her, his body colliding with the upper cabinets. The pot simmered behind him, meat bubbling in its black belly. The small blade wouldn't do enough damage to take him down before he reacted, but it would hurt plenty. That's all she wanted him to see—the threat of more pain.

Her hand hovered over the knife, and Blue pressed himself as far away from her as he could get. His chest heaved, his blood painted the floor, and Molly thought, *This could be it.*

Blue gasped as her hand darted past the knife and grabbed the paper towels instead. She pulled off several sheets and handed them to him. He considered her for a moment before jerking them away and pressing them to his injury. She saw the wound, then, and knew it'd do best with stitches. And also, that he would never get them.

Molly grabbed the knife, flipped the short blade toward herself, and offered him the handle. "Careful," she said, and it was everything she had to keep the smile off her face.

He jerked back. Then, when he realized the blade wasn't directed toward him, he reached out and snatched it away.

"Keep pressure on it," she said, walking back to her seat. "And keep it elevated."

Molly had grown up with the best of everything, and that included a doctor that made house calls to those rich enough to afford the luxury of skipping disease-filled waiting rooms. Every sniffle, headache, and bruise sent her mother running for the phone. Her favorite parts of the doctor's visits, because they were rarely needed, were asking him questions about the human body. About all those bloody, thumping parts that wormed together to make people operate.

He'd always humored her and gave her lollipops that tasted how Lysol smelled.

She waited while Blue sat down and got himself together. He was so quiet that she wondered, for a moment, if he had died. Could it be that easy?

But then she saw him. He stood up, fumbled once, and

leaned against the counter, staring at her. He held the towels to his hand and watched her and watched her, as if he were trying to figure her out.

She was not what he expected, she knew. And that was the point.

He took a step toward her, and Molly tensed. She had controlled the moment before, but now he was armed again. He was her keeper again. But that was always how this was going to go.

He took another step and reached out his left hand to lay the knife on the counter. Her eyes snapped to it as if it were a snake, rattling the tip of its tail, reminding you of its venom even as you backed away.

He walked toward her slowly, as she had done him, and then bent down, keeping his inky, painted eyes on hers. She tried to see past the mesh covering to the color of his irises, but he seemed to understand what she was doing and dropped his head.

Then he dropped to one knee.

Then the other.

Molly's mouth fell open as he stayed like that, kneeling next to her. What did he want from her? What should she do now? The gash in his hand was forgotten as he bowed his head and let his arms fall loose by his sides.

He made a strange sound and then bent at the waist. All Molly could think as she watched him fold into himself was that he seemed tired. So very tired.

She knew the feeling.

Gently, moving slower than seemed humanly possible, Blue turned his head sideways and laid it, softly, softly, on her lap.

She froze.

It was the first time he'd ever touched her in this way, and she had to play this very carefully. Her life depended on it.

She raised one trembling hand and placed it on his head.

He raised his arms and wrapped them around her legs, gripping her tighter than he ever had that knife.

She placed her other hand on the back of his neck and, after squeezing her eyes closed, said, "Shhhhhh. It's okay."

He wept.

She knew how hard he fought the reaction, but he released those tears anyway.

They stayed that way for a long time.

Her hands on him.

His hands on her.

And just like that, here was Molly's opportunity to unfold the next piece of her plan. She wet her lips, guarded her heart, and said, "You are so sad. So very sad."

He tightened his grip on her legs, and his head grew heavier.

Molly took a steadying breath and said, "You've been sad for such a long time. I can feel it seeping from every part of you."

She wasn't certain whether she was correct, but she suspected she was. It didn't matter. Daddy taught her how easily influenced people were. Tell them they seemed happy, and they brightened. Ask them what's wrong, and they searched themselves until they found an answer.

Studies show, Daddy said, *that people's moods alter to match what others see in them.*

The fingers on Molly's hand twitched as they crawled toward Blue's mask. Before she could convince herself to stop, she slipped those fingers beneath the mask and swam them through his hair.

She gasped at the feel of him.

At the soft locks gripped in her palm.

And though he jerked beneath her touch, he didn't pull away.

"Shhh," she said again as she stroked his hair. "Shhhh."

He held on to her as if she were the only thing in the world worth having. And as she gently soothed him, she reminded herself that she hated him. That she would, most certainly, kill him.

Then she reminded herself again.

Just to be safe.

NOW

I wait for Rhana in the parking lot.

I know what car she drives—a Ford Mustang, custom painted pink because that's the girl she is. Ten minutes before school starts, she shows with another student I'd seen around campus.

When the girl steps out and I see the flash of blond, my heart leaps. From this distance, the girl looks exactly like Molly.

Could it be? I think.

But of course it isn't her.

When Rhana spots me, I wave. She frowns and tells the girl she'll catch up with her later. The girl looks at me as she passes by, and my skin tightens as a chill rushes over me. Even her eyes are similar.

I watch her go before turning my gaze on Rhana.

"A replacement?" I ask.

Rhana grimaces. "What are you talking about?"

I shake my head. "Nothing."

Rhana pulls her bag up farther onto her shoulder and sighs. "What do you want, Cobain?"

"Do you know where Molly is?" I ask, cutting past the bullshit.

Rhana frowns. "You're asking *me* that question?"

"I am," I say. "I know you were jealous of her."

"Jealous? Of Molly?" Rhana releases a sharp laugh. "Look, you want to know what I really think? Who cares where she went? We're all better off with her gone. That chick was crazy."

I frown. "I thought you two were friends."

"Yeah, we were. And then I told her I didn't want to hang out anymore because she was always hiding crap from me. She's got, like…major issues, and I'm allergic to drama."

I shake my head because this isn't adding up. "Molly said she stopped hanging out with *you*."

Rhana looks past me at the school, like she's running out of patience. Or, maybe she wants to ensure we don't have an audience. "I'm sure she did. She said a lot of things. Mostly whatever got her what she wanted."

I look up and away, pretending that what she says next won't bother me either way. "What did she say about me?"

Rhana's face softens. "That you were nice. That you were infatuated." Rhana bites her lip. "And that you talked about money a lot."

"Money?"

Rhana rolls her hand. "How broke your parents were. How you wanted more money than you were making at the gym. How you were going to get rich no matter what. I don't know. She made it seem like it's all you ever talked about."

My teeth snap together, and I look down, utterly confused.

"Were you?" Rhana asks. "I mean, are you like that? I know your family probably doesn't have a lot, but I didn't…I don't know. I'm sorry about the things I said about you." Her voice lowers. "I'm sure she told you."

I scowl at her. Molly hadn't said anything, but of course

her friends were telling her to stay away from me. Still, it stings.

"After she broke up with you, I felt really bad about it. I kept wondering if it was because everyone talked crap about you. I mean, what if she really was happy and we made her think she wasn't?" Rhana dug her finger into her ear. "You seemed so weird afterward that I almost…I don't know."

I take a step back, my mind spinning around this information. Molly told Rhana she dumped me. She *lied*. My hand goes to my stomach, and I feel…almost sick. That's the third person that's said she broke up with me. But, of course, she didn't.

Right?

I clench my eyes shut. Open them. Do my damnedest to stay calm as I say, "Rhana, Molly and I never broke up."

Rhana narrows her eyes. "What are you talking about?"

"I mean, we were together up until the moment she left."

"Together, where?" Rhana pauses. "She said you'd never even been to her house. I mean, are you sure she *invited* you to hang out? You didn't just show up and—"

"Listen to me. Listen. We *never* broke up." I say it louder than I mean to. "We were in love. I think."

The last part is too quiet, and I see the doubt solidifying on Rhana's face. "I…I've got to go, Cobain. I'm sorry about Molly and whatever, but I've got to get to class."

"Rhana, wait." I grab her arm. It's a mistake.

Rhana tears away from me like I'm contaminated. Looks at me with big, accusatory eyes. Any trace of pity is gone from her gaze.

"Don't follow me," she snaps.

I watch her as she strides away and think about the things she said. She didn't like Molly as much as I believed. Molly hadn't fooled everyone like I thought, either. I think on Rhana's version of our relationship, too, but that's not what I dwell on most.

If Rhana had anything to do with Molly vanishing, then she'd be moronic to talk negatively about her. Rhana is cleared, in my mind. Which leaves few people to check out. And if none of them did it, I'll know Molly ran away.

That should make me feel relieved, considering the alternative. But instead, I feel mixed up. Jittery.

Like I need to run and never stop.

THEN

*Y*ou invited me to your house.

Your mom almost never left, but that day, she had somewhere to be.

We skipped school, remember? We were too excited to sit in class knowing what awaited us. So we took off. I'd never been more nervous in my life. I wasn't certain what would happen. But I knew what I *wanted* to happen. I knew I wanted you. All of you. And it seemed you wanted me, too.

We walked straight to your house, and you let me in like it was your name on that mortgage and not your mother's. You started to walk down the hallway to your room but held up a finger when I started to follow.

"Just…just wait in here for a minute, okay?"

I would have waited until there was gray in my hair. Until the end of time. I couldn't imagine waiting for anything better than what I figured you were doing—preparing for me.

When the door to your room opened, I straightened like a soldier. I was ready for you. Ready for anything you'd have me do.

You raised a long, slender finger and curled it toward yourself.

I'd never moved quicker in my entire life.

I entered your room in time to see you glide toward your bed, wearing a white nightgown that drove me to madness. When you turned, the smile on your face was shy, and I couldn't tell whether you put it there for my sake or if it was sincere.

You stopped in front of your mattress and said, "Come here." There was urgency in the way you spoke, in the way you moved as if you were afraid you'd back out of what you had in mind.

I was there before you could take another breath.

You wrapped your arms around my neck and pulled my mouth to yours with little warning. I kissed you, and my nerves melted away. I found my courage in the way you shook between my hands. In the uncertain glint in your eye.

You'd never done this before, I realized.

I would be your first.

I was afraid of how I would feel after this. Like you were mine. Like I had *made* you mine. That was wrong. Wrong, wrong, wrong.

But you felt so right.

You threaded your fingers through my hair, and I gripped your back tighter. Pulled you against me. Our bodies pressed together, filling each other's slopes and valleys. We didn't stay like that for long before you broke away from me.

You laid yourself on the bed like an offering. One I was supposed to unwrap and devour. I climbed on top of you, and you reached for my jeans. I had *those* words on my lips again, but I wouldn't speak them. I knew I shouldn't. Instead, I stood up and slipped out of my jeans, pulled off my shirt, and stared at you. Your hair fanned over the bed, so white it lit my heart on fire and sent those flames crawling across my skin.

You pulled up your nightgown, and I watched as, inch by inch, you exposed your knees, your thighs, your hips. I hooked my arms beneath yours and moved you farther up on the bed, then I climbed after you. You seemed so fragile beneath me. My body swallowed yours, and you disappeared under the armor I'd worked so hard to accumulate. Is that what you wanted? To disappear?

You weren't as fragile as you seemed that night.

I knew perfectly well that I was lying in bed with a viper.

I kissed you anyway. And I lifted that nightgown over your head and trailed my lips down the delicate skin on your neck. Then I took your tightened nipple into my mouth and nearly lost my mind to the moment. Felt myself pushing against you with impatience.

But you were the impatient one. Tugging on my boxers with anxious fingers. Digging your nails into my back. Wrapping your legs around my waist and inviting the thrust of my hips.

Once this was over, we wouldn't be the same. We would be bound. I wanted that so badly that every part of me ached. But that was the problem. You made dormant pieces of me spark to life, and it wasn't enough to connect our bodies.

I wanted to hear you say it.

I knew you felt it.

I reached down and slipped your underwear off, holding your ankle in my hand, and I guided one leg and then the other upward and then down. You watched me, and I could feel some part of you pushing its way out, its desperate arms stretched toward me. Time and again, you towed that part of yourself back inside. Gave me a false smile.

"I know you're scared," I said, breaking our vow of silence.

You shook your head, and that false smile widened. "I'm not."

"You're putting your body into this, but not your head. Why?"

You grabbed my face and stared intently into my eyes, but that only made it worse. I could see the lie so plainly. "I'm here."

"You're falling in love with me," I said, taking my boxers off. Keeping you beneath me. Hanging on to the hope that you'd admit what I needed to hear.

You closed your eyes and released a small gasp when you felt me, unclothed, uninhibited, pressing between your legs. We were so close, so close, and yet that unsaid thing hung between us.

I kissed the bottom lip of your open mouth, and then kissed your eyes, too. They opened beneath my touch.

I found your stare and said, "Listen to me."

"I'm listening," you whispered.

"I love you."

You smiled, but you were only placating me.

"I love the girl you hide inside. The one you're so afraid to show the world. Afraid because it would make you vulnerable." I pressed closer to you. Not enough. Not nearly enough. "I love the girl you show the world, too. The manipulation and the kindness. Your hard edges and your soft ones.

"I don't know if someone made you this way, or if you did this on your own." I shook my head. "It doesn't matter. I love you. I love your fucked-up pieces. Every last one of them."

I reached down and gathered myself. Put it against you and gave another small thrust. Almost there this time. Almost.

"Tell me, Molly," I said against your neck. "Tell me what I want to hear."

When you didn't respond, I lifted my head and searched your face.

"Be vulnerable. Just once."

Your bottom lip trembled. It belied the confidence in your gaze.

You pulled me tighter, opened your legs wider, and said, "I am."

But that's not what I meant, and you knew it. I wanted your body, but I wanted your mind, too. I wanted to strap on a headlight and explore every last part of you—the crevices in your brain and the lines of your body.

But you were holding me back.

Holding yourself back.

Getting up from the bed took a Herculean effort. My body wanted you more than it had ever wanted anything. More than it ever wanted food, or sleep, or sunlight. More than it wanted to grow and protect the raw, fragile interior parts of me.

But my brain wanted *you*. It wanted to know I was safe here. And right then, I wasn't.

You sat up and pulled a blanket over yourself. You must have felt exposed. But you couldn't possibly have felt as exposed as I did. I think my organs were showing.

"Cobain, wait," you said. "Wait, don't go. Don't be upset."

I turned to pull on my clothes.

I heard you rising from the bed. You were angry now. I could feel it radiating from your body. It warmed the room. Scorched the walls. Singed the hair on my arms.

"Don't walk out on me," you said, but I was already halfway to the door. You'd broken the bones of my rib cage to get at what lay inside. But you wouldn't do the same for me.

"I'm in pieces, Cobain," you said, your voice becoming hysterical. "You've ripped me to pieces. You think I wanted that? You think I wanted to come undone? I was barely holding on as it was."

I opened the door and turned back.

You were crying. I wanted to hold you in my arms and

protect you from anything or anyone that would hurt you this way again. But I was hurting, too.

"I want all of you, Molly," I said.

Your face changed from sadness and fear to anger. You were furious that I was doing this to you. That I was opening you up.

You ran toward me with that anger contorting your features. I opened my arms to you. Ready to still your turmoil or to push you away. I wasn't sure which. I just knew you were running and I was anticipating and the world was holding its breath because we were about to—

Crash.

NOW

*O*ur garage smells like mold, but it's my only refuge from the world, so I can't complain.

My dad is gone, repairing a ride at a carnival that will start touring come spring. My mother is still here, but she'll be on her way out soon, and I certainly don't want to rehash what happened between Holt and me. So I'm in hiding, with the garage door closed because it's too damn cold outside, using the bench press I carried home from a neighbor's house three blocks down. They'd thrown it by the curb—their trash, my sanctuary.

I slide a forty-five on one side, and a thirty-five and a ten on the other, because those are the only weights I have. With the bar, it's 135 pounds. I can do more, but this is enough to take the edge off.

I clamp the weights in place, remove my shirt, and throw it in the corner. The chill hits me, but I'll warm up soon enough. I lie down on the bench, and instantly, my brain settles on this task. It focuses on my hands gripping that cold bar. The feel of lifting the weights off the rack. The satisfying pressure on my chest and triceps.

I bring the bar down to my pecs and breathe my way back up, keeping my wrists locked, controlling my head so it doesn't press into the bench.

I bring the bar down again. And again.

In between reps, my mind betrays me. It's supposed to remain quiet. That's our arrangement. I provide the body fuel, and it repays me with blessed silence. But each time I get that bar back up, my mind asks a question.

Did Molly break up with me that afternoon we almost slept together?

Bar down.

Bar up.

Did I misread that last kiss before I left?

Bar down.

Bar up.

She never mentioned a breakup after that, did she?

Bar down.

Bar up.

What was it she said the next morning at school?

Bar down.

Bar up.

She said she belonged to me.

The stress of it all pushes down, down, down on my chest and throat until I feel like I can't breathe, until my vision grows blurry. I sit up, gasping, my lungs burning from the cold winter air. Clenching my eyes shut like I did that day with Molly in the forest, I slow my breaths.

Then I shoot to my feet and go back inside for a drink of water, trying to erase the sensation from my mind.

Trying to get ahold of myself, for fuck's sake.

MOLLY

Blue took to sleeping outside her room.

He did it on accident the first time, Molly decided, after she'd sung longer than she normally did. At first, she thought she was imagining the gentle sound of him breathing deeply. She kept singing, softer, as she crossed the room, her footsteps trepid, until she was able to see him through the slot he'd left open.

He slept on his side, his arms folded across his chest, his head resting on a stair. The mask he wore slipped up a fraction, and she spotted the stubble on his jawline. Her heart leaped at the color—black.

She knew the color of his hair now.

It was such a simple thing, but these pieces, they were everything. Especially those she discovered without his awareness.

The color of his hair didn't answer that ultimate question, but it got her closer.

She feared she knew what she would ultimately find beneath that mask.

Was she certain she wanted to know?

Yes. Yes, of course she was.

When he fell asleep outside her door a second time, she was certain it wasn't accidental. Blue hadn't seemed to hate her when he took her from that convenience store, she thought. The kidnapping didn't even seem to *be* about her, regardless of what the dusty dresses and wilting flowers suggested.

But whatever his reason was for taking her, it was changing.

It was daylight now, and Molly stretched toward her bathroom window, causing small bruises to bloom along her wrists. She was so close to the glass. Six inches. Maybe less. She did this several times a day. It kept her sane to attempt a quiet escape, even if she knew it was futile.

She curled her fingers toward the world beyond—toward that rectangular painting of blues and browns and snowfall whites. Her chin trembled as she thought of *him*. She remembered what she'd told Rhana about what had happened between her and Cobain, and how it split her heart into two irreparable pieces to do so.

She was a survivalist, and so she tried to forgive herself. All she'd wanted was freedom. Freedom from her father. And her mother. But the closer she got to Cobain, the further she tumbled into a cardboard box that held only her. Only him. Suddenly, she didn't want freedom if he wasn't a part of that new equation.

But was that really freedom?

She'd seen what she was doing to him, of course. He was unraveling. At first a quiet, lonely boy who kept his head down, and then, slowly, a man who fought for what he wanted. He'd had cracks, her Cobain. He'd filled them with mortar, but she… she had chiseled away at them until his entire body became unstable.

She dreamed of him every night now. And when she woke, she cried.

Her arms dropped to her sides, and she fought to keep herself contained. Her eyes lowered, and she stared at her wrists. At the tiny bubbles of blood rising beneath her bonds.

Molly heard the door unlock behind her, and she twirled around, hiding her arms behind her back.

Blue stood in her doorway, seeming more confident than he had in the past.

He walked toward her with powerful steps, but she didn't shrink away. She knew how he felt about her.

Blue cut the restraints and waved her toward the stairs.

When they arrived in the hallway, he opened his arms as if to say—left or right? Living room or kitchen?

Molly stepped to the left because she remembered that's where the front door was. He followed after her and stood in the doorway as she examined the room. A floral couch. An empty mantle. A coffee table. A lamp without a bulb. All of it suffocating under a blanket of dust. All of it devoid of life.

She turned to look at Blue, her head full of wishes.

He went to the front door and double-checked the lock, a bolt that would only open with a key. She was certain he did it only to show her she couldn't escape. He touched a flat hand to his chest and jabbed a thumb at the kitchen. His hand was still bandaged, but it didn't bleed through anymore. He hadn't cooked anything since his injury, and she hoped that changed today. Her stomach rumbled at the thought of a warm meal. A glass of milk. Normally, she didn't like milk. But the thought of it now, creamy and thick and cold in a tall glass, made her mouth water.

Molly started to follow him, knowing he would never leave her unattended. But he stopped and held another hand out. Waved it around the room.

Stay here, if you want.

Her jaw went slack as he left the room. Almost immediately,

she was searching the space again, looking for a way out. As the clanging of pots and pans colliding reached her ears, she rushed to the first window she saw and attempted to lift the glass. It was painted shut, and so she ran to the next window. And the next. Four in all, and none lifted so much as an inch. She couldn't break one, or he'd hear, so something else, then.

Her eyes snapped to the fireplace. Could she climb up it?

She began to cross the space in a frenzy when a *bang* sounded through the room.

Her heart soared into her throat as she whipped around, expecting to find Blue. But it seemed he was still engrossed in cooking. Molly went to the nearest window, looked out, and found the source of the sound she'd heard. Her eyes fell upon a bird on the ground, beak opening and closing. It flapped its wings vigorously at first, and then slower. And then not at all.

What window had it slammed into? Her eyes went to the door again, and this time she noticed the small rectangle of glass above it. The same size and shape as the one in the basement.

She took five quick steps toward the kitchen and listened.

What sounded like humming drifted from where he worked.

Molly raced toward the couch and shoved it across the floor, her pulse beating so hard she was afraid she'd faint. Would he ever bring her above ground again or take his eyes off her? She couldn't gamble losing this chance for a head start.

She leaped onto the couch and reached for the handle on the window and cranked the lever.

It opened.

Tears welled in her eyes, and her heart exploded with the possibility of escape. Maybe she wasn't her father after all. Maybe she could just leave and never look back. Tell the cops what happened like a good girl. Forgive. Forget.

Her true self scoffed even as she cranked the lever faster and faster. As she grabbed the edge of the window and lifted herself off the couch. Her feet pin-wheeled against the wall as she pushed herself higher.

She got her shoulders through. Then her chest. She could feel the cold. Could hear the birds.

She reached her stomach, and though she heard a noise behind her, she bit back a scream and struggled the rest of the way through. Fell headfirst toward the ground. She broke her fall with her hands, and pain rocketed up her arms.

Didn't matter.

She was on her feet.

Running, running, running.

How far did she get before that front door swung open? Ten steps? Twenty?

She glanced over her shoulder and saw him racing toward her, and instantly, she switched from a physical escape to a mental one.

She stopped in place and said, "I just wanted to help it."

She knew he wouldn't understand, wouldn't care.

He charged toward her, and she backed up, hands raised, stumbling over her own feet. Her back pressed into a tree, and he pressed against her. Invading her space. Invading her senses. He grabbed her wrists and pinned them against the grating bark.

She shook her head, and he reached up to take her face in his hand. For one terrifying moment, she thought he would lift his mask and kiss her. If he so much as leaned in, she would tear his eyes out. Even if he killed her, she would die inflicting as much pain on him as she could.

"I was trying—"

He released one of her arms and covered her lips with his finger.

Cautiously, Molly lifted her free hand and took his hand in her own. His head whipped toward the place where she touched him. "I wanted to help it. I didn't think you would let me outside."

His head tilted ever so slightly, as if trying to piece together what she was saying.

She released his hand and pointed toward the bird lying still beneath a window. "The bird. I wanted to help the bird."

She stared at him, afraid to say anything that would strain his belief any further.

He kept a firm grip on her wrist, dragged her toward the bird, and bent down.

She bent, too, and examined the tiny creature. One beady, black eye gazed up at her, and its tiny breast heaved with fear. "It's still alive," she exclaimed. "Can we help it?"

She hadn't meant what she'd said about escaping to help the bird. He must have known that. But the more she looked at that frightened thing lying in the dirt, the more she wanted to do something. She *needed* it to be okay.

Pensively, Molly reached out to take the bird into her hand. She touched one finger to its warm body, stroked its gray feathers, and went to pick it up. Blue grabbed her wrist and hauled her to her feet before she could.

He spun her toward him and shot a pointed look at the window over the door. Before she could say another word, Blue hauled her toward the cabin.

"No, wait," she said. "Let me take the bird."

He nudged her in the back to keep her moving, but the farther she got from the injured animal, the more hysterical she grew.

"I can help it," she said as they reached the stairs.

He grabbed his voice manipulator from a nearby table and nudged her onward, making it more than evident that he didn't believe her. That this was her punishment for leaving the confines of the cabin.

"Please bring it to me," she pleaded. "Blue, *please*."

He opened the door at the bottom of the stairs and pushed her inside. Then, with his entire body filling the doorway, he brought that black device to his lips. "It's going to die," he said, as if death didn't matter at all. As if it were as simple a thing as jam on bread.

"It's not," she contested. "It's not. I can keep it alive."

He shut the door. Locked it.

"It's not going to die," she screamed. "It's not going to die! It's not going to die!"

She beat her hands against the door until they grew numb. Until her legs collapsed beneath her and she could only hug her knees to her chest. Rocking. Back and forth, back and forth. Repeating those words.

"It's not going to die."

"It's not going to die."

And then, a simple change right before she fell into an agitated sleep on the floor.

"You're going to die."

THEN

*M*y world tilted the moment you walked in that front door.
I'd been waiting for you in the cafeteria, sitting two
seats down with your friends because I knew that's where
you'd go. You walked in, and it felt like the floor slid to the
right, like a boat hitting high tide. Like the table lurched across
the room and slammed into the wall. People went with those
tables, and Styrofoam trays of scrambled eggs and limp toast
fell to the floor.

The room went quiet as you strode forward, your eyes on
mine.

My scalp tingled with anticipation. Where did we stand
after last night? I didn't know. It made me sick not to know.

Your eyes darted toward the back of the school, and I
walked after you, hoping it was a subtle signal to follow along.
I imagined that with every step we took away from the dining
hall, the cafeteria righted itself a little bit more. Tables returned
to their proper places. Kids found their seats. And food returned
to plates, tasting exactly the same as it had moments earlier.

You let the doors to the morning air close behind us, and

then you kissed me.

I'd never felt such relief in my entire eighteen years on this planet.

"I'm sorry," you said.

"Me, too," I replied.

"You have to understand. My heart…" You touched that place between your breasts. "It's my compass. It can't guide me if it's distracted." You reached up and touched my face. "Do you understand?"

I wasn't sure I did, but I found myself nodding along.

You smiled and scratched the stubble on my jawline. "I belong to you. I am yours."

Something in your gaze flickered as soon as those words left your mouth. Like you wanted them back. But no way would I give them to you.

"Cobain, listen," you said.

But I didn't want to hear it. I was too afraid of what you'd say. Too worried you'd reclaim what you'd just said. Because you would do something like that, Molly. You would chase *I belong to you* with *But I belong to everyone else, too.*

And I couldn't hear it. I'd scared you last night, or maybe you'd scared yourself. Either way, I couldn't handle the repercussions.

The bell rang, and my body buzzed at the chance to escape.

"I can't be late again," I said. "Mr. Freedman will have my ass."

I turned and walked away from you. Didn't even look back.

Maybe by the time we saw each other again, I reasoned, you would have moved past last night. I'd say something like, "Let's just move past this, all right? Let's go to the park and make up stories about the little kids. Pick which ones will become veterinarians, and which ones will become serial killers."

And you'd say, "I get the good swing."

And I'd say, "You always get the good swing."

And you'd say, "I love you, too, Cobain. I don't know why I haven't said it before."

I'd take your hand, and you'd take mine, and I'd make you repeat what you said about being mine.

NOW

*D*uane's apartment complex is everything I remember it being.

A lima bean shaped pool sits between the buildings, and people stand around it with drinks in their hands as music throbs from the speakers. It's the middle of winter, and yet these people want so badly to be seen. They need to be seen.

And I need safe passage to Duane's front door.

I pull my hoodie over my head and stuff my hands into my pockets. Keep my shoulders hunched as I stride up the stairs. Large metal numbers scream from the doors, and I can still smell the fumes from the freshly painted brick. This complex is a mirage, two stories of outdated living arrangements neatly orchestrated to appear trendy. But it's as fake as the people living in it.

I knock once on Duane's door and wait, recalling the time Molly and I came here for a party—her idea, not mine—and how we both left early, smelling like weed and Funyuns and laughing so hard we nearly rolled down the stairs.

When no one opens up, I glance around and knock harder.

I'm peeking through the blinds when the door swings open. A deeply tanned guy steps out, pulling a T-shirt down over impressive abs. I kind of want to ask him where he works out.

"What's up?" he says.

Behind him, another guy asks who it is. The voice doesn't belong to Duane.

The guy at the door evaluates me. "No one," he says over his shoulder.

"I'm looking for Duane," I say. "He home?"

Confusion knits his brows together, and he shakes his head. "There's no Duane here, but I get some of his mail sometimes. I think he moved."

"When?"

The guy frowns. "I don't know, man. Can I help you?"

"Charlie?" the guy inside says.

"No, I'm cool," I respond.

"If you say so." He closes the door.

I walk the two and a half miles to Steel, unsure what I'm planning to do when I arrive, since Chad told me that if I stepped foot on his property again, he'd sue me. But I have to know. If Duane is gone, and Molly is gone…

My vision blurs with fury just imagining it.

I wait along the street, hidden by a row of cars, and glance over as gym patrons come and go. I find myself evaluating their physiques. Coming up with workout plans for their body types. I decide I should focus on myself, and I start going through what I need to do next time I find myself at the school gym. Can I chance going in there again after everything with Nixon and Jet and Coach?

I run my hands through my hair and tug. I'm slowly losing everything I care about, and I didn't have that much to begin with.

After an hour of pacing, the sun begins to set, and I finally see what I'm looking for. A girl walks out wearing a maroon collared shirt and khaki shorts. She's removing her name tag and striding toward her car. She's got her keys jammed between her fingers the way Molly used to do. The girl looks to her left and her right, just waiting to use those keys as a weapon if she must.

I step out in front of her. "Hey."

She brings her hand up a fraction of an inch.

I raise my own hands. "Sorry, didn't mean to startle you."

Her eyes narrow. She's young, but older than me. Of course, I'm bigger.

Why does that matter?

"I was wondering if Duane still works here?"

The girl unlocks her car. A lock of dark hair falls along her cheek. She's got big eyes. Nice big eyes. "Not sure. You can go and talk to Chad inside. He's the manager."

She's nervous around me, and I wonder why. Am I really so threatening? Everyone seems to think I am lately.

"I used to work here," I offer.

This seems to settle her nerves. She smiles. I like her smile. But it isn't Molly's smile. "Oh, really?" she says. "I just started. It's pretty cool. I get to work out for free, and Chad lets me take as long as I want for lunch."

"But you don't know Duane?" I ask.

She hesitates, and I see that she knows more than she initially let on.

"We're friends," I push. "But I haven't seen him in a while."

What would Molly do?

I frown. Run a hand through my hair. "I'm kind of worried. The two of us were more than friends, if I'm being honest."

Molly would be proud.

"Oh, okay. Well." The girl looks back at the gym. It's gotten darker, and those metallic letters are now backlit in blue. I can hear the music from out here. It's subtle, but it makes my muscles ache with the need to move. She makes a face like she's telling me something she shouldn't. "I think he took off. Went to Thailand. I guess he didn't put in his notice, so Chad was pretty pissed about it. That's what this guy Aaron told me, anyway."

"When?" I ask, stepping toward her. "When did he take off?"

My entire body tenses, awaiting her response. Calculating how long Molly's been gone.

She scrunches up her face. "Uh, right before I got hired. So…a week ago? I think he called Chad collect from Thailand, but Chad wouldn't accept the charges."

I have to laugh then, because only Duane would first skip town without word and then try to call collect from another freaking country.

"Did you…did you want to come back to work at Steel?" the girl ventures. "Like I said, I haven't been there long, but I could—"

"No," I say. "No, that's okay. But maybe don't tell Chad you saw me."

The concern rushes back to her eyes. "Okay. Hey, sorry, I've got to run. Sorry about you and Duane. You're better off, if what Aaron tells me is true."

I watch as she gets into her car and drives away. She glances back once to see if I'm still there.

I almost wave.

After she'd gone, my eyes flick to that glowing *Steel* sign. I think about what she said. That Duane left town long after Molly did. I have serious doubts that Molly went to Thailand. Whether she sent that letter to her mom herself, or someone else did, in the end it was mailed inside the U.S. So, no, I don't think Duane has any idea where Molly is. He probably doesn't even know she's missing.

It hits me, then, just how absurd it would have been if he

had. I mean, why did I even suspect him of anything at all? Because he thought my girlfriend was attractive?

What about Jet? Because she embarrassed him?

And Nixon? Because he was male and her friend?

Rhana? Because I thought she was jealous of Molly?

Her mom? Because she smothered her daughter?

My brother? Because he asked about her?

The reporter? Because he took a photo of us?

I've pointed fingers in as many directions as I could to avoid the inevitable. That maybe, just maybe, Molly really did just leave me. Maybe, in the end, Molly only did what she did because she is everything that reporter insinuated she was. Unpredictable. Manipulative.

Just like her father.

The other alternative is that she was taken. But my list of suspects has shriveled to exactly zero, and I'm no closer to finding out what happened to my girlfriend.

It just doesn't make sense.

Nothing makes sense!

Except, that is, the line from her letter.

My compass is broken.

I finally remember how she referred to her heart as her compass.

So her heart is broken, is it?

An answer, at long last.

But it's an answer that leads to yet another question—

Am I the one who broke it?

MOLLY

*H*e brought her the bird.

It lived after all, and so he placed it inside a small rusted cage and hung it from the ceiling. Molly could hardly sleep at night since its arrival. She feared it would disappear when she wasn't looking.

She loved the bird, but it hurt her to see it. To be reminded of the outside. Of beautiful things, and unexpected things. She had to escape. She could no longer be patient. And so when he brought her another dress—this one with plastic flower buttons—she asked him a single question.

"Can we spend the night together?"

He'd been watching the bird, but he turned to look at her when she asked this. He didn't respond, and so she asked a different way.

"I've missed singing to you," she said. "You haven't come to me in several nights."

He looked up at the bird as if saying she had plenty of company.

"It's not the same," she said in a rush when he moved

toward the door. "I need human companionship. I know you understand that."

He stopped in the doorway and kicked the door open a little wider with his boot. An invitation.

"Blue," she said when he started to go up the stairs without her.

He turned around, impatient, and then remembered her bound wrists. He came toward her with his knife to cut them. She wondered how much more of the unbreakable plastic rope he had. An infinite amount, she decided. Enough to lasso the moon. To pull it toward him and bind it so that no light shone from the heavens at night.

He reached up to cut the ties, and she pressed against him. Blue grew still. As soon as her arm was free, she wrapped it around him. Hugged their bodies close.

She knew it was no longer a gamble.

He wouldn't touch her.

He seemed to fight for breath before reaching up to cut her other bond. She threw that arm around him too and breathed *thank you* into his broad chest. Then, just as quickly, she released his torso, went to the bathroom, and slipped on her new dress. She passed him by once she had it on, knowing he watched every step she took, and walked ahead of him and out the door. She climbed the stairs with confidence, her purple dress cascading over the steps as she rose higher and higher, a velvet moon in her own right.

When they arrived at the top of the stairs, she went to the thing she remembered seeing—a record player in the living room, with stacks of vinyl beneath it. She crouched down to take one, but Blue grabbed her wrist.

These meant something to him, she realized.

"It's okay," she said, because she had to make progress. And she needed to set the stage.

Don't ever try and sway someone without first tending to ambiance, Mockingbird. Don't simply ask for what you want. Sweep them away into a production of your own creation.

He released her and backed away. As she pulled the record from its sleeve and placed it on the turntable—fumbling over how to get it started—she noticed the window over the door had been boarded over. Her stomach churned as she remembered what was at stake.

He watched her as "House of the Rising Sun" began to play, and she sat on the couch, sweeping her dress beneath her. Unsure what to do with himself, he leaned against the wall opposite her. Folded his arms across his chest.

Blue glanced toward the kitchen, and she knew he was thinking of cooking something. That was his default when things grew tense. It kept his hands busy.

But Molly had other uses for those hands tonight.

"I had a friend once," she said, and Blue looked back to her. "A *real* friend. She used to come to my window at night, and I'd crawl out to meet her. We'd go anywhere. Everywhere. It would be so quiet. When I was with her, it felt like everything that was happening at my house slipped away. We didn't go to the same school. We didn't even live in the same neighborhood. She would ride her bike three miles to come see me at night."

Blue watched her closely, not uttering a single word. Though he always wore that wretched mask, she tried to imagine his face. Wondered if he wet his lips. Or chewed the inside of his cheek or furrowed his brow.

"I met her at the park, mostly because my dad hated the park. He always said it was a place the rich paid for and the poor overused. But I loved it." She smiled, sadness twisting her bones. "And I think I loved her, too."

Blue slid down the wall until his legs were held protectively in front of his body. He rested his forearms on his knees and kept his eyes on her.

"One day, she told me she'd be gone soon. I thought she meant her family was moving." Molly shook her head. "We lay side by side beneath this perfect night sky, and I stared at the stars, and I thought, 'If she leaves, I'll kill myself. I can't exist without her.' I kissed her then, thinking that's what she wanted. But she knew I was doing that for her sake."

She dropped her head and fought to regain her composure. She took three deep breaths, and when she raised her head again, the record was ready to change sides. She rose and strode across the room as if she'd lived in this home her entire life and knew the exact places the boards would creak beneath her feet.

She turned the record, and her eyes fell on the floor.

Then they fell on Blue.

Swallowing, she walked toward him. Stopped before him as he looked up at her. She held out her hand. He recoiled, and then seemed to realize what she was offering. He shook his head.

"You brought me here against my will," she said with unintended ferociousness. "And now you refuse to touch me?"

He stared at her face, and then looked back at her hand.

And he took it.

She helped pull him to his feet, imagined shoving him back down when he was halfway up. Imagined crashing her heel into his nose a thousand times until that mask was impaled through his skull.

She smiled at him.

She stretched his hand out to the right, and when he didn't make a move to do it himself, she placed his left lightly on her hip. The music played, and with his body stiff, awkward, Molly led their feet across the floor.

As one song led to another, Molly struggled to find the words to say what needed to be said. Finally, as she worked through these things in her mind, Blue found the courage to move his hand a little farther around her waist, and to pull her an almost imperceptible distance closer.

Now, she thought to herself.

Molly stepped toward him and bit back bile as she laid her head on his shoulder. He flinched but didn't pull away. The music played, and the room tilted, and his hands burned holes through her skin.

She raised her mouth to his ear, and she said, "I know why you brought me here."

His feet slowed, but she pushed against him, led him into another turn about the room, and he followed her like the clouds chasing the sun across an ever-blue sky.

"The sadness you're feeling fills this house. I'm drowning in it."

He tensed, but she only danced closer.

"I know what you want to do," she said, filling his head. Infiltrating his mind. "But you're afraid to leap. And you don't want to leap alone."

Blue pulled back and watched her face.

"You wanted someone who could care for you," she stated. "And when the time comes, you wanted someone strong enough to not back out."

Molly wrapped a hand around the back of his head. Touched her lips to the plastic where his ear lay, tasted the chemicals on her tongue. "I don't want to be the one to kill you," she said. "But I know it's what you want."

He struggled against her. But not hard enough.

"You want release," she continued, pressing their heads together. "And I will give it to you. Just not quite yet."

His hands relaxed on her as he took in what she was saying. What she was injecting, like a vial of poison, straight into his bulging, blue vein.

"Not yet, Blue," she whispered, and swayed with him and swayed with him. "But soon."

She could almost feel him soaking up her words. Making them his own to have and to hold. It would take him time to accept his fate as one of his own invention, and so she knew to give him time.

Slowly, his hands tightened around her. And as the music played, he allowed himself to bend his head toward her shoulder. She felt his back quivering with emotion, and a smile flashed across her face.

But as he held her closer, and closer, and the emotion overtook his body, her smile dropped away. His sadness seeped into her, and she felt her own despair—despair she'd carried her whole life—reach out to embrace his own.

She found herself holding Blue differently.

Almost immediately, she recognized what was happening to her. She'd been trapped here too long. Had only this person for company. This person who listened to her. Who cooked for her. Who brought her birds to sing away the loneliness. This person who scared her. And feared her.

She knew what it was called when, in order to survive the mental turmoil, a victim forgave the fact that they'd been taken captive.

That's what this was, she told herself.

It wasn't because she was so royally fucked up by her father that she craved real emotion, regardless of the delivery.

Blue held her tight.

And Molly held him tighter still.

And the two danced long after the music ended.

NOW

"Thanks for coming in, Cobain," Detective Hernandez says. "Didn't really seem like you gave me much of a choice," I snap, tiring of these meetings. "Have you figured out what happened to Molly?"

"That's what I'd like to talk to you about."

I lean back, hoping beyond measure that they're about to give me a name or an address. Something that will tell me they've finally figured out where she is and that she's safe. And that they're *this close* to bringing her home. Is that too much to ask?

"What happened at the party the night before Molly disappeared?" she asks me.

I freeze.

I mean, I fucking *freeze*.

She already knows the answer.

I hesitate too long, and then want to punch myself in the face when I blurt, "I wouldn't know. I wasn't there."

I fidget under her stare because if she finds out I just lied, this won't look good. But it was just a fight. A bigger fight than we had at Molly's house that day we skipped school, sure. But a fight all the same. I try to appear confident.

She smiles. "I have no fewer than six witnesses who tell us differently."

I clench my hands into fists beneath the table and keep my mouth shut.

The detective studies my face. Dissects my reaction. "One of those same witnesses informed us that you and Molly were engaged in quite the heated argument."

Fucking Nixon.

She nearly smiles. I can see how badly she wants to. Clearly, she knows I've figured out who she's talking about.

"We called him to ensure he didn't have anything else he cared to share." She shrugs one shoulder. "Just covering bases, of course."

She leans forward, her fingers splayed across a facedown piece of white paper. "I can understand how upset you were. Molly had just broken up with you. Maybe you saw her with another person that night. Must have been hard to see your ex-girlfriend there, having a good time, and you weren't the one with her."

My mind clicks on trees in a forest, growing too tall, too thick. Crowding each other for space to breathe.

I clench my eyes against the image as a storm of denial floods my system. Even now—even with all these eyes on me, with all these fingers ready to point me out in a lineup—even then, it's impossible to accept that I did something to my own girlfriend, one of the only people to ever truly see me.

I know I shouldn't say it.

I know they won't believe it.

And yet I find myself throwing a Hail Mary anyway.

"Molly and I weren't broken up," I say.

Too loudly, and without enough confidence.

Glances are exchanged. Lips press together.

Detective Hernandez opens the red bag.

Inside is a phone. I've seen it before, I think.

"Recognize this phone?" she asks.

I shrug.

"It's Molly's best friend's phone. Rhana?"

I shake my head because I already I know what's coming. All I had were the words from Coach and Rhana, but I'm about to see the physical proof. And it won't look good for me.

In a desperate effort to deflect the pain of what's about to happen, and how it will make me look, I say, "Do you know Molly's father is in jail? He took money from people and talked this guy into killing himself. Have you guys looked into him?"

The detectives share another glance.

"We're not at liberty to discuss the details of the case with you. Let's concentrate on the questions we have for you today."

It isn't so much what they say as it is the looks on their faces. They already know about Molly's dad. They know, they've looked into it, and they've ruled out him being tied to Molly's disappearance.

But then, who does that leave?

The possible answer to that question makes me feel sick.

Detective Hernandez turns the phone on, taps until she finds what she's looking for, and turns it toward me.

My heart jackhammers in my chest, and my palms start to sweat.

Molly's name is at the top of the text exchange, and on the left side, in green, is a message bubble from Molly—

I broke up with Cobain last night.

Went horribly. I think he pretty much hates me now.

My face scrunches with pain. I'm not sure I believed Rhana when she told me. I'm not sure I believed Coach Miller, either. But there's no denying it now. Molly told Rhana—she told *everyone*—that we broke up. That little green bubble feels like a sucker punch to the jaw. The solidity of it rocks the ground beneath my feet. Because Rhana's words are one thing, but seeing Molly's is another.

"Perhaps…" Detective Hernandez ventures, "you truly *don't* remember what happened to Molly. But maybe you have pieces. Pieces we can work with."

Because she thinks I'm crazy. They all do. That's what she doesn't add.

Is this why my father told me about the medical records? What do they already know?

Maybe to try one last time to convince them, myself, *everybody*—like a man with his toes at the precipice of madness trying to keep his balance—I say, "I didn't hurt Molly. I *was* at the party, and Molly and I had an argument, but that doesn't mean I hurt her. No matter what any of your witnesses said. And whatever she told Rhana doesn't mean anything, either, because she was with me that night of her own free will. She wanted to be with me. And I wanted to be with her. And if you did even an ounce of digging into who Molly is, you'd know she'd weave a thousand different stories for a thousand different people." *Even me.*

A shard of pain rips through my chest. But it's the truth.

I suck in a deep breath, press my back against the chair, and raise my head. "I didn't hurt Molly. No matter what you say, no matter what you show me, I'll keep telling you what I know in my gut. I wouldn't have hurt Molly. I *loved* her."

Detective Hernandez tilts her head to the side and stares at me, and I stare right back. When it's clear she isn't buying what I've just said, I stand up. "I'm leaving now, and I'm not coming back again. I don't know why I agreed to come this time."

"No one forced you here," she says. "This time."

There's no mistaking the threat. I stand there, shaking with anger. And fear. Terrified that they're a breath away from locking me behind bars and leaving the real criminal—if there even is one—out there.

Detective Tehrani is the one who says, finally, "Go on, then."

I spin on my heel to leave, but Detective Hernandez's voice rings out after me.

"I think it's time you get that lawyer, Cobain."

My dad is standing in the lobby when I get there. He's yelling at the lady at the front desk about parental rights and lawyers, and she's explaining that I came voluntarily, that I haven't been arrested, and he's saying, *Well, he won't be coming* voluntarily *again, and, by the way, my wife and I won't be answering any of your goddamned questions, either, so stop calling.*

How in the hell did he know to find me here?

"Dad, Dad," I say, grabbing his arm. "It's okay. Let's go."

My dad frowns and points at the lady. "I'll be back."

He walks me all the way to the car without a word, because his anger already found a target inside that station. I wish he'd say something to me. *Anything.* His silence allows Detective Hernandez's words to ring through my skull.

Lawyer.

Lawyer.

Time to get that lawyer.

THEN

Something ugly lingered between us.

I knew what I needed to do to bring us closer again, so I grabbed my bag and shoved in a pair of gloves and a mask. It must have been from Halloween, that mask, hidden in a box in our garage.

I grabbed something else, too. Something shiny and glittery and empowering. Something that should have been used to make meals for four in a quiet kitchen. Instead, I slipped it into my bag for another purpose.

My dad was in the living room as I headed toward the door. He stood in front of the window staring outside like he just remembered there was an entire world beyond caramel corn and buzzing rides.

"Taking the car?" he asked when he saw me.

"If it's all right."

"Sure. But be back soon, okay? Your mom will be home for dinner."

He said it with such optimism. As if my mother's presence at the dinner table was the start of something new, something better.

"Sure," I said.

And then I left with my mother's knife.

A knife I planned to use.

I hopped in the car and pulled out of the driveway. My knuckles whitened as I gripped the steering wheel and drove to Steel and then parked down the street. I knew Duane would be coming out soon.

When he appeared carrying the bag, I readied myself. Chad was an idiot for allowing Duane to drop the money at the bank. He should have paid for a pickup service, but that would have cut into his bottom line, and his only aspiration in life was for the owner to pat him on the back and invite him over for dinner twice a year. A dinner Chad would talk about for days because *Fitz has an indoor pool. A goddamned indoor pool with heaters and pink LED lights and a surround sound system and…you guys have got to see it.*

I followed Duane and thought about you lying on a hotel bed covered in cash like they show in the movies. You'd be undressed and reaching for me, and I'd bend you over because that's what you'd want after what I did for us. Fear mixed with adrenaline, and I felt myself grow hard.

Duane parked near the bank slot at the mall. Near, but not near enough. He should have pulled right up to the deposit pull, but he didn't, because he's a cocky bastard.

I left my car on the street and softly closed the door behind me. Then I ran through the lot, ducking between the cars. Duane walked slowly, keeping his eyes on the phone in his hand.

I shouldn't have been this excited, but I couldn't stop thinking about my training at Steel. It was Duane who showed me how to run the register and how to do the paperwork for a new patron and set up their keycard. He did this thing every time I had to ask a question twice. He laughed. Every single time, he'd give a short, sharp laugh. Maybe he didn't mean it the way it felt, but it still humiliated me.

It would be me who laughed this time.

When I was no more than ten feet away, I stepped out from between the cars. Glancing around, I ensured no one was watching, and then grabbed him from behind. Shoved him to the ground. Before he could make a sound, I leaped on his back and held the flat of the knife against his cheek.

"Don't say a word," I hissed, ensuring my voice sounded different.

Duane rolled over and looked up at my mask. His eyes filled with horror as I grabbed the bag from beside him, stood, and kicked his phone away.

I danced from foot to foot, thinking I needed to do something else. Say something else. Guilt flooded me as I watched a dark, wet spot bloom between his legs.

"Don't do anything, man." His voice shook, and it broke something inside me that I figured was unbreakable. "I've got a girl."

I've got a girl, too, I thought to myself. *And we need this.*

As much as I hated Duane, I didn't like seeing him this way, scooting backward along the pavement, his eyes swollen with fear, his hands reaching for—

He pulled a gun.

"Oh, shit," I said and turned to run.

"Cobain," he yelled.

And I stopped. Like an idiot.

"I fucking *knew* it. What the *fuck*, man?"

I turned around and watched as Duane leaned over, put his hand on his knee, and caught his breath as he kept that gun trained on me.

"Did you think you'd get away with this shit?" he asked. "Why do you think Chad has me take the cash instead of you?"

He waved the gun as if to answer his own question, and

my stomach lurched.

He tipped the gun toward himself. "Throw the bag over here and drop that pitiful knife."

I did both, and after he picked up the bag, he held it in front of his crotch.

He stood there staring at me for a long time. So long that I finally said, "This was a mistake. I'm just going to go. I'm sorry. I didn't—"

"Shut up, I'm thinking," he yelled, and then spotted a woman walking to her car beneath the mall parking lights. She didn't look in our direction, but he still lowered his gun next to his leg.

He watched her until she got in her car, backed up, and pulled away. Then he looked at me and said, "Okay. Okay, here's how this is going to go. Lucky for me, this is the biggest haul of the week. So I'm going to take a few hundred, and tomorrow you're going to change your name on the close-out sheet so it looks like you did the last count."

"Fuck," I said under my breath.

"Chad will think you stole it, but he won't be able to prove it. You'll be canned, and I'll be a grand richer. Win, win."

"Duane," I tried.

He lifted the gun a second time. "There's another way this can go."

I raised my hands and turned to go as Duane watched. I glanced back once and saw him scrambling for his phone that had fallen beneath a car, then caught the sound of a zipper being pulled.

I walked faster.

I was almost back to my dad's car, wondering how the hell I screwed this up, when I heard Duane say, "Say hi to Molly for me. I'm sure she'd be real proud of her dirtbag boyfriend now."

I almost turned back.

I almost forgot about the gun and charged him. Almost took the cash and what was left of his pride. But instead, I climbed in my car and sped away. As I hit the highway, I slammed my fist into the steering wheel.

"Fuck," I yelled. "*Fuuuuuck!*"

I was going to lose my job.

I was going to lose you, Molly.

I was going to lose everything I'd grown to care about.

My phone vibrated, and I glanced down. It was you. You were going to be late coming over. You were grabbing ice cream with Rhana and Nixon.

Fucking Nixon, I thought.

Fucking Rhana.

If you and I broke up, you'd have them.

And I'd be left alone.

Again.

NOW

*I*t's dark outside as I lie in bed, remembering the life I nearly stole for Molly and me.

It was supposed to be the two of us together with that money. I was going to steal the cash, and she was going to meet me at a gas station. We'd take her mom's car as far as we could, and then dump it and take the bus. Molly's favorite thing was imagining the place we'd have together. What color she would paint the walls. What kind of couch we'd buy together. She liked to take walks and stare through people's windows. Watch them making dinner, make note of something they had inside their home that we'd need.

I imagined I'd get a new job at another gym. Eventually, I'd start buying art online. I'd learn something about art. Or maybe I'd realize I liked the idea of being an art dealer more than actually being one. That was something I'd figure out in our life together.

Either way, that dream died when I lost my job. When I lost our chance at getting away easily. I didn't tell her I failed at robbing Duane, so why did she run without me? She should have been waiting. I promised her I'd get it.

Why didn't she believe me?

Frustration grows inside my gut, parasitic. As I'm slipping into a fitful sleep, my mind's needle snags on the vinyl, the lyrics repeating until I'm a moment from snapping—

Trees, green trees.

The smell of water.

A white dog.

Barking.

Breathlessness.

My hands on Molly, shaking.

My hands on Molly, shaking.

My hands on Molly's...neck?

I bolt upright in bed, sweat drenching my body. What the fuck?

It takes me half an hour to calm down enough to chance closing my eyes again. And then, finally, release. I succumb to sleep.

But when I wake, the images are still there.

And they scare the hell out of me.

PART IV

where did you
sleep last night

MOLLY

Blue treated her differently after the night they danced. He brought her gifts—smooth stones from the lake, or pinecones that filled her room with an earthy aroma. He let her out of her room more often but stayed nearby.

It was on one of these days that he brought her to the water. He wrapped her in a coat and slipped boots that were two sizes too big onto her feet, made comfortable with a pair of thick black socks.

Blue motioned for her to sit on a fallen log, and she obliged. He sat next to her and stared toward the water. She watched his face, her eyes tracing the lines of his mask. When she realized he hadn't brought along the contraption to manipulate his voice, her pulse picked up. She'd have to get him to speak. If she could hear his voice, she'd know.

But didn't she already know?

"It's beautiful out here, don't you think?" she asked.

But he only nodded.

Molly thought of her father. Dug deep into the recesses of her brain to produce a nugget of twisted teachings.

People are desperate to speak of themselves, Molly. And there's no way to get someone to open up faster than to present an opinion on something they feel passionately about. Then— and here's the real lesson, baby girl—then you must pretend to come to their side. When they feel they've won you over, two things happen: they like you better than they did before, and they feel guilty for convincing you. That's when you can ask for what it is you really want.

What was it she really wanted?

Freedom.

But could she simply ask for it? Would that even satisfy her at this point in the game? Because that's what this was…a game.

Molly pulled her hair over her shoulder and narrowed her eyes at the water. "Some people wouldn't appreciate all this beauty." She gave him a small smile. "Or how to just sit quietly and appreciate what it is they have."

She folded her hands in her lap. "I knew a girl at school who never appreciated anything. She would complain about *everything*. One time she said it irritated her when she got too much ice cream on a cone. That she'd have to dump some out so it wouldn't melt everywhere before she could eat it. Can you believe that? Complaining because someone gave you too much ice cream? That can't be a thing."

Blue scratched his wrist and continued staring forward.

"Daddy always said everyone begins the race at the starting line. And when the gun fires, some people run, and some find excuses for why they can't keep up even though they've got two good legs."

Blue cracked his neck, and Molly weighed her next words carefully.

"Out here, you're really reminded to just be appreciative. And to stop making excuses."

Blue held up a hand, silently telling her that was enough.

But she was far from done.

"What? I thought you liked me to talk."

Blue shrugged.

"You don't agree with what I'm saying?"

When he didn't respond, she added, "I would've thought you'd agree. You seem like a take-charge kind of person. I mean, you took me because you knew I could help you. You choose to be alone because you want to be. Other people have friends and family and a normal life because that's what they want." Molly looked at the water and fought to hide her grin. "That's just not what you want."

Blue looked away from her, and she could feel the anger rolling off him. Of course he wanted friends. Of course he wanted family. He burned with loneliness so deeply he could thaw this pond if he merely brushed his knuckles against the surface.

Molly hesitated. One beat. Two. Ten.

Then she shook her head and said, "Actually, you know what? My dad is full of crap. That's exactly what people say when they're at an advantage. Some people fight for what they want their whole lives and don't win a single, solitary thing for their efforts."

Blue looked at her.

"You disagree?"

He shook his head.

Of course he agreed with that. She'd said it for his sake.

She nodded. "My dad's an asshole."

Truth.

"You're never really free of your parents, are you?" she added.

Blue hung his head, and Molly wet her lips. This was the moment. Her throat grew tight, and she struggled to get the words out. What was it that she wanted? What would he give her? She thought of the bird. She hated it. She loved it. She'd die if she had to return to a time before she had company. But last night, as it tucked its head beneath its wing, she thought of those bars. And how she was the one keeping it trapped. It no longer needed to be contained. Its wing was long-healed, she was sure.

But it was hers.

It was hers, hers, hers.

"We should release the bird," she whispered.

Blue looked at her.

"I want to release the bird."

Blue looked back at the house as if he could see the small sparrow from their place on the ground. He stared into the distance for a long time, and then rose to his feet. He seemed to contemplate something for more than a moment, and then offered her his gloved hand.

She looked at it, remembered the feel of it around her waist as they danced, and then took it. He led her back to the house, and she watched his back with an imperious smile. She had succeeded in this small feat. It gave her hope that she would ultimately convince him to let her go.

Blue led her down to her room, and she walked toward the birdcage. Her heart ached as the creature gave a pleasant chirp in greeting. Or maybe in fear. She wasn't sure.

Her hands were almost on the cage when she felt Blue grab her wrist and wind something around it.

She glanced down to see the plastic ties.

"What are you doing?" she asked.

He reached to attach the other end to the ceiling, and then reached for her opposite wrist. She held it behind her back.

"You said that…you said—"

He ripped her arm in front of her and bound it as she remembered he'd never said a word. He was more perceptive than she gave him credit for.

"I asked for one little thing!" she roared.

But didn't her daddy say to never ask? To only vocalize a need and let someone fill that need on his or her own?

Blue walked toward the door, and Molly tried to push down her rage. She tried and failed.

"You fuck!" she screamed. "You selfish *fuck*! I am not yours to keep here like some dog."

He looked back at her, and her eyes widened. She reduced the volume of her voice. "I can't help you unless you give me some wiggle room."

He closed the door.

"I'm sorry," Molly yelled. "Please, Blue. Please don't leave me down here."

When she heard the door at the top of the stairs slam shut, she went wild. Thrashed against the restraints like freedom lay only a few feet away. Because it did, just beyond that window. She pulled until her wrists opened and bled. Until pain racked her insides and threatened to upend her stomach. She yanked and pulled and stretched like a rabid animal. And when she finally collapsed onto the ground, she cried.

She cried because she needed her Cobain back. The boy who cared about her. The boy who saw her as she was and wouldn't let her go. She missed him so much her heart dripped like melting wax. Like a candle left burning too long without quiet lips to extinguish the flame.

Where was he now? What was he doing? Was he closer than she realized? So close she could dance with him as the record player turned?

Those questions drove her mad.

She listened for Blue's footsteps above her, tried to recognize the rhythm of his gait.

Cobain.

Blue.

Cobain.

Blue.

Slowly, she lifted her head to look at the bird. It stared back at her with an eye that held far too much comprehension. She rushed toward the cage, and the bird flew against the bars.

"Shh," Molly said. "I'm going to help you."

I'm going to help you, I'm going to help you, I'm going to help you.

The reality of where she was—and the loss of control—was hitting her. Dizziness swept through her head, making the room tilt. She told herself she could manipulate Blue into submission. But was it true? Was it ever true for a single second?

She grabbed the cage and opened the door. Watched with delight as the bird flew around the room, knocking against the walls, searching for a place to perch. It came to rest on the table near her bed.

"That's good," Molly said, hysterical. "Stay there."

Her eyes fell on the cage, and before she could entertain a rational thought, she grabbed the thin, brittle bars and pulled on them. When they didn't budge, she sat on the floor, put the cage between her boots, and pulled backward with both hands.

The wire bent to her will.

She laughed and pulled harder. Pulled until she was sure the metal would slice right through her skin like a fork piercing melon. When the wire broke away from the cage, the momentum threw her backward. Her head clunked against the concrete floor, and she had to bite down against the pain.

She checked her head for blood. Checked her hands to ensure they still worked.

Then she bounded to her feet and raced toward the window. She got as close as she could, her hip brushing the sink, and then she got to work on the wire.

She spread it out, long and hopeful, and stretched it toward the window. It tapped against the hook that opened the window, but the wire gave way when she pressed.

The bird produced a small sound behind her, and she said, "Don't worry. I'm going to get it."

Molly pulled the wire toward her and bent the end until it made a hook and then reached back out with it. It took an infinite number of tries until, at last, it hooked around the handle and stayed put while she guided the wire to the right.

The window unlocked and popped open. Just a fraction of an inch, but Molly hung her head with triumph and rejoiced.

Then she stuck the wire back out and slammed it against the glass. Over and over again so that it opened a little farther each time.

The door at the top of the stairs opened, and panic lit up her insides so that she glowed like those lightning bugs beyond her rectangular porthole to the world.

Molly raced toward the bird. She wanted to release it with her hands. To feel the flutter of its wings as she launched it toward safety. But the bird needed no prodding and flew on its own. It bashed against the walls twice more as footsteps thundered down the stairs. Then it reached the bathroom.

As the downstairs door flew open, the bird perched on the toilet.

"Go!" Molly screamed and ran at it as Blue reached for her.

The bird flew.

The bird flew straight out that open window and sailed toward the winter sun.

Blue's arms came around her, and she laughed like a lunatic. Laughed until her body slumped to the ground. He released her and raced toward the window. When the lock slid back into place, the last of Molly's laughter fell away.

He turned his eyes on her in time to see her rise to her feet.

For her to hold that wire in front of her like a child's toy sword.

Her face twisted with desperation, and she said, carefully, so very carefully, "You were afraid of what freeing the bird meant." She motioned toward the window. "But I'll be here to—"

Blue rushed toward her, and she raised the wire, though she knew it would do nothing to stop him. He shoved it aside, and as it clattered to the floor, he grasped her face in his hands, breathing hard as he stared down at her. He was a foot taller than she was. Maybe more than a foot. Maybe his shoulders brushed the stars at night.

"Don't," she said, but she didn't know what she was trying to stop.

He released her roughly and marched toward the door. Slammed it closed.

Later, much later, as Molly listened for the sound of her bird, she heard a different noise. She jolted up in bed and turned to see Blue outside her window. He lowered his face and peered at her from the other side of the glass.

Then he leaned back, and a thick board took the place of his silhouette.

She heard the sound of nails.

And she knew that, though she'd tried to spin that bird flying away as a symbol of his own impending, contrived suicide, he'd interpreted it much differently.

Molly was becoming quite important to Blue, she realized.

And as slender gray nails were driven into the siding, she learned just how afraid he was of losing her.

NOW

I wake to flashing lights.

They're painting my room red, red, red.

My dad shoves my bedroom door open. "Cobain! Cobain, get dressed!"

I pull on a T-shirt, jeans, and tennis shoes and try to think clearly. But I can't because I just woke up and my dad is yelling and our front door is exploding and I know, I *know*, that this is it.

My mom appears in the hallway, grabbing at my shoulders, asking what I did.

I don't know what I did. I don't know, *I don't know*.

I hear a sound at the back door and realize they're about to break the door down. That's how serious they are.

I run to the front, shouldering my dad out of the way, telling my mom I'm sorry. I'm so sorry. Even though I can't be sure what I'm sorry for.

An officer I don't recognize reaches in and grabs me as soon as the door is open.

"Cobain Kelly?" she says. "You're under arrest for the kidnapping of Molly Bates. You have the right to remain silent."

Cold cuffs snapping around my wrists.

"Anything you say can and will be used against you in a court of law."

A hard shove toward the waiting patrol car.

"You have the right to an attorney."

Words of warning shouted at my mother, who is racing toward me.

"If you cannot afford an attorney, one will be provided for you."

Door opening, a hand guiding my head down, leather seats stinking of piss and sour vomit.

"Do you understand the rights I have just read to you?"

She looks like a nice woman. Good laugh lines around her mouth.

"Fuck you," I say.

She smiles, and I feel like the criminal they believe I am.

My dad runs toward the car, his finger waving in people's faces. He tries to tell me something, but the cop slams my door closed. Thank God for that.

The cop gets in the driver's seat, and a man slides in on the passenger side. Other police officers, maybe five of them, get in different cars and pull away. Man, I must be dangerous if it takes this many to bring me in. I wonder if they drew straws at the station to see who would get to cuff me. I like to think when the woman won, she pretended to celebrate but secretly dreaded doing it.

I need to know what the police have on me.

I tap on the plastic that divides me from the cops up front. The guy turns around, and the woman looks in her rearview mirror.

"Where are Detectives Hernandez and Tehrani?" I ask.

The man stares at me for a moment longer and then turns back around.

I grow frustrated. *My* cops would have answered me. They would tell me what's going on.

I realize that's bad—that I've developed a sense of camaraderie with police officers who in no way have my best interest at heart.

"Am I going to jail?" I ask.

The word strikes fear through my body. For some strange reason, my terror isn't from a fear of being caged, but rather the fear of growing smaller. Of not being able to lift, to grow. I'll shrivel to half my size. I won't be able to protect myself. I will become a target.

When we get to the station, the female officer grabs my arm and hauls me out. She's stronger than she looks. I respect that about her. I wonder what she's like in bed. I wonder what the hell is wrong with me.

The woman leads me to the same office I was questioned inside of a few days ago. I see the girl who led me out the one time. Her mouth turns downward like she's disappointed to see me here again.

You and me both.

The woman puts me into a chair and re-cuffs my hands so they're in front of me. The male officer stands close by in case I try something.

Will I try something?

Yeah, I might.

When the two officers leave and Detective Tehrani enters, I breathe a sigh of relief.

"What's going on?" I ask him.

But he doesn't respond. There's a change in his demeanor. His shoulders are tenser. The line between his eyes deeper. There's the start of a beard where there wasn't one before.

He sits across from me and looks as if he's debating confessing something. Something inside him must win, because he says to me, "I have a daughter, you know that? Different school."

I realize he means we're about the same age.

I realize he sees me as what could have been a predator to *his* baby girl.

Detective Tehrani stares me down, and I realize he's lost something. Last time I saw him, there was hopefulness in his eyes. Now it looks like he knows better.

I lower my eyes to the table and think of Molly. Of what she'd do when I was nervous about something. I imagine her lifting my hand to her mouth and touching her lips to each fingertip. Then she'd wrap her hand around one of my fingers and squeeze. Then she'd do the next one, and the next one— thumb to pinkie, and back again. Over and over, and then… she'd skip one. It drove me crazy when she skipped squeezing one of my fingers. But the anticipation always took my mind off what plagued me. Instead, I'd focus on those steady squeezes. On the reassurance of her skin on mine. On the game.

I look down at my hand and wish, more than I've wished for anything in my entire life, that she would squeeze my fingers and that would be enough to make this all go away. I feel alone. I feel so fucking *alone*.

Detective Hernandez comes into the room, and I try to stand up against the restraints. I don't know why. I'm desperate for anyone to remind me that I'm not a monster. But Detective Tehrani says, "Sit down," in a gruff voice I didn't know he had.

Detective Hernandez takes a seat across from me, and I follow her lead. She hasn't shown the disgust for me that the other detective has yet, and so I look to her for guidance.

"Cobain," she says with tiredness in her heavy brown eyes. "We've spoken with Jet about the day you met Molly."

My eyes seal shut, and I force air through my nostrils.

"Sounded pretty violent, which is of course much different than the story you told us."

I don't respond. Nothing I say could help at this point.

Detective Hernandez leans back, like what she has up her sleeve next is even worse.

I can't wait.

"We also talked to your former boss at…" She checks her notepad to ensure she gets it right. "…at Steel. It appears several hundred dollars went missing, and immediately after that, you were let go."

I'm having trouble getting enough oxygen in this room. I think the walls are moving closer, the lights getting brighter. Am I imagining that? I have to be imagining that.

"You needed that money so you could take Molly." She nods along to her own story. "Maybe you just planned to keep her somewhere, but something went wrong."

I start to defend myself, but how can I do that? I have no arguments left.

"Cobain, I'm going to ask you this very simply, and I'd like it if you gave me a simple answer." Detective Hernandez locks her eyes on me. "Do you know where Molly is?"

I look at her for a long time. She opens her arms wide on the table, shakes her head once or twice. She wants so badly for me to surprise her. I want to surprise her, too.

But I can't.

"No."

She breathes forcefully through her nostrils and then waves at someone behind a mirror. I wonder how many people are watching me from behind there. Am I putting on a good performance? Do they believe I'm innocent? Because if they knew the random shit playing on repeat in my head, they'd want to dice my brain up and slide it beneath a microscope. Label it *EVIDENCE*.

Green trees.

Blue water.

A white dog.

Barking.

The smell of water.

Breathlessness.

Something in my peripheral, flying closer—

A crow.

A person comes in carrying a red bag and a tablet. It's a young guy with zits around his jawline that bulge red and white. Patriotic. He places both items on the table, then walks back out of the room.

Detective Hernandez asks me one last question. "Cobain, do you have anything at all you'd like to tell us? This is your last chance."

I look at the bag. The tablet. *No matter what you say,* they say, *we will destroy you.*

And so I stay quiet, my mind racing, fear making my fingers and toes go numb.

Detective Hernandez sighs, dejected, and slides the tablet toward her. She enters a password to unlock the thing, clicks a few buttons, and then turns it so I can see.

"I think it's time we show you this," she says firmly. "We got it this morning."

My hands start to shake, and my entire body feels electric. I have no idea what to expect. No idea what to believe. I don't know how I got here, how this all happened.

How is this happening?

I don't know anything anymore.

Except that they're looking at me like I'm a monster.

Let's see if they're right.

The video starts to play, and I watch the night of Molly's disappearance unfold.

THEN

*Y*ou took me to a party.

I'm not even sure you wanted to. You'd been distant ever since I came to your room, despite what you'd said the next morning. I'd thought a lot about how I'd screwed up that day at your house. I should have just kept my mouth shut. I should have used that mouth to taste every last part of your body.

Despite the crap that happened, I couldn't keep my eyes off your legs. You wore a skirt, and blue tights I wanted to tear off with my teeth. I wanted to trail my lips up the insides of your thighs and spread your legs with my hands and hold them open—wide open—against the ground.

I wanted us to connect again. I wanted you to stop looking at me with this expression that said I was ripping you into pieces. Because you were the one ripping me apart, Molly. It was you.

I reached over and grabbed your hand, and you gave me a smile that stretched from your chin to your hairline...but it skipped your eyes.

You were worried about something, I knew. So I took your fingers in my hand and tried to do the squeeze tactic like you did on me. After a few times, you clenched your hand around mine, shook it playfully, and put your hand back on the steering wheel.

I wanted to turn the wheel and drive us both into a tree to get your attention.

If you knew the kind of stuff I thought, would you have been in the car with me?

Maybe you *did* know.

Maybe that's why you ran.

The party was in a field outside an abandoned house. We'd been there before. There was a man who lived an acre away who would sometimes come up the road yelling for us to get out of there. We'd run or drive away as fast as we could. I sometimes wondered who had more fun in those moments—us, or the man who got to feel like a big shot.

As we stood around the fire, you reached over and planted a kiss on my mouth. It was a surface level kiss, like you were kissing my lips, but not *me*. But then you pulled back, and the smile on your face faded. You looked at me differently then, and I wrapped my arm around your waist.

"Molly," I said. "What the fuck is going on with us?"

It smelled of campfire smoke, and the taste of beer clung to my lips, and yours, too.

Your eyes lowered.

"I'm going to get us that cash," I said, not telling you I'd lost my chance.

You looked at me. "You would, wouldn't you? Just because I asked."

I grabbed your shoulders. "Because I want to get out of here, too. And yes, because you're unhappy here. Your dad—"

You held a finger to my lips.

Grabbed my hand.

Led me to the house.

I'd like to say I was surprised by what you were about to do.

But I knew. I knew, and I felt myself grow hard before you even walked inside that abandoned house and shut the door behind us.

There was another couple leaning against the wall, hands down pants, hands up shirts. The guy looked over the girl's shoulder at me, frowned, and returned to the girl.

Molly led me to the back and down a couple of steps into a sunken living room. It was impossibly dark, but I could see the smoke that stained the walls from people lighting fires to keep warm. It was a miracle this house had any stand left in its old bones.

I took your face in my hands and kissed you. You released your weight into my arms, and I held you up. I would never let you go again. Your arms rose to wrap around my shoulders and gripped the muscles there. You trailed your hands down my arms and my back, feeling me. I was so much bigger than you, and it struck me how much you must trust me to allow me access to your body. In the dark. In the quiet. With the closest person several rooms away, distracted.

You stepped back and started to remove your shirt, but I was there to do it for you. I bent and trailed kisses along your stomach as I lifted the fabric and threw it to the side. Then I reached for your skirt, unzipped the side, and suppressed a groan as you shimmied out of it.

I removed my jacket, shirt, and jeans and shivered before you because it was cold as shit, but I planned on keeping you warm. I planned on doing so many unspeakable things to you.

I lifted you off your feet and laid you on top of my jacket. Goose bumps raced across your skin, and I was there with my mouth. With my weight.

I leaned back to remove those tights, and as your leg slipped from each hole, you locked eyes with me.

"Cobain," you said.

I shook my head, and you quieted. I didn't need you to say

it anymore. I knew how you felt now. You couldn't have hidden it if you tried. And my God, how you tried. It was all over your face right then—your fear, your love.

I lowered myself between your knees and kissed you again. You wrapped your legs around me, and I wrapped myself around you, and I think the house finally was engulfed in flames, at long last. Taken by the night. Taken to the ground.

You arched your back, and I slipped my hand between your shoulder blades. Your bra came away in my hand.

We pressed our bodies together, and our breath came faster, our fingers dug deeper. You reached down to push off my boxers, but there was no time for that. I had to have you, Molly. And you needed me, too. I knew because you said, *I need you, I need you, I need you* against my neck.

So I pulled myself out of my boxers and pushed your underwear to the side, and I slipped my fingers between your legs to make sure you were ready. And you were. Your legs parted farther, and you threw your head back, and I sank into you.

The last of you became the best of me inside that house, on that soot-covered floor with the stars burning outside a broken window.

And I loved you, Molly.

I loved you, Molly.

I *loved* you.

So I held you tight and rocked against you and drank in every bit you offered to me that night. And when it was over, and I collapsed beside you, and you slung a thin, white-as-fog leg over my torso, I thought I might want to die that way. Happy. In your arms. Knowing you loved me back. Certain nothing would ever come close to touching this moment we'd shared.

And then you looked at me with eyes so green that Spanish moss clung to the edges, and you said—

"We can't be together anymore, Cobain."

MOLLY

Molly dreamed about that night with Cobain and woke with an ache between her legs. When she remembered where she was, however, the want died.

She hadn't seen the light outside in three days. A sliver slipped in through the cracks—enough to tell her whether it was day or night—but it wasn't enough.

She'd lost his trust.

He wasn't angry that she'd freed the bird, exactly. It was that she'd made a decision that he hadn't initiated or authorized.

This was about control, she reminded herself.

And if she was to stand a chance, she had to give him a sense of reclaiming it.

And so her mind began to turn in circles like a carousel, wide-toothed horses and griffins spinning round her brain.

She stayed in the shadows for one day and part of another one, and when the idea finally came to her, she smiled. This would go against everything her father had ever taught her, and if she failed, well, he just might kill her.

But at least this thing would come to an end, at long last.

When Blue finally appeared in her doorway carrying a tray, she came to him softly. As softly as a lion. She reached out, claws retracted, and took the food. Shoved it into her mouth and ate furiously, her eyes locked on his. The crusty bread filled her mouth and slid down her throat. She reached for the strawberry preserves next. Ate them with a spoon straight from the dusty mason jar.

When she finished, he lifted the tray and made for the door.

He meant to leave her down here again. But she was done with such games.

"I planned to kill you," she said, climbing to her feet.

Blue stopped.

"I was going to talk you into killing yourself."

He turned to look at her.

"My father was a master manipulator." She nodded to show him it was true. "Once, he even talked an employee of his into blowing his head off. That's Daddy for you." She pointed at Blue. "And I was going to do the same to you. I still could. You wouldn't even know it, and I would be doing it."

Blue's grip on the tray tightened. Molly wondered if he was angry or afraid. Probably a little of both.

"But I don't want to be like him. And I'll be honest, I don't want to be here, either. All I really want to be is out there."

She motioned toward the boarded window.

"One day," she said simply, "I'll escape. And I'll never know who you are. Not for sure. I'll tell the police what I know. They'll find you. And neither of us will be better for the experience. I'll live every day afraid that it'll happen again. That someone will rob me of my independence. And you'll live every day behind bars, wondering why you did all this."

Molly stepped toward him. "But this could go differently. You could be honest with me for once. I could show you who I really am. And you could show me, too."

Blue's hands shook, and the silver utensils on the tray rattled ever so slightly against the dishes.

"I'll remove my mask," she said softly. "If you'll remove yours."

Blue studied her for a long moment. Then he crossed the room, slowly, and set the tray down on her bed. He looked down at her bed, seemed to think about her lying beneath those blankets. With one uncertain hand, he leaned down to smooth out the wrinkles.

Then he looked at her, removed the voice changing device from his pocket, and brought it to his mouth.

And he said—

"Molly."

She squeezed her eyes shut against the emotion that rolled inside of her.

He'd never said her name, and she'd never said it, either. He *knew* her. This person who violated her basic human rights *knew* her. But of course he did. There was a difference, however, between suspecting something and having it confirmed.

Was this boy who spoke her name the same boy she'd touched in the school hallway? The same one who held her hand at the fair? The same one who held her body in that old, decaying house?

She thought she knew the answer.

"All this time," she said to him. She fought back the tears and tried again. "All this time I've been talking you into leaping over the ledge, but it's me who's been waiting for someone to come along and push me."

He reached for her, but she backed away.

"I don't want to be comforted," she said as tears rolled over her cheeks and fell to her chest. "I want you to finish this. I want you to take away my pain."

Blue's hand dropped to his side.

"I haven't been happy in a long time," she said. "And I'm tired of trying. So just do it."

Blue sat down on her bed and put his head between his hands. And as Molly fought back tears and tidal waves of emotion nearly knocked her off her feet, she wondered if she was still pretending.

THEN

*A*s we lay in that abandoned house, as my world rocked from what you'd just said, you got up and put on your bra. Then you grabbed your shirt and skirt and jacket and boots. I lay on the ground, exposed, confused.

Angry.

"What are you talking about?" I demanded because I couldn't repeat it. Repeating it would make it real.

You shook your head and looked at me directly. Any emotion you might have had on your face while I laid on top of you, pushing myself inside of you, had vanished. You looked like a machine in the moonlight that cut through the window.

"We just can't do this anymore," you said.

"Do what?" I asked. "Be happy?"

"I've got to go." You grabbed something from the floor. Your purse? Had you brought a purse in with you?

You turned your back on me and started toward a door that led to the back of the house, then turned toward the place we'd come in through. I guess you figured you could appear through the front entrance with your head held high. Even after you'd screwed the school weirdo and left him nude on the dirty floor. *Especially* because you'd left him nude on the floor.

"Don't walk out on me," I said, and I heard the warning in my voice. But what would I really do if you did? I wasn't sure.

You stopped in the doorway long enough for me to pull on my jeans.

Something inaudible escaped your mouth.

"What?" I asked, afraid to come near you. Afraid you'd run.

Afraid I'd chase you to the ends of the earth and set the path on fire to ensure you couldn't double back.

"Then don't let me," you said, louder this time.

"Don't let you what?" I ask, stupidly. So fucking stupidly.

You sighed and made to leave.

I took your arm and turned you around. "Is that what you want?" I asked. "You want me to force you to stay with me? Are you that fucked up?"

Tears filled your eyes, and I felt myself drowning. Felt like I couldn't fill my damn lungs.

You shook your head. "Never mind. Never mind."

I shook mine, too. "'Never mind, never mind. Don't let me leave, Cobain. Never mind. Take me away from here. Never mind. Come over to my house and fuck me, but only if you can do it without giving a shit.'"

I grasped your face, and you cried harder. "I love you, Molly. I fucking *love* you, and there's nothing you can do to change that."

"But I don't love you," you whispered.

But the opposite screamed in your eyes.

You reached up to grab my hands. Pulled them away from your face.

Then you shoved me, *hard*. I stumbled back a few steps, startled by your strength.

"You're better off without me," you said, your lip curled in anger.

You turned to walk out, but I jumped into your path, because honestly, if you walked out on me after what just happened between us on the floor of this house, I'd combust.

"Tell me you want me to leave you alone and I will," I challenged.

"Get out of my way," you replied.

"No," I said.

"Cobain."

"Molly."

You shoved me again.

I didn't move a fucking inch.

Your eyes flicked toward the back wall, and I should have seen it coming. Should have, but didn't.

You ran.

You ran, and for all my strength, I didn't have half your agility or speed.

You were out the door in a flash, and I was chasing after you.

In a matter of seconds, you'd cut through the trees, your stocking-free legs ripping through the underbrush.

Every turn you made, I made. Every stone you leaped over, I flew over as well.

I didn't know what I'd do when I caught you.

But I knew you were crazy. Crazier than me. And beautiful as your white hair sliced through the darkness. I was chasing a toxic addiction. A mindless tornado. A possible sociopath. I should stop, I knew. Let you run until you leaped off a cliff and your broken body lay at the bottom. But I knew I'd never stop. And if that cliff came into view and I saw you fly through the air like a gazelle, I'd leap right over the edge with you.

"Molly!" I roared.

Do you remember me roaring your name?

I remember, Molly.

I remember growing more frenzied the farther you ran. I

remember a new sound.

Someone else?

Someone else.

The ground tore open my feet as I raced after you, but the pain escaped me. All I could think of was catching up to you. All I could think of was holding you in my arms and kissing you and telling you, *It's okay. See? I didn't let you go. That's what you wanted. You wanted me to keep you, and that's what I'm gonna do and is that a sound no it's just me and you forever, forever.*

I caught you.

I hugged you to my chest.

I may have held you too tightly.

I may have yelled too loudly.

I pulled you away, and I was so angry and so in love and so full of emotions that needed an outlet.

"Let her go."

My mind cleared, and I realized I was standing—barefoot, shirtless, jacketless—in the heart of winter, and Nixon was going, *What the fuck, man?*

And you were going, *We had a fight. It's okay, Nixon. It's okay.*

And I was going *Molly, listen to me.*

"I'm sorry, Cobain," you said. Those were the first words that really stopped the world from spinning.

"Let's go back to the house," Nixon said.

I started to come, too, one hand on my head, and Nixon said, "No, man. You stay back here for a while. Give her some space."

And I looked at Nixon, who was applying for a weight-lifting scholarship at the Air Force Academy where he'd be third-generation alumni, and said, "I'll tell Coach what you're taking."

Nixon's brow furrowed and then smoothed in one heartbeat. "You can be a real asshole, you know that?"

"Only if pushed."

He touched your back and said, "Come on."

"Molly," I tried.

But you didn't even look at me.

I stayed in the trees longer than I needed to. Long enough that my skin went numb from the cold, and I wondered if maybe I ought to just stay out there forever. Then I remembered what you said—

But I don't love you.

And so I took a breath and headed out of the trees because I needed to hear the truth slip from your mouth. Just once.

Except that was the last time I talked to you, Molly. The last word you heard from me was your name. Remember how I said it? As if my heart had grown too big for my body?

And you know what? The last word you said was my name, too.

I'm sorry, *Cobain.*

After you disappeared, I thought of the way you said it. Like you truly were sorry. Like you loved me, but that wasn't enough. Or maybe it was *too* much. Yeah, I think that's closer.

But don't worry, Molly, because I know why you left without me.

It took me a while to get there, but now I know.

MOLLY

She'd planned to betray him.

Her Cobain. Her heart. He didn't have her devotion at first, of course. She'd protected it well. She told herself sacrifices had to be made if she were to escape her mother, and her father's bloody, manipulative legacy. But first, she had to succumb to his ways. And so on the first day of school, she searched for someone who would help her escape this life she despised so deeply that her bones wept.

She thought she'd found that person when she met Rhana.

But then there was Cobain with his sad eyes. With his Herculean size and hands that seemed like they could be soft or lethal, depending on who he turned them on.

She'd waited for someone like him for fourteen months as her mother's obsession with her grew, as she drowned in her mother's home with the reminder of her father lingering in every last corner, and then there Cobain was on the first day of her new school.

So she'd grasped his face and said, "There you are."

His cheeks felt rough in her hands. She'd wanted to kiss the look of surprise off his mouth. She would have done anything to put a leash on that beast. But it was her in the end who wore the collar. Because she fell in love with him. She fell apart for him.

That heart she protected so fiercely—her compass—guided her to him now. Every day. Every night. And so after that night in the abandoned house, she knew she couldn't manipulate him any longer, even if it meant heading out on her own without the resources she needed. Even if it meant forgetting her plans to take the cash he planned to steal and disappear.

She could have gotten away with it, too. She'd already told everyone they'd broken up. His insistence that they were still together would make him seem untethered. The police would believe the strange, quiet kid had taken the money, and that his ex-girlfriend had left, in part, to get away from him. Even if they did believe she was involved, she'd be long gone, and they'd have a perfectly good suspect to take the fall.

The thought made her feel like shit, like maybe she was her father's daughter after all if she could let this happen, but she was fighting for survival. Because if she'd stayed with her mother in that house, well…the dark thoughts that plagued her would have eventually done her in.

In the end, she had left the city, left Cobain, because she was slowly ruining him. She'd seen the changes. The silent, forgotten boy changing into someone who would stop at nothing to pursue her happiness, and his own.

She'd seen the way he looked at her.

At first, with fascination. And then lust.

And then…with something fiercer.

Protectiveness.

Love.

For once, Molly had cared about something more than her survival. She cared about the way he smiled, though he hated when she forced it out of him. She cared about the way he chewed his fingernails to bits, and the way he'd grab her face and scratch it with the dark stubble on his jawline until she squealed. She cared about his genuine heart. And his hands, warm on her body. And his addiction to ketchup, even though the stuff was mostly sugar, and she'd told him that a dozen times.

She cared about the guarded way he looked at the world.

And the way he'd trusted her so entirely, though she'd done little to deserve it.

She cared about Cobain.

She *loved* Cobain.

And so she had left him before he did something disastrous. It seemed that she wasn't her father's daughter after all. At least not in totality.

What had it accomplished, though?

What had she done to them both by leaving?

Blue placed his hand on her arm and led her up the stairs and into a room she'd never seen before. Her eyes fell on the bed, blankets rumpled, a bedside lamp made of glass that reflected her numbness. There was a pile of clothes on the floor, and an oil painting of a nude woman that would bring Cobain both happiness and frustration—happiness because he loved art, frustration because he didn't understand it and feared he never would.

Blue led Molly to a closet and threw open the doors. He pulled a string, and light poured over a closet packed with T-shirts, blouses, slacks, a few pairs of jeans, and then…a dozen or more dresses. They belonged to an older woman—she could tell from the fabric and patterns. But there were a few that even a young girl like herself would worship.

Molly wished she could meet the woman who would keep such lovely things at a cabin in the middle of the woods. Did Blue know her?

Molly's eyes shifted to him. He waved a tired hand toward

the closet, indicating she should pick for herself this time.

How kind.

She was allowed to choose her own funeral garb.

She thumbed through the hangers until she found an emerald green dress. It was floor-length with an empire waist and capped sleeves. It would match her eyes.

She pulled off the dirtied striped dress she wore and threw it to the floor. And though she didn't care if he was, she glanced over to see if he watched her.

He did.

Her eyes moved to the bathroom. "I want to take a shower."

He tilted his head as if in a question.

"Without restraints," she clarified.

He thought about her request and then nodded. When she tried to close the door between them, though, he grabbed it and shook his head.

He turned around, indicating that he wouldn't watch.

When she removed her underwear and bra and stepped into the warm water, a gasp of ecstasy escaped her. She was able to wash her hair and her body without wrestling plastic cords like some marionette in a stage comedy.

The terrycloth towel felt like a cloud around her torso when she was done, and she felt—for the first time in a long time—happy. Because by giving him the control he sought to regain, she was actually taking a piece for herself. It was a gamble, she reminded herself. But where was the fun in living without it?

That was her father talking.

Molly slipped on the dress and took her time braiding her hair off to one side. Then she pulled open a drawer and rummaged for the makeup she suspected she would find. It was old and caked, all of it, but the pigment remained strong, and so she rubbed blush into her cheeks and swept lipstick across her mouth. She even found eyeliner with enough life left to give her the dark, dangerous look she sought.

When she appeared in the doorway, Blue rose to his feet.

That was the reaction she needed, but she realized as she dressed that she was doing it more for herself than for him. It felt therapeutic, to do something for her own happiness versus trying to affect someone else in some way. Was this the first time she'd done that?

Blue left the room and went to the kitchen, and she followed him out. He'd set a table for them with white dishes covered in indeterminate meat drowning in black sauce. Stiff green beans and mashed potatoes lay beside the meat, and two goblets of wine sat proudly above the plates.

There were cloth napkins. And polished silverware. And two pillar candles with flickering flames. As Molly took her seat, Blue put a record on the player and laid the red needle on its spinning face.

Molly smiled, because what else could she do?

As they ate in silence, Molly looked through the window. Her eyes fell on the white van. If she died tonight, would they ever find her body? Or would they only find that blasted van? This claustrophobic cabin? The room where he'd kept her?

"Where do you get this food from?" she asked, trying to make conversation.

But he didn't respond, and she didn't really care about the answer anyway.

When they were done eating, they left the plates where they were, because what was the point of cleaning them?

Molly took Blue's hand, and they danced in the living room as they had done several nights ago. But this time, Molly didn't do it for any other reason than to cling to the last person she might ever touch. Her concept of what was right and what was wrong was slipping, she knew. All she could focus on now were her immediate needs.

I need to feel cared for.

I need to have human interaction.

So they danced until the record skipped to a stop, and Blue flipped it over. Then they joined hands again and took more turns around the room. When the record stopped a second time, though, they lifted their heads and looked at each other.

It was time.

They both knew it.

And so Molly took his hand and asked, "Are you ready?"

He watched her for a long moment before nodding.

She took his hand and led him toward the door. He unlocked it quietly and led her out into the night in silence, over the snow. Long before they reached the pond, Molly's body shook from the cold. When they stood with their toes at the edge of the water, she turned and looked at him.

"Are you sure you want to do this?" she asked.

She knew she shouldn't push, but when he didn't reply, she said, "I know this was the reason you found me. I needed to do this with someone else. I've thought about it for so long. I'm just so tired of being sad."

His eyes fell to the ground, and she added, softly, with her gaze landing on the cabin, "They'll find us eventually, and then we'll have lost this moment."

He raised his head.

"This is our choice," Molly said.

He looked out at the water and removed his shoes.

She did the same.

They were still holding hands.

Molly turned to him and said, "Once we're out there, you'll have to take it off."

Blue looked at her and then back at the water. He swallowed. Even in the moonlight, she could see how nervous he was. How ridiculous, she thought. They were about to kill themselves, and he was worried about how she'd react when she saw him.

He shouldn't have worried, though, because she already knew.

It was in the way he walked.

In the way his shoulders moved.

It was in the way he lifted a fork to his mouth, and the way he stared at the sky when he was thinking. It was in the way he clapped his hands together when he was angry, and the way he held her when they danced.

It was in the way he looked at her when she sang.

It was in the way he gripped her hand just now.

It was in the way he pushed her against that tree and clasped her face between his hands.

She knew who he was.

Though she hoped she was wrong.

Or maybe that was a lie, too.

NOW

I lean closer to the tablet and realize I'm watching what must be security camera footage.

The lens is directed at a parking lot, and static licks through the screen every few seconds. My stomach threatens to upend itself as vehicles come and go. What's the last thing I ate? Peanut butter on stale bread because we'd been out of jelly for two weeks. A couple of guilt-laced oatmeal cookies Mom made late at night.

Finally, I see Molly's car appear.

"The cuffs," I bark, thrashing my hands against the restraints.

Detective Hernandez nods to Tehrani, and he removes them with a frown.

I immediately snatch the tablet and lift it so I can see better. My heart slams against my rib cage as Molly sits in her car for a few moments. I wonder what she's doing. Waiting for me? Is she waiting for me? Is this the gas station we were supposed to meet at? I don't think it is.

Finally, she steps out. Her white hair is loose around her shoulders, and she's wearing my favorite sweater—black with an animated rainbow over her left breast.

Molly, my girlfriend, someone I haven't seen in over a month, walks past the screen. It's blurry, but I know it's her. I know the way she walks. The way her hips move as she covers ground.

She vanishes inside the store, and a moment later a white van pulls up next to Molly's car.

Saliva pools in my mouth as I fight nausea.

The driver is wearing a baseball cap. He looks at Molly's car, and then at the doors to the convenience store.

He's waiting for her.

This prick is *waiting* for my girlfriend.

Molly appears from the store carrying something. I narrow my eyes to figure out what it is. For some reason, I feel like if I don't know what she's carrying, then nothing that happens next will make sense. Maybe it's something Molly would never buy. Maybe it's something for this guy in the van.

The bag is yellow.

It's peanut M&Ms.

When I realize this, I have to squeeze my eyes shut. I shake with anxiety, my teeth chattering inside my head. When I first met Molly, I figured she must not eat much. How else could she look so skeletal? But the truth was Molly ate more than any human being her size ever should—hot dogs, chili cheese fries, root beer floats, mozzarella sticks, buttered popcorn, pork tacos, fried chicken salads with extra ranch dressing. Anything and everything I ate, and sometimes more.

After every meal, no matter how far we had to walk to get them, she'd demand peanut M&Ms.

She opens the bag as she walks to her car. Tears the end off and, as I almost smile because I know it's coming, sticks it into her back pocket.

The guy gets out of the van.

I grip the tablet tighter and pull it so close to my face that my eyes water trying to take in all the tiny details the grainy footage doesn't show. I want to scream for Molly to run back inside. For her to pay attention. But she rounds the van anyway, and a second later, the guy walks after her. I hold my breath hoping this plays out differently, knowing it won't. I stare at the screen, willing Molly to appear again. Hoping to see her kissing this guy because that's better than the alternative.

But neither of those things happens. What does happen is Molly disappears from view, and then there is only the guy, holding the bag of M&Ms up to his mouth. And that's where the scene freezes. Detective Hernandez reaches over and taps the screen once, twice, and then the guy's face is *right there,* and it's like staring into a fucking mirror.

This guy, he looks just like me.

This guy, he is built just like me.

This guy…he is me. And there's no possibility left that exists that says I didn't have something to do with Molly disappearing.

"Did you move her car afterward?" Detective Hernandez asks, and I can tell she's upset they don't have that footage.

"Since we've had a tail on you," Detective Tehrani says, "and you haven't once visited a place she might be, we have to assume she's dead."

"You what?" I say. "*Dead?*"

"There's some evidence," Detective Hernandez interjects, "that leads us to believe we're looking for…" She hesitates. "Cobain, we're going to provide a court-appointed attorney for you, but if you wish, you can speak to us now. You can tell us where Molly is, so we can go and find her."

Green trees.

Blue water.

White dog.

Black crow.

Pressure.

Pressure.

Detective Hernandez lowers her voice, but that doesn't hide the sliver of hopefulness in her voice. "Cobain, is Molly still alive? Just tell us that. Detective Tehrani and I have been led to believe she's not, but perhaps she's just hurt somewhere. Or maybe she's okay, but you couldn't face being around her. Could you just tell us—"

A girl opens the door to our room, and I run.

I don't plan anything besides using my size to sledgehammer my way out of here.

I slam into the girl that opened the door, and she falls to the ground. I want to apologize and give her a hand up, but it's better I don't touch her. It's better that I don't touch anyone ever again. But I can touch this gun.

I grab the gun from an officer crossing my path. He's got his hands on a perpetrator, and now I've got my hands on his weapon. I point it at him. Flick my hand toward the door.

"Open it," I instruct, feeling like an imposter. My hands sweat, and my arms shake, and I'm terrified I'll drop the gun and it'll go off.

The officer raises his hands and says calmly, "Don't hurt anyone, okay?"

He walks to the door and swipes a card so that it opens.

"Give me the gun back before you go," he asks, and I've got to give him credit for trying.

There's a woman inside the lobby with a red-faced kid. She's demanding to see her boyfriend, but when she sees me, she picks up the kid and jumps back. I want to stop and assure her I'm not dangerous. But that's not true, now is it? I thought I wasn't a threat to anyone, especially Molly. I believed it until the very end.

But I was wrong.

I push through the glass doors and pass two officers, point my gun in their direction, and holler, "Get down now!"

Arms raised.

Stomachs touching the ground.

Not even a second of hesitation.

I imagine they have wives at home that need their husbands. Chubby-cheeked babies that can't lose their daddies.

"I'm sorry," I say, and start running.

I cross an intersection and hop over a fence. I don't know where I'm going.

Sure I do.

Sure I do.

NOW

I keep running, glancing over my shoulder to ensure the police haven't found me.

Green trees.

Blue water.

White dog.

I go to shove the gun into my jeans and feel something wedged into my pocket. My phone! I wonder if it's still on. When was the last time I paid the bill? Two months ago? But I prepaid for a month up front.

When I reach the train tracks, I collapse and put my head between my knees. Gasp for air. Grab at my throat because this can't be happening. All this time, I was chasing leads. Hoping it'd turn out that someone else had taken Molly, and that I could be the one to rescue her. Or that she had simply taken off on her own to start a new life with no strings.

But that was my face I saw.

Black crow.

Pressure.

My dad yelling.

Those were my arms that threw Molly into that white van. Where did I even get that van? How did I know how to find her? I have so many questions that may never be answered because there is a hole in my memory. A hole that widened as I fell deeper and deeper in love with Molly.

I reach for my phone, and as my hand shakes, I dial my brother's number. What if he doesn't pick up? What will I do here alone with this gun?

My brother answers on the fourth ring, and I lose my shit. I can barely respond when he asks, for the third time, if I'm there.

"I'm here," I finally manage.

He hesitates, hearing the wobble in my voice. "Cobain, what's wrong?"

"I did something to Molly," I say, hardly able to choke the words out.

Holt doesn't respond for several seconds, then he asks, "Where are you?"

I'm afraid to tell him. What if he calls the cops? I guess it doesn't matter. I have to trust him. Besides, they'll find me eventually.

"I'm in town," he says. "Are you?"

His words sucker punch me. He's here seeing his friends and didn't bother coming by the house. I don't blame him, but it doesn't stop the hurt.

"Yeah," I say in a near whisper. "I'm at the tracks."

"Don't move," he orders. "I'm coming there. Cobain, don't do anything until I get there, okay? I'm going to help you."

I have to grit my teeth to keep from crying and shake my head.

"Ten minutes," he says, and I can hear the keys jingle as he jumps into his truck.

I hang up and wait.

I stare at the gun.

Just to see, I lift the barrel to my lips. Open my mouth just a touch, then rip my arm back down and shake with fear.

Green trees.

Blue water.

White dog.

Black crow.

My dad yelling.

My vision blurring.

"Cobain."

I glance up and imagine what I must look like—red eyes, red face, shock and desperation and mania twisting my face into one he doesn't recognize.

He's so much smaller than me.

Alarmingly thin.

How can he possibly care for us both? I'm the stronger one. I'm the one who should be helping him. Didn't I get bigger and bigger so I could feel half as good as my older brother?

Holt sees the gun and stops.

I lay it down beside me and cover it with my hand to show him I don't intend to use it. At least, not yet.

He swallows what must be a substantial amount of trepidation and sits down beside me.

"What happened?" he asks.

"They showed me footage of me taking Molly," I say.

"Are you sure—"

"I'm sure."

He nods and takes a deep breath. Puts his hand on my back. "Fuck. *Fuck*."

His hand on my back is what does it. I drop my head and fight against the tears. Think of Molly. The way she streaked my face with pickle juice and kissed it off. Her laugh that most often sounded suppressed, and the booming, earth-shattering one she reserved for when I tickled it out of her. Her nails, always chipped. Her smile, mischievous. Her heart, only half awake.

The way her head felt on my chest.

The way she felt on the inside.

The way I felt when I was with her—worthy, seen.

What is wrong with me?

What am I forgetting?

Why is this hole only appearing now?

I haven't had holes since I was a kid.

Or have I?

Maybe there have always been holes, and I simply filled them.

Filled them with convenient lies.

Filled them with partial truths.

Filled them, because the truth was too unbearable.

Green trees.

Blue water.

A dog barking.

My mind stutters and skips.

And then I know.

I know.

Holy shit. Oh fuck, *no*.

All the pieces slide into place, the holes filling with new information—

Green grass.

Blue water.

A dog barking.

My father running toward me, yelling.

A gunshot.

"Holt," I say, in a voice that isn't my own.

He looks at me with concern for my wellbeing, and then slowly, so gut-wrenchingly slowly, his face changes into concern for himself. Maybe that's because I'm lifting the gun from the ground and placing it on my lap.

Maybe that's because I'm getting to my feet and keeping my gun pressed against my leg.

Holt gets to his own feet, his eyes locked on the weapon in my hand. "What are you doing?"

"You've never really been there for me," I say, accusation twisting my words.

Holt's hands come up like he's been afraid of this moment for a long time. "What are you talking about? I've always been there for you." Holt hesitates. "Brother, we're going to figure this situation out together. I'm going to be with you—"

"You're always running off to be with your friends," I say, feeling the blood simmering in my veins. Not sure what I'm doing, but unable to stop the escalation. Because I'm remembering my childhood now. Remembering how Holt *always* resented me, and not the other way around.

"You never cared about me." I lift the gun.

Fear lights up my brother's face. His eyes are so big I think they might roll from his head and land in the palm of his hand like a pair of dice—snake eyes.

"Cobain, holy shit, what are you doing?"

"You were always jealous that Dad liked me best," I say.

Holt's face twists with confusion. "You...you always said Dad favored *me*. Now you're saying it's the other way around? Cobain, just put the gun down. *Please!*"

I shake my head. "I remembered everything wrong. It was too hard to remember it the way it was. It was too hard to remember the truth." I straighten my arm, stare down the length of my weapon to the fear locking my brother's body in place. "You never cared about me."

"I *loved* you!" he roars. "No one cared about you more than me!"

My voice is a lesson in control. "No one cared about me *less* than you."

I search the side of the gun until I find the safety. Click it off. Holt looks like he might run.

I've never seen terror like this before.

And I'm asking myself, *What am I doing, what am I doing?*

But I have to be sure about him.

I take aim with purpose, hold the gun with both hands, and ask him one question.

"When is your birthday?"

Holt's face contorts with confusion. "What? Cobain, put the gun down. What the fuck, man? You're my brother!"

"When is your birthday?"

"Cobain, stop. Please, for fuck's sake, I'm your family! I'm the one who—"

"WHEN IS YOUR GODDAMNED BIRTHDAY, BIG BROTHER?"

He holds his hands out in front of him, shaking from head to toe. In the distance, I think I hear a train. Is that a train or is the sound in my head?

Slowly, Holt begins to lower his arms. And even slower, a smile parts his face. He laughs, once, and it echoes the crazy I feel inside.

"You got me," he says at last. "I can't remember my fucking birthday."

I shoot him.

Blood sprays across my face, but that can't be right.

That shouldn't be what's happening right now!

He stumbles back two sharp steps and then falls, and then I know for certain that a train is coming, and I'm going to throw myself beneath those rusted wheels.

I rush to his side, dropping the gun, dropping to my knees. I take his head in my hands and hold it in my lap as he sputters. When he smiles, his teeth are laced with blood.

"Holt!" I shout. "Oh my God, Holt. Please, God. You're

going to be okay. I fucked up. I thought I knew, but… Oh God, oh fuck!" I release him and reach for my phone, my fingers fumbling to call for help.

But he reaches up to stop me.

"Cobain," he says with a wheeze that cuts through every vital organ in my body. "Cobain, say it."

"I'm sorry," I say. "I'm sorry, I'm sorry. Oh fuck! Holt. You're bleeding so much."

I press down on his chest, and he covers my hand with his.

"Say it," he repeats.

And I know I need to because he doesn't have much time left. Already, the color has drained from his face, and his too-thin body somehow appears even more emaciated.

Holt fights to take a breath, squeezes his eyes shut, and grips my hands with sudden intensity.

"Say it!" he demands, and blood splatters my face.

The train is coming closer, but there's no whistle this time. Just the *thunk-thunk* of the beast barreling toward us.

I put my hand to his cheek and bite down against the tears filling my eyes.

"You never really cared about me…" I begin.

Holt nods and coughs.

"You never really cared about me," I say. "Because you were never here."

Holt smiles.

"You've never been here," I continue.

Holt's eyes bore into mine. Eyes I've seen every day since I was born. But those eyes changed when I turned seven, didn't they? They used to be brown. And now they're blue.

I *made* them blue because that seemed a nicer color.

"You went away when I was seven," I say, and now the tears are pouring down my face. Because I remember him—my big brother, the way he was before.

Holt pulls in a deep breath and releases it as if by me saying this, he is finally free.

"You went away," I say. "And I'm the reason you're not here anymore."

The train flies by, and as the wind slaps against my face, I stand and watch the cars race past.

I try and count them, but I'm too dizzy. The world is going much too fast.

When it finally stops, I look down at where my brother's body lies.

But it's gone.

Of course it is gone, because it was never there to begin with. Not for a long, long time. I forgot his birthday. I remembered most things about him, but not his birthday. If I didn't know it, then he couldn't have known it either.

So many lies have been told since I met Molly, but the first of them, the last of them, was the one I told myself.

I know what I am capable of now.

I know I will not be the hero in this story.

I will not wear a cape and rush in to save Molly in the end.

No, I am the one who has taken her.

I am capable of anything, really.

If I killed my own brother, what would I do to a girl who planned to betray me?

My head snaps up.

I know where Molly is.

I know where I took her.

THEN

I remember a day with you, Molly.

Do you remember it, too? It's one of many, not a particularly exciting day. We went to the train tracks, and I was surprised you wanted to go to my spot, because you always wanted to go to the park instead.

We sat on the tracks, and you seemed to be waiting for something.

"Do you ever think about things too much?" you asked as rain drizzled over your shoulders.

"Yeah," I said.

You nodded and looked down the tracks again.

"I get sad sometimes," you admitted quietly, and I could tell it was probably the hardest thing you'd ever said aloud.

"I know."

You looked at me, surprised. "You do?"

"Yeah, I see it."

You smiled then. "No, you don't, because I never get sad. I was just playing."

I studied your face until your smile faded away.

"Sometimes I just hate myself," you confessed.

I took your hand, but you wouldn't look at me. You kept looking into the distance, waiting for something, and a wave of uneasiness crept over me.

"Hey, let's get out of here," I said to you.

But you shook your head, and tears filled your eyes.

"Molly, get up," I ordered.

When you didn't move, I grabbed you and hauled you into my arms. You wrapped your legs around me and kissed me and kissed me and took my mind and my heart straight into your mouth.

You bit my bottom lip hard enough that I pulled back, and I saw that you were smiling again. You just needed reminding that I was here, I guess. That you weren't alone. You were always saying that—*don't ever let me go.*

I used to think you meant to never break up with you, no matter how crazy you acted.

But now I think you might have meant something else.

You were looking for a way out, weren't you, Molly?

On the other side of the world.

Or on the other side of this life.

MOLLY

Molly took the first step into the water, and Blue followed her out.

Blue gasped. Molly cinched her eyes shut against the sound, and then took another step. He matched her progression, but with each step, he gripped her hand tighter.

"I'm scared," Molly said, because it was true. Oh God, how it was true.

She had to do this.

This was her only chance at surviving him.

And so she hauled her dress higher with her left hand and held firm to him with her right and took another step and then another. When the black water licked at her chest and his waist, she said it again. "It's time to take it off." After a moment, she added, "I won't back out as long as you don't."

He lifted a hand to his mask and paused.

"Together," Molly said as her teeth chattered.

Her body was numb in the frigid water, her shuddering breath filled with heart-pounding fear. Already, they'd been in the water too long. Much, much too long.

Blue released her hand and raised both to his mask.

Then, as the moon slipped closer, Blue removed his disguise.

"I knew it was you," Molly whispered, but still, she could hardly believe it.

She dropped her head and released a muffled cry. Then, remembering what had to be done, she raised her eyes and reached for his hand in the water.

He raised a surprised eyebrow at her touch, like he was shocked she'd still touch him after seeing his face.

But she'd known all along, in a way.

She just wasn't sure until this very moment.

"I don't know which name to call you now," she said.

Instead of responding, he kissed her.

And she let him. In fact, she may have kissed him back. She may have.

It was the least she could do, she thought, *since she was about to kill him.*

NOW

When I was a kid, we used to go to a lake house. I remember it because that's where I killed my brother. It's a perfect place to hide a kidnapped girl. Or a body. I can't remember the address, though. How is that possible if I'd already taken her there?

I have to call my mother. I have to know why I hurt my own brother. And I can't get to Molly without a vehicle or knowing where the house is.

And so I crouch behind our neighbor's fence across the street, dial our home phone, and cringe when my mom answers.

I can hear it in her voice right away.

She knows what I did at the station.

Hell, cops are probably in the house with her.

"Mom," I say, "I know what happened."

"Cobain? Cobain, where are you? Why did you take that man's gun? Don't do anything with it, okay? Tell me where you are."

"I know what I did to Holt," I say.

My mom doesn't respond. I listen for someone to tell her

to keep talking, but I don't hear anything. What's more, I don't see anyone, either.

"Cobain, what are you talking about?"

"I know he wasn't there," I yell, and then remember that I'm too close to the house to chance being so loud. I duck behind some bushes and see my mother standing in the window. My heart clenches at the sight of her. I want her to hug me so badly. To tell me everything will be okay. I wonder how it felt to watch her only son fight someone who wasn't there. To listen to conversations held with ghosts. How painful must it have been?

My mom covers her mouth with her hand.

"I know I kept him in my head because I couldn't handle the truth."

My mom's head drops. "It was so hard. Pretending. Trying to play along. Your doctor told us we should, but it was so hard, baby. We didn't know if you'd ever remember the truth of what happened. And then Holt finally started going away, and we thought…we could just move past it. Then you met Molly, and he came back." My mom pauses. "Cobain, where are you? You need to come home. You've got to talk to these people and—"

Green trees.

Blue water.

White dog.

Black crow.

In the distance, a cabin.

Pressure.

And then—

A gunshot.

"I killed him, didn't I?" I say. "I killed him at that house in the woods. I remember the house. I remember the water."

"Killed him? *You?*"

The surprise in my mom's voice raises goose bumps along my arms.

"Oh, Cobain, you didn't kill your brother. You didn't even try to hurt him. You were just playing around like you always did, and he got upset. He jumped on top of you and…he started to…" My mom's voice breaks. "His hands were around your throat, and we couldn't get him off you, and so your daddy… he had his gun with him and…"

My mom cries again, and I put the pieces together.

My father's unrelenting hope in me. His unwavering belief that he had to kill one son to protect the other. And that I was worth the sacrifice.

"It was Dad," I say.

"What?" my mom gasps. "No. No one killed Holt, Cobain. He's still alive."

Her words slam into me. Nearly take me to the ground.

Holt is alive.

Holt is out there.

"We had to put him in a facility to help him," my mom continues. "We didn't have a choice. He was never… It was hurting all of us."

"Mom," I say, so quietly I almost can't hear my own voice. "When is the last time you saw him?"

Mom vanishes from the window, and it takes a moment for her to answer, her words swimming in tears. "It's hard to visit him. It's just so hard. I have to keep myself busy so I don't—"

She breaks off in a sob, and I nearly drop the phone.

"Mom, where is the lake house we used to go to?

"Aunt Nancy's house?" she asks. "Cobain, where are you? You need to come—"

"*Where is the house, Mom?*"

"I…I can't…" She thinks to herself. "Woodling Road? No, Woodbine. In Reading. Is that where—"

I hang up and race toward the house, keeping low.

I know what lies inside that garage.

I roll open the door as quietly as possible, moving faster than I ever have, and see a black truck inside.

Holt's truck.

No, *my* truck.

I jump inside, find the keys in the ignition, and barrel from the garage and onto the road. Only five minutes pass before I see and hear the red lights behind me. It doesn't matter. They'll never find the place before I do. A drive that should take twenty minutes or more takes only ten. Houses whip by through my windows, giving way to trees arching over an ever-thinning road.

Two lanes narrow to one.

Pavement morphs into dirt.

A cloud kicks up from my tires as I jam my foot down to the floor, and the officer behind me gives chase. That cop will soon turn into two. Or three. Or a dozen. I have to lose him before that happens.

I wait until it's almost too late to make the turn and then hit the brake and slide to the left until my tires catch. Then I'm off.

The officer has to stop and back up, but he's on me again. His lights flash, his siren wails, and I realize with a sinking feeling that I might not outrun him. That I haven't been here in years and may miss the turns myself.

But, no, as I get closer, I'm recognizing things.

A field with a broken windmill.

The house with the wraparound porch.

The long barbed wire fence that used to hold two gray horses.

I make another sudden left turn, and this time the officer takes longer to back up and hit the gas. I consider taking wrong turns, any turns, just to widen that gap. But I'll risk losing myself and losing Molly.

So I press down on the accelerator and keep gunning it. My hands are slick. My heart is explosive. And I just don't know what I'll do if he runs me off this road. They'll never believe me. At the very least, it would take them too long to take action and find her—the way I will, right now, no matter what.

I'm coming, Molly.

The last turn is a narrow split between fences. I take the turn, and after slamming into one of the fences, the cop takes it, too. I pull in a shaky breath, steady my hands, and ready myself to play the only card I have.

We crash into the heart of the forest, the trees and brush so thick my only prayer is to stay on the dirt road. I remember this. I remember. But do I remember well enough?

I have a few crucial seconds. Just enough time to throw him off my trail. I arrive at the split I knew was coming and tear down the dirt path, then I throw the truck in reverse until I reach the split again—a split you'd only notice if you'd been here before. This time I drive in the other direction, cutting through the foliage.

When the officer whips around the bend, I kill the engine and clutch the steering wheel until I'm afraid my knuckles will split open. With any luck, he'll see the dust I kicked up and assume that's the direction I went. It's the only clear road with enough turns and hills to have hidden my truck from immediate view. The path I'm on is hardly a path at all, just two tracks where tires have flattened the weeds and brush.

Holt has been coming and going, I realize.

When I don't hear the officer's approach, I breathe a sigh of relief and start my truck. Then I roll farther until I see the outline of a house squatting in the distance. My throat tightens, but it isn't the sight of the cabin that destroys me, or the memories that come flooding back.

It's the white van parked out front.

I get out of my truck, kicking myself for leaving the gun at the train tracks. I take one step onto the soil, and I'm slammed with a memory so heavy, my knees nearly buckle.

I'm playing with my brother near the cabin. My aunt is there. She's very thin. Too thin, Dad keeps saying, and he seems sad.

Dad asks if I want to play baseball.

"There's no bat," Holt says. "No ball."

Dad shrugs. Messes my hair. "Cobain could probably knock one to the pond with a tree branch and a stone. Wanna give it a try, kiddo?"

Dad slings his arm around me.

Dad hugs me to him.

When Dad isn't looking, I glance at my brother. The look on his face is there. The one that scares me. The one he reserves for me late at night. Mom told me to stay away from him when he gets like that. Said sometimes he gets frustrated that things don't come as easy to him as they do me, and that makes him sad. And because he doesn't know how to process his sadness, he gets angry. So that's how I always thought of my brother.

Holt, happy.

Or Holt, blue.

More often than not, he was Holt Blue.

MOLLY

Molly took his hand, and together they waded farther into the water.

When she felt her feet sweep from the dirt floor, she panicked. But then his arm was there, wrapping around her, and he said, "Together."

Her eyes enlarged at the sound of his voice. It was so much like Cobain's, but not quite. He looked so much like him, but not quite. Moved and ate and danced like Cobain, but not quite. He still had the same eyes she saw in that photo of him with Cobain, though—the brown of a grizzly bear hide.

She remembered how the photos had suddenly stopped when Cobain and his brother were young. How Cobain said he got "messed up in the head," around that time. It took her a long time to recall these things. To fill the holes. She still didn't know everything, but she knew enough.

What happened between the brothers to make one hate the other this much?

Would she live long enough to find out?

Molly closed her eyes and imagined it was Cobain's arm

that held her. It wasn't him who stole her away from the life she had. And that meant he was still back there, wondering why she left him.

She nodded once because she couldn't keep her head above water anymore.

Holt pulled his legs up, and the two floated toward the bottom. Molly opened her eyes and saw him watching her face. His eyes were unbearably large with fear. Was it even possible to keep themselves down there? Would human nature cause them to burst to the top for a lungful of air whether or not they were intent on ever breathing again?

Holt took her to the bottom, and Molly readied herself to pretend she was a corpse. She wouldn't let him drown her. She wouldn't die this way. Not with his arms around her. Not with him looking at her like she was the only thing that mattered. She wouldn't breathe her last breath beside the brother of the only boy she'd ever loved.

But as the cold seeped deep into her muscles and her lungs began to burn for oxygen, she wondered what death awaited her if she resurfaced? Cancer, fifty years from now? A car crash two years out of college? A heart attack, though she'd never had the signs? One way or another she'd return to the earth the same way she came. Wouldn't it be easier for this to be it?

Her mind grew fuzzy.

Molly had never in her life felt so much pain, and then, in a rush of adrenaline, it left her. She was left with only peace. Her heart beat in her ears, and her eyelids began to flutter. She was frozen, suspended in time.

Holt jerked, and his eyes fluttered, too. His legs kicked as if he wanted to resurface but his body wouldn't cooperate. His entire body jerked again, and his arms released her.

The world lost all dimensionality. Became a path forking in the woods. One path led to the unknown—filled with some happiness, but also heartache and pain. On the other was only peace.

Was this the cold whispering in her ear? Wishing only to keep her body for itself? To suck on her marrow and lick the salt from her skin?

Or was this something darker still? Was it her past that told her to succumb to the icy waters, or was it her version of the future? Had she really sunk below the tide to kill him, or to do to herself what she'd always thought of in her quietest moments?

She closed her eyes to see how it felt, and her body floated toward the bottom until her back touched the silt. The pain from the cold had long vanished. Now it was only her heart thumping far too slowly, her lungs squeezing, searching for air. Finding none and slowly relaxing. Her gaze flicked to Holt, and she watched as his eyes slipped closed. Twice he clawed at the water as if trying to find a way up. But he'd waited too long. Maybe she had, too.

That final thought was her undoing. That she no longer had a choice. Nothing scared Molly more than exhausted options.

With a determined start, she told her body to kick upward. But her legs didn't comply. And when she screamed internally for her arms to swim, they only brushed loosely against her sides.

This was how Molly Bates would die, and only when she realized that did she grasp how deeply she wanted to live. This was supposed to be a murder, not a suicide. She opened her mouth and found her throat still worked. Molly watched, half lucid, as little bubbles raced from her mouth to the surface.

Her body jerked the way Holt's had, and Cobain's face flashed in her mind. She loved him. Maybe she only knew that for certain at that moment. When her life was slipping away. When she had only death's hand left to hold.

Her heart—her compass—had been broken when she left. But it wasn't Cobain who broke it.

She'd done that to herself.

Her body jerked a second time, and agony rocked through her. A shot of adrenaline surged from toes to nose—her body's final stand—and Molly captured it. She maneuvered her feet beneath her, and, feeling as if her spine would snap in two, she shot upward. On her way to the surface, she saw Holt's body dragging along the ground, rocked gently back and forth like a newborn baby.

When Molly surfaced, she filled her lungs so mightily that every creature on earth lost their breath for a moment. Then she gasped for a second and third time, and the world was put right again.

She cried from fear and from the cold and because she wasn't certain that she could make it to shore. She couldn't feel her arms as they reached out and tugged at the water, and it may have been her imagination, but she felt much farther away than when they'd dunked themselves under.

She made it a few feet before she turned back and watched the place from which she came. For one mind-warping moment, she considered going back for Cobain's brother. Could she really leave him there to slowly decompose beneath the water and slushy ice?

She turned and swam for shore.

The jerky movements sent blood coursing through her body, warming her if only enough to reach land. When her feet touched the muddy bottom, she cried out. Hung her head and wept. She'd killed someone. She killed someone, and she'd nearly let herself die along with him.

Molly collapsed onto the ground and groaned like a dying animal. But she wasn't dying. She was alive. Just look at the color returning to her ice-kissed skin. Just look at the way her chest heaved for more, *more*.

She fumbled onto her back and stared at the sky, thinking only one word over and over and over and over and over and over and over and over and over—

Freedom.

Molly sat up.

And she saw him.

Cobain's brother stood hip-deep in the water, teeth chattering, body shaking. The embodiment of rage.

Molly's heart shotgunned in her chest.

She scrambled backward as he powered toward her, his torso cutting through the pond. It bowed to him—the water and the ice and the entire kingdom of trees that witnessed his furious approach.

"Together," he said, his voice holding a dangerous growl. "You…said…together."

His words were broken from the cold.

She was broken from the cold.

But she found her feet anyway. Rose, stumbled twice, and then began to run.

He ran, too.

NOW

I run faster as I try to remember real Holt versus Holt from my imagination. When I push open the front door, I'm assaulted by the smell of dust. I search the room—the sagging couch, the sofa chair, the record player Holt always loved toying with.

I find a door to another set of stairs and take them down. I'm so terrified of seeing my brother that I'm afraid I'll collapse. But there's anger there, too. Because this guy I no longer know took something important to me. He took the *most* important thing.

When I reach the bottom of the stairs, I have to steady myself against the wall. Another memory comes crashing to the forefront of my mind.

The crack of the stone being thrown through the forest of green, green trees, a white dog chasing after it.

"What did I say?" My father booms. "A stick and a stone and he's Joe DiMaggio here."

My dad has a can of Coke in his hand and a baseball cap

on his head, and he smiles like he's never had a bad day in his entire life.

I glance at Holt, who is picking up sticks, too. They are sharper than the dull one I hold. They are thin and narrow and pointed at one end. If a tree had teeth, they would look like that, I decide.

Holt points at me with one of the sticks.

He points, and he smiles.

I run to Dad, who throws his arm around me and asks, "What's wrong, kiddo?"

When my eyes fall on Holt, Dad frowns. "Holt," he hollers. "Stop hiding and get out here. Wanna try and hit one?" He takes the limb I'm holding and shows it to Holt.

Holt looks at my dad, looks at me, and then sinks deeper into the trees.

Dad runs a hand through his hair and sighs with frustration. His unbreakable smile has shattered.

Dad says, "Just ignore him. Let's keep practicing, huh?"

I run to find another stone to crack through the whispering trees.

I step across the filthy floor, steeling myself against the sight of the cords hanging from the ceiling. They've been cut, dozens of them, so that they drape down, everywhere. Dresses litter the ground, and my lip curls in fury.

I turn and race up the stairs. If the van is still parked out front, they've got to be here somewhere. I freeze when I get to the landing, and my eyes fall on the kitchen table. I hold my breath and cross the room. My eyes flick across the food, the silverware, the candles. The setting looks more like a ceremony than a dinner.

I swat away a fly buzzing around the half-eaten food, browning at the edges.

It's been sitting here, spoiling, all day. Maybe longer. As panic rockets through me, a sound snaps outside the cabin.

I turn and race toward it.

MOLLY

The branches tore at Molly's frozen dress as she crashed through the woods.

He was a bear in pursuit, following every turn she made, nostrils flaring. It was like he could sense her everywhere. On his clothes, on his skin, in his head. She was a part of him now, and he would never let her go.

Together, she'd said, and he would ensure it stayed that way.

Molly ran faster, her feet tearing open, leaving scarlet droplets of blood in the snow. No matter how hard she pushed herself, he pushed harder. It came down to who wanted what more.

Molly wanted freedom.

But he wanted Molly.

And love always triumphed in the end.

Molly saw a cavernous space in the hillside up ahead and ran for it. She was two steps away from the hiding spot when he wrapped his arms around her and lifted her from the ground.

She screamed.

He laughed.

Molly kicked her legs backward, but he only scooped them into his other arm and pinned them against his chest. He carried her like a new bride, but she was no longer playing games. Now he would know she was a fighter.

She slammed her head sideways and cracked her skull against his.

With a grunt of pain, he dropped her to the ground.

He covered his face, his hands full of blood.

She ran, bypassing the cave.

In a matter of seconds, he was on her again. As she screamed, he bellowed, "You said *together*."

"I didn't mean it!"

"Yes, you did!"

She broke away and made it three steps before his body collided with hers. She turned and punched him in the side of the head, and he smiled in amusement before pinning her against the tree.

Her hands were restrained on either side of her, and he pressed his body against hers. He bent at the knees, laid his head on her shoulder, his lips just brushing her neck. "You nearly talked me into *killing* myself. That isn't some survivalist bullshit—that's called being a psychopath."

Molly brought her knee up with monumental force, and he bent at the waist, groaning.

She ran, her head tipped toward the sky, and when she heard him coming, she slipped behind a tree to catch her breath.

"I'll find you, Molly," he called out. "I'll always find you."

NOW

I run outside, searching for the source of the sound.
       She's nearby. I can sense her. Can feel her in the snow
and in the dead, twisting trees. I feel something else, too—
something I haven't felt for nine long years.

   "Want to try and catch some supper?" Dad asks.

   I look to the pond. "Out there?"

   *Dad laughs, and the sound fills me with happiness. "Yes, out
there. Go on, and I'll catch up with the poles."*

   *I run as fast as I can because Dad loves to see me run fast.
As my aunt's dog chases after me, Mom calls out to be careful. I
wave at her over my shoulder. She smiles and waves back and
guides my aunt into a chair on the porch.*

   *When I get to the pond, I throw a rock into the blue water.
The white dog disappears into the brush, sniffing after some
animal. I try to skip the rock like Dad does, but it only sinks to
the bottom.*

   *"You've got to throw it sideways," my brother says, startling
me.*

I turn and find him slipping out from between the trees. "I can show you how, but you'll have to get closer to the water."

I look behind him, trying to find my dad, but don't catch sight of him.

Holt looks for him, too, and seems pleased when he doesn't see him coming.

Mom says to stay away from Holt when he gets funny, but I don't think I can get past him. I'm faster, but he's got longer legs, and he's older by three years.

Holt comes two steps closer.

Then he lunges.

My head snaps up when I spot movement between the trees.

I put my head down and run, unafraid because I'm not his little brother anymore.

I made sure of that.

MOLLY

Molly shook from the cold and the fear as she hid, her back pressed against the tree.

"When I saw you and my brother together, it made me sick," he said as he searched for her. "Here I was on the streets after the shithole my parents stuck me in closed down, and there was my fucking golden-boy brother with his happy little girlfriend. Then I decided, fuck it, you know? I'm just going to take what I should've always had."

Holt rounded the tree. "I never expected to find my carbon copy, though. And yet here you are."

Molly screamed and raced toward the van, but he was on her in an instant. He wrestled her until her back pressed against the cold metal.

"I am *nothing* like you," Molly spat.

"Yes, you are. You're as messed up as I am." But then his eyes flashed, and for a moment, the person she'd spent these last few weeks with came back. His head dropped, and he turned his face away from her. The uncertainty and pain returned to him.

"You don't even know my name," he said.

"I don't *want* to know it."

"Holt," he said, his voice gentle. "Say it."

Molly smiled. "Blue."

He shook his head. "No, say my real name."

"Blue," she said, her grin widening. "Blue, Blue, Blue. What a stupid fucking name, Blue."

He pulled her away from the van and pushed her back against it. It hardly rattled her, but there was no mistaking the warning.

"You won't hurt me," she challenged.

He searched her face, and what she saw in his eyes shook her confidence.

"You care about me," he said, delivering his own challenge. "Admit it."

Molly leveled him with a look. "Listen to me when I tell you this. Listen *very* carefully. Are you listening?"

He nodded, his desperation broadcast for all the world to hear.

"I don't care about you," she said, her voice unwavering. "I *never* cared about you. Every time I touched you, I envisioned your death. Every time I sang for you, I imagined watching the life leave your body. You locked me away with no thought of what that would do to me." Molly leaned closer. "You *disgust* me."

He released her, the surprise in his eyes so profound that it stole Molly's breath away.

She took several steps away from him, her heart leaping at the possibility of escape. But then he looked down. Said with sudden clarity, "I thought you were like me. But you're not. You're like *him*."

When he looked up again, it wasn't with intrigue.

It was with decisiveness.

He was going to kill her.

"Holt, wait," she said.

Didn't matter.

He rushed toward her.

NOW

I hear Molly. Hear her screaming.

I power toward the sound of her.

"Molly!" I roar.

Holt's body slams into mine beside the water. His hands find my throat, and he squeezes.

"They used to love me," he tells me.

He's crying, and I am, too. Or I would be if I could get enough air.

I claw at his fingers, at his face, but he only clenches his hands tighter, the pressure on my neck becoming unbearable. Blackness creeps in at the corners of my vision, and I hear Holt saying, "I love you, too, but no one will love me as long as you're here."

I kick and thrash, but he is so much bigger than me. I don't even fully understand death, but I know I'm crashing toward it. I know, and all I can think of is my mom. I want my mom.

I realize as I look into my brother's face, as he cries and pushes down, that he wants my mom, too. That's why he's hurting me.

"I'm sorry," he says as the world begins to fade away.

I remember a crow flying across a cloudless sky.

I remember the sound of a dog barking.

I remember the blast of my dad firing a gun into the air, and moments later, his hands ripping my brother away.

He beat him.

He beat him so badly I thought he was dead.

He beat him until my mother screamed and my aunt collapsed, and then he kicked his son once more.

Molly screams louder when she hears me coming. I see a flash of her between the trees. Someone is on top of her.

I yell her name again and run faster, and then she's on her feet, and the person on top of her is racing in the opposite direction.

She barrels toward me, and when our bodies crash together, everything is right again for one moment in time.

"Cobain!" she screams, tears cutting streaks down her dirtied face. She's soaking wet and freezing in my arms.

"I'm here," I say against her neck even as my entire body throbs with anger. I want to end the person who did this to her.

"It's your brother." Molly turns in my arms, her terrified eyes searching for him. "He's the one who—"

When I hear footfalls crunching through the snow, I know it is him.

I *feel* that it's him.

I release Molly, push her behind me, and turn to face my brother.

He appears from the trees, his head tilted to one side, and it's like I'm back beside that pond skipping rocks.

He looks like me, his face shaped only a touch differently.

His eyes brown to my blue.

No wonder even I thought I was seeing myself on the gas

station security footage. The resemblance is uncanny.

As he strides closer, I take in his build, so different than the thin, unintimidating brother I'd created in my mind. The real Holt is big. Big like me. I can imagine him spending his days at the hospital working to grow larger. I can imagine him doing pull-ups and push-ups and crunches and using his body weight to grow wider, stronger. I imagine him doing all that so that when this day came, when he faced me again, he'd be ready.

Well, I'm ready, too.

He looks at Molly. "Get away from her."

I'm shocked that these are the first words from his mouth. It takes me a second to recover.

"Don't come any closer," I warn.

Holt produces a blade from behind his back. "What are you going to do, little brother? Beat me until I can't see out of either eye? Kick me so that two of my ribs break? Hide in your room as Dad berates me because I'm not a shining star like his *other* son?"

"I'm not scared of you, Holt," I say.

Holt takes three barreling steps forward, but Molly steps out from behind me and holds up her hand.

"Stop," she says. "Just let us go, Holt. *Please*."

"Molly," he says. "I'm far from finished with you."

It's the way he says her name, like he really *knows* her.

I can't bear it.

It reaches into my head and twists my brain into knots, and I have to silence his voice. I have to silence this person who drove me to madness these last nine years.

I charge him, slamming into him with every fear I've held since Molly vanished.

He flies backward, and his head hits a rock with a sickening crack. When he lifts up, he leaves blood splattered across the stone. He remembers the knife and raises it above his head.

"Holt, no!" Molly screams, and he hesitates just long enough for me to smash my forehead into his.

Molly takes off running.

Holt panics as she leaves and brings the knife down. I grab his wrist a second before he plunges it into my side, and we roll across the ground. He manages to get on top of me and drives the blade closer to my throat.

But this is not how this is ending.

I bring my elbow up fast and hard and hit him clean across the face. He rocks to the side, and I hit him a second time so that he gets off of me. I snatch the weapon by the blade, and he rips it backward, tearing open my skin.

I howl with pain and anticipate the blade sliding between my ribs. But when I straighten, I see Holt straining to hear something.

An engine.

A car.

Molly's in the van.

Molly's going to run!

I want to roar with triumph, but my brother starts running toward the van, yelling her name.

I race after him, clutching my hand, calling him a coward. Trying to goad him into fighting me instead of chasing after Molly.

We reach the clearing, and I see the van.

It's facing Holt, and Molly is behind the steering wheel with a smile that looks more than a little deranged.

She points at Holt and then slams on the accelerator.

The van bolts forward, and though at first it seems Holt will run, in the end, he opens his arms wide.

"Do it," I shout. "Don't stop!"

Molly barrels closer to him, and I wonder what it will do to me to see my girlfriend kill my brother.

Holt keeps his eyes glued to Molly's face and steps toward the vehicle. He's actually walking *into* his own death.

Molly's scream erupts from the open window as she jerks the wheel at the last moment and sends the van crashing into a tree instead of Holt. Steam rises from the engine, and Holt races toward the driver's seat.

What the hell is happening here?

I cut off his path and barrel into him. He drops the knife, but instead of diving for it, he turns and races toward the water.

"Stay there," I yell to Molly before running after Holt, leaving the knife behind.

"Holt!" I plunge into the woods, the moonlight cutting a path between the trees. As I grow closer to the lake, my footsteps slow. I realize I'm enjoying this. It's therapeutic in a way that ten months of therapy never was. I didn't need talk therapy. I didn't need white pills in white cups. I needed this. The chase. The conquest.

The finality that would come when two brothers who've always hated each other collided at last.

NOW

I spot him hiding behind a boulder on the beach and stalk toward him.

"What are you doing back there, brother?" I ask. "Trying to skip rocks? I can show you how, but you'll have to come closer."

Holt stands up, facing me head on.

He smiles.

"Dad's not here to save you now, Cobain," he says, stepping out from behind the rock. There's blood on his shoulders. There's blood on my hands. There's no telling how much more blood will spill tonight.

I raise a finger and curl it toward myself.

Holt strides toward me.

When he gets close enough, Holt gives one arrogant cock of his chin as if saying, *Let's go*. He's ready for this.

I am, too.

I lunge at him.

Together, we go to the ground. He attempts to crawl on top of me, but I bring my leg up and knee him in the face. He groans as his shattered nose takes another direct hit.

Blood sprays across my face. I wipe it with the back of my hand and stand over him, ready to end this. He groans, and then swings his own leg around, knocking me behind the knees.

I crumble, and this time he is able to clamber on top of me.

He delivers two punches to the side of my head, and my ear rings from the impact.

"She…isn't…yours…anymore," he grunts as he hits me.

His words send a tidal wave of fury coursing through me. I grab for his throat, and his eyes flash with surprise. The reaction scratches some desperate, childlike itch inside me, and I find myself taking hold with my other hand.

He claws at my hands, throws his fist out to try and hit me again. But I lean just far enough away to avoid the blows and maintain my grasp on his neck.

He starts to sink to the side, and I follow him there. Soon, it's me on top. Me with the advantage. I press my hands down harder, my fingertips touching on either side of his neck.

He flops like a beached fish, his eyes bulging. I imagine if I swam my finger inside his mouth, I'd find a hook and lure.

Holt grabs on to my wrists and squeezes. His mouth opens and closes in desperation, as if in a silent attempt to reason with me.

I tighten my hold in response.

I push down with every ounce of weight I carry and imagine the things he might have done to Molly. I imagine his mouth on her skin. Her breasts in his hands. His hand fumbling for his zipper. The grunts he made as he rocked inside of her.

An animalistic sound escapes my lips, and I shake his neck.

Nine years ago, it was him on top.

But now it's me who is in control.

"You tried to kill me," I say, and I push down, down. "You took away my parents. You took away my girlfriend."

Holt opens his mouth to the sky and makes silent gasping

motions. Then he reaches back and clocks me against the face. I wasn't ready for the hit, and so I lose my hold. Just a bit. But he's weak from lack of oxygen, and I reclaim my grip in a matter of seconds.

This time, I will not let up.

No matter how hard he hits me.

No matter how strongly he fights back.

Even if I remember my mother and father saying, quietly, when he wasn't around, "He's sick, Cobain. We take care of each other when we're sick, right? We have to be patient with him, even when it's hard."

Holt seems to make a decision beneath me. He releases my wrists and reaches up, and for a moment I'm certain he's going to attempt hitting me again.

Let him try.

Instead, his hands grab my cheeks, and his eyes meet mine. Eyes that are starting to roll inside his skull. He opens his mouth to say something, but of course, there is no air. I'm holding it in the palms of my hands and refuse to return it.

He grips my face tighter.

And then closes his eyes.

His head falls to his side.

His body collapses.

And I cry out and leap off of him while there's still time and throw my face into my hands because he is my brother. He is my brother, goddammit.

And sometimes he was Holt, happy.

"Cobain," Molly says, and my head snaps up.

I spin around to see her, and I imagine what I must look like in her eyes. Crazy, unmanageable, not at all like the boy she imagined me to be.

Those green eyes stay locked on mine, and I find myself entranced.

"It's okay," she says. "Everything is going to be okay now." I watch the way her lips move as she speaks—a tiny heart-shaped weapon that could kill me with only a few words. I search her eyes, and they tell me everything I suspected. That she loves me. That she was only scared. I hate her for turning her manipulation on me, but what happened to her here was because she knew me.

Molly lays a hand on my chest and nudges me farther away from my brother. "Do you have your phone?"

I nod. "In the truck. I don't know if it will—"

"Go get it," she interrupts. "Call the police, and let's get out of here."

I grab her elbow. "Come with me. I'm not leaving you alone."

She nudges me a second time. Her eyes have hardened like two marbles tucked inside her skull. The sight of them sends a chill over my body. "Go," she insists. "I need to do something first."

I glance down at Holt. He lies unconscious on the ground, and I know he won't be getting up anytime soon.

I nod once at Molly and then run toward my truck.

I'm not sure what makes me turn back—the fear of her vanishing before my eyes, most likely. Regardless, I glance over my shoulder and stop cold.

Holt is waking up.

Molly is standing over him.

Molly has the knife in her hand.

I step toward her as my pulse kicks along my neck.

She points the knife toward him and says something. Then she gets down on her knees and lays the blade against his neck.

"Molly," I say, but I'm not sure why I say it. My brother hates me. And I love her. This could be the perfect end to this nightmare.

But even as I think this, something unnamable rolls in my stomach. I don't want this blood on her hands. And I don't want to watch my brother die, either, even if I thought I did.

A sound crashes over my shoulder, and I turn to find three police cruisers pulling in next to my truck. Doors fly open, and guns are drawn, and officers move in toward the scene.

"Molly," I say again, louder, and watch as she gets to her feet.

She says one last thing as the officers yell for her to *get back, drop the weapon, get on the ground!*

Holt sees the police.

Holt sees Molly.

Resentment twists his face, and he dives toward Molly. He rips the knife from her unsuspecting grasp and lifts it into the air as the police yell and I yell, too, and the entire world pivots one-quarter inch to the right.

A shot is fired.

NOW

Blood bursts from Holt's shoulder.

The police are there in an instant. They are hauling him up, calling for an ambulance, grabbing Molly and me and pulling us away from the scene. Detectives Hernandez and Tehrani are there. They are asking, *Are you two okay? Are you okay?* And to me they say, *Your mother told us everything*, and to Molly, they add, *We're calling your mom to let her know we've got you.*

At this, Molly clenches her eyes shut. When she reopens them, her gaze falls on me. She breaks away from Detective Hernandez and moves toward me like it's the first time she's seen me. She throws herself into my arms, and I wrap her up. I'm afraid I'll never let her go. I'm afraid I'll squeeze the life out of her right after I've found her alive.

"Cobain," she says, and grabs my face to make me understand.

"I know." I take the blanket Detective Tehrani hands me and wrap it around Molly's shoulders. She lays her head against my chest, and I am whole again.

Detective Hernandez puts a comforting hand on Molly's back and asks, "Molly, I know what you've been through has been very hard. But I need to ask if Holt Kelly is the person who brought you here, and if he did so against your will."

Molly glances up, and she searches for Holt. When she finds him, their eyes meet. Holt looks at her with such anger and such *longing* that a chill rushes across my skin.

"Molly," he roars. "*Molly!*"

There's a strange look in her eyes as she watches the police dragging him away. There's anger on her face to be sure, but there's also something…softer. Understanding. She doesn't look at him like a monster but as someone who needs help. It's the same look I saw on my parents' faces growing up. When I look at him now—when I *really* look at him—I don't see Holt, happy and Holt, blue. I only see my brother. I am not afraid of him anymore. I am afraid of his illness.

It's different.

As Holt calls Molly's name over and over and reaches for her as the police struggle to get him into cuffs, her face twists with conflict.

"Molly?" I say.

"Yes, that's him," she answers the detective suddenly. "And yes, he took me against my will." She glances at me and then at Detective Hernandez. "What will happen to him?"

"He'll be in our custody until he goes to trial," Detective Hernandez says. "Don't worry. He won't be getting near you again."

Molly's gaze flicks to Holt once again, and I pull her tighter as they put a hand on Holt's head and push him into the car. He's still calling her name. Saying he's sorry. Saying he needs to tell her something. Saying, "That's my brother. He's my *brother!*"

His words drift down to the pond, lift that forgotten blade, and drive it into my chest.

"You got her?" Detective Hernandez asks me.

I pull myself together and nod. She jogs over to where Detective Tehrani is closing the car door on a man I'll never think of as my brother.

Molly wraps her hand around the arch of my neck and brings me back to her. She looks...sad.

"Are you okay?" I ask.

She gives me a weak smile and nods. "I am now."

And then, she says something I don't expect but always felt blazing across every inch of her. "Cobain, I love you. I'm so sorry I told you I didn't. I'm so sorry for everything."

I grasp her face in my hands and say the things I've imagined telling her since that night in the woods. "I know. And I'll never let anything bad happen to you ever again. We'll be happy. I promise."

Tears prick her eyes, and I know, *I know*, words alone won't be enough. She's heard too many words, too many lies. So have I. Our lives are full of them.

How did we even get here? Would any of this have happened if we'd been honest with each other? Of all the lies, both big and small, which one hurt us the worst?

Was it when I lied to the police about how we met? They might not have doubted me if I'd told the truth.

Was it my dad lying about the dog I remembered? Or my mom playing along when Holt and I got into that fight? Would I have figured everything out sooner if they hadn't let me believe my own lies?

Maybe it was that jerkoff, Duane, lying about who really took that money.

Then again, that lie saved me from a lot worse.

Was it your lie, Molly? The one where you told everyone you'd broken up with me? Would everyone have still thought I was crazy if you'd just admitted you loved me?

You lied to me about that, too.

Or maybe this was all *my* fault. Wasn't the biggest lie mine? *I'm your brother. If you can't trust me, who can you trust?*

So many lies. More than any of us can count. And with every lie, we had a chance to make things right. How could we have been so stupid?

I'd like to say it's all behind us.

But, of course, I'd be lying.

"We'll be happy," I repeat, "and I'll love you back. Every part of you."

Molly tugs my face toward hers, and our lips meet. There's desperation in our kiss, and tenderness, and I feel all the things she's never said aloud but offered to me anyway. I feel her considering this future I've painted, and I feel it when she pulls back and looks at me with eyes that have no hidden agenda.

In that moment, I forget about my brother. I forget about the police officers calling to one another, and the cold working its way into my bones. I forget about the messy lives that await us at home, and our imperfect families and imperfect pasts. I forget about all of it and stare down into this strange girl's eyes, naked to me at last.

I kiss her lips, soft, quick, and lift my mouth to her ear and say, "There you are."

ACKNOWLEDGMENTS

We Told Six Lies is my ninth published book, and it sure gave me a run for my money (edit for cliché). The characters, the points of view, the time jumps, the twist…it made for one hell of a project. A project I wouldn't have conquered without my writing warrior and editor, Heather Howland. From initial idea to final draft, Heather was at my side, pushing me to tighten the story, to close loopholes, and to answer questions. And just when we thought we were done, one of us would find another inconsistency. Hey, Heather, we finally finished this wicked book! Kylo Ren would be proud.

Thank you to my family (special shout out to Mama), to my fans (V Mafia forever!), and to my friends, old and new. And of course to Lindsay Cummings, always, for being my writing BFF. Did we start a company together? Pretty sure we did. Bring on the Scribbler tattoos!

Thank you to my daughter, Luci—who this morning carried around an earthworm that I'm most certain is now postmortem—thank you for asking me to make up stories for you every night. "Not from a book, Mommy. You say one!" An enormous thank you to my husband, Ryan, for your continued support and faith in my writing. I didn't think I'd make it through this book, but you did. You always do. I love you.

Love to my cousin Kristina who I am looking forward to seeing more often. What a beautiful family and life you have! Love to my aunts and uncles, who I think about often, even with many miles between us. Love to my cousin Reed who I've adored since I was a child. I love your art, your brain, and our two-hour phone calls. If I carve a class 5 river through Dallas, will you come live next door to me? And finally, love and a final farewell to my cousin Wayne who will always be with us in memory and spirit. To those who have felt your loss the deepest, I am so sorry. I wish there were more I could do than dedicate this book to you.

To my readers—those who know me intimately, those who follow me online, and those who are reading my work for the first time—life is short and beautiful and messy. Appreciate every moment. Mad love to every last one of you.

If you enjoyed Victoria Scott's
We Told Six Lies,
you'll love
Violet Grenade.

AVAILABLE NOW!

Her name is Domino Ray.

But the voice inside her head has a different name.

When the mysterious Ms. Karina finds Domino in an alleyway, she offers her a position at her girls' home in secluded West Texas. With no alternatives and an agenda of her own, Domino accepts. It isn't long before she is fighting her way up the ranks to gain the woman's approval…and falling for Cain, the mysterious boy living in the basement.

But the home has horrible secrets. So do the girls living there. So does Cain.

Escaping is harder than Domino expects, though, because Ms. Karina doesn't like to lose inventory. But then, she doesn't know about the danger living inside Domino's mind.

She doesn't know about Wilson.

PART I

DOMINO'S RULES
FOR LIVING ON THE STREET

1. Stick by people worth knowing.
2. Take care of yourself first.
3. Always wear armor.
4. When in doubt, run.
5. Roll the dice.

CHAPTER 1

PRYING EYES

People say blondes have more fun.

Please.

I snatch the wig off my head and toss it toward Greg. He catches it like a fly ball, his eyes never leaving my face. Leaning over in the chair, I dig through the pile of wigs he's brought me.

Brunette?

Redhead?

My fingers land on hot pink tresses that fall in long, sexy waves. Bingo, my friend, bingo. I slide the wig over my head, pull the straps until it's snug, and flip my head up like I'm a starlet in a soft-core porn. "Well?"

Greg claps his hands slowly, as if he's got all the time in the world. Judging by the lines around his eyes, I'm not sure that's true. "Fan*ta*stic."

"I'll take it." My thighs create a sucking sound against the leather chair as I stand. I like the sound, I decide. It makes it seem as if I have a little meat on my bones like a real woman. But a quick glance in the mirror tells me I'm still the shapeless girl I woke up as.

Greg fidgets as I stare at myself. Finally, in an attempt to make me feel better, he says, "Looks like you've put on some weight."

I smile at the lie and click toward the checkout counter in my super-duper high heels, the ones that make me look a hand taller than the five feet I stand. The second I think about my height, I hear Dizzy's taunting in my head: *five feet, my ass*.

"I am five feet," I grumble.

"What?" the counter girl asks.

I look up at her. She must be Greg's new girl. "Nothing," I answer. "How much?"

She clicks a few buttons on the register with shiny purple nails. I'm pleased that she chose a fun shade instead of the typical pink or red or—dare I speak it—a French manicure.

"Twenty-one dollars and forty-four cents," she announces. I glance at Greg, who's busy replacing the wigs onto creepy mannequin heads. I clear my throat. When he doesn't hear me, or pretends not to hear me, I decide to pay the full amount. He usually hooks me up with a discount, which he should, considering I'm here every week. I dig into my pocket for the cash, knowing Dizzy would give me hell for paying at all.

When I glance up at the cashier, she's looking at the underside of my left forearm, at the crisscrossed scars that nestle there. I instinctually pull it against my side. The girl straightens, realizing I've caught her staring. I think we're done with this awkward moment, but the girl isn't going to let this slide.

"What happened to your arm?" she whispers, as if that helps.

I shake my head, hoping that'll deter her from asking anything else. No such luck.

"It looks like you got in an accident or something."

I meet her eyes, my blood boiling, wanting so badly to shut her up. Instead, I slap the money on the counter and grab my pink wig. The bell chimes as I push open the glass door. "I'll be by next week."

On the streets of Detroit, the heat comes in waves. The

pink faux hair dampens from my sweaty palm, and I silently curse the sun. It's so hot in the dead of summer that people are practically immobile. They sit on chairs outside their homes, and on benches near stores, and on the cracked sidewalks. And. They. Don't. Move.

Except, that is, to gawk as I pass by.

They ogle the blue wig falling past my shoulders and down my back, the one I'll replace tonight with the gem in my hand. They stare at my tattoo, the way it slithers down my exposed side. And they narrow their eyes at my pierced lip and wonder where else I may be pierced. What else I'm hiding.

They come to a conclusion: I am a freak.

And they are right.

I head down the sidewalk toward our home, the place where Dizzy and I live. The house doesn't really belong to us, but in this part of town it doesn't matter. No one cares. Certainly not the police. They have bigger problems to worry about than teenage kids squatting in an abandoned house.

Nearing our block, I notice a parked sedan. A guy leans against the side, smoking a cigarette. When he notices me, he nods. I put my head down and walk faster. If Dizzy were here, I'd lift my chin and lock eyes with the man. But he's not, so I don't.

I hear a whistle, and my head jerks back in the man's direction. He's smiling at me. It's not a terrible smile. He's got a mouthful of teeth. That's something. He turns so his body faces mine, and watches as I walk past. The man looks to be in his mid-twenties. He's wearing dark jeans and a proud white shirt, and even from here I can tell his nose is too big for his face. His cigarette dangles between his fingertips as he raises his arm and waves.

I wave back.

His eyes narrow when he sees the underside of my arm.

I rip my hand down and walk faster. I don't want to see his reaction, but I can't help looking up one last time.

The lazy smile is gone from his face. A look of satisfaction has taken its place. He pulls a phone from his back pocket and makes a call, eyeing every step I take.

If I didn't know better, I'd think he just found something he'd been searching for.

I rush toward the end of the street, glancing at a nonexistent watch on my wrist like I have somewhere important to be. Behind me, I can feel the guy watching. I don't know why he looked at me the way he did, but I don't like it. Dizzy and I work hard to ensure no one notices us. The tattoos, the piercings, the loud clothing—you'd think it's to attract attention, but it has the opposite effect. It shows the world we're abnormal, and the world looks away.

Twice I look over my shoulder to check if I'm being followed. There's no one there either time, and I begin to feel like an idiot.

No one wants to follow you, Domino.

No one except a particularly determined social worker who's approached me more than once. This neighborhood is part of her territory, and underage strays are her passion.

Just thinking about the woman sends shivers down my spine. Her frizzy blond hair, the way her arms seem too long for her body like she wants nothing more than to snare me in them. Twice now she's followed me as I made my way home, speaking softly in her tweed business suit and scuffed black heels. I could hear what she was saying, but I didn't want to hear it. She's a paper pusher. Someone who pretends to care. In the end, I'd be another tick mark in her body count. Another dog off the streets, shoved into a kennel.

That's when they'd find out who I really am. What I am.

And then the badness would come.

Standing outside our house, I feel relief. Gray paint peels in frenzied curls, and the front light is broken. The grass is dead and half the windows are covered with boards. But the bones are strong. The house stands three stories tall and is an old Victorian build. This part of Detroit used to be glamorous, where all the rich people lived. But they built too close to the ghetto, hoping against hope that this section of the city would turn around. The opposite happened. The slums grew arms and legs and crawled toward their shiny homes and manicured lawns, and then swallowed them whole without remorse.

And now Dizzy and I have a home that used to be beautiful.

"What are you doing?" someone calls from the upstairs window.

I raise a hand to shade my eyes from the sun. When I see Dizzy's face, I have to stop myself from smiling. Instead, I shake my head as if I'm disappointed to be home and head toward the door.

"It's Friday, Buttercup, you know what that means." Somewhere above me, I hear Dizzy howl long and energetic like a prideful wolf.

I want to tell him not to call me Buttercup, that my name is Domino. But I don't. I just curl my hands into tight fists. I open my mouth wide.

And I howl right back.

CHAPTER 2

SEE DIZZY FLY

Dizzy throws open the door and rushes toward me.

"Stop," I yell, holding my arms out.

"I won't!"

The street-lamp-of-a-guy flips me over his shoulder and barrels into the house. I laugh when he tosses me onto a couch that may or may not harbor the Ebola virus. He places one long, skinny finger on my nose. "Where have we wanted to go for the last two months?"

I slap his hand away. "I don't know. Where?"

He taps his temple and bobs his head, dark curls bouncing against brown skin. "Think, Buttercup. Think."

So I do. My brain goes tick, tick, tick. And then my face pulls together and I crane my neck to the side. "Are you saying what I think you're saying?"

Dizzy jumps onto the makeshift coffee table we constructed and pretends to pound the surface with a king's staff. "Here ye, hear ye. I pronounce tonight the night we wreak Havoc."

"Havoc?" I say quietly. "No one gets in that club."

He nods and his curls kiss his long lashes. "I met someone who knows someone who said he could do something for someone like me."

"We're going to Havoc," I say again, because saying it again makes it real.

Dizzy raises his arms into the air, and I know that's my cue to react. I stand up and spring onto the couch. Then I jump up and down and he grabs my hands. He leaps onto the crusty couch beside me and we go up and down screaming that we're going to Havoc. That we're going to party like beasts, because we are beasts. I throw my arms around him before I remember that we don't do that. I hate being close to people and he hates being confined and this isn't okay.

"Gross. Get off me," he yells. "I can't breathe. I can't breathe!"

I let go, gladly, and Dizzy leaps back onto the floor. He looks like a spider doing it, all arms and legs. He's certainly as thin as one.

His brown eyes spark beneath thick, caterpillar eyebrows. "Get ready," he orders. Then he dashes up the stairs, each step burping from the weight.

I step down from the couch. Going to Havoc isn't that big of a deal for most people. I get that. But this is my life now, has been for the last year. Sometimes going somewhere new—somewhere that'll let people like Dizzy and me in—is everything. It's a shiny penny fresh off the press, a black swan among white. It's nothing groundbreaking. But it is.

I wash my hair and body as best I can using the bottles of water and bar of soap Dizzy stole from the gas station. The drain slurps it down and sighs as I massage my scalp. Next to me on a rusted towel hook, my pink wig waves hello. She's ready to go, she tells me. She can't wait to be worn like the crown she is.

I tell her to hold her damn horses because I'm washing

my hair in a sink.

Wrapping a towel that's seen better days around my head, I step out of the bathroom and into what's been my room for the last ten months. Ten months. I've lived with Dizzy for nearly a year, and I could count the things I know about him on my pencil-thin fingers.

When he was sixteen, his mom put him and his older brother on a plane from Iran bound for America. The pair landed in Philadelphia, and eventually Dizzy ended up here. He never talks about his brother, and I don't ask. I know he enjoys Twizzlers and blue ballpoint pens and crisp, white shoelaces. I know because he steals those things most often.

I've never seen anyone steal something the way Dizzy does. Once before, when I was at a department store, I spotted a pair of kids working together to pinch a yellow Nike hoodie. One kid distracted the associate, asking for help to get something down off the wall, while the other slipped the hoodie inside his leather jacket. They got away with it. I remember wanting to follow them. See what they did next.

Dizzy doesn't work that way. He doesn't distract or scheme. He just slips by what he wants like a ghost, and it's gone. Anything he wants, gone. Dizzy never takes more than he needs, but he needs a lot.

I met him at an arcade. I was playing Pac-Man when I saw him across the room. He was almost as thin as I was, and his nails told me everything I needed to know. He was like me — homeless. I've met homeless people who try to scrub away the streets. It never works. The human body has too many crevices, too many places for grime to settle. You can see it in the small lines of their faces and in their palms and elbows. And you can see it in their nails.

Dizzy's nails were atrocious. He didn't try to scrub away the street. He embraced it. I needed someone like that. As I watched, the long-legged, dark-skinned man-boy swiped a red can of soda from the bar. The soda was there. The soda was gone. If I hadn't been watching closely, I might have believed he was made of magic—Dracula strikes Detroit.

That day in the arcade, Dizzy met my stare with a boldness I admired. I eyed the place where the soda had been, and he smiled. Then he turned and swept out the door. With the rang-tanging of arcade games behind me, I followed him. I followed him then, and I follow him now. He's my person. Not that I need one.

I startle when I spot my person standing in the bedroom doorway.

His eyes widen as if he just remembered I'm a girl. Tugging the towel around my body tighter, I avert my gaze. "What are you looking at?"

"I forget sometimes," he says softly. "What you look like."

He means without my makeup. Without my rainbow wigs and chains and piercings. He means me as I am right now: Domino, in the nude. "Stop staring at me, perv."

"I know you hate it when I—"

"Stop," I say. "Just don't."

He holds up his hands in defeat. "I'm ready to go when you are."

I move to my closet—a pile of clothes on the floor that Dizzy stole for me—and bend to dig through it. Behind me, I hear him turn to leave.

"You are so beautiful," he says under his breath before he's gone.

I almost charge after him. I almost beat his chest and scratch his face with my dirtied nails. Anything to make him regret what he said. But I just tighten my hands into fists and I count—one, two, three...ten.

Now my blood is even Steven, and everything's going to

be okay. It's just Dizzy. His words are easy enough to forget. I smile like I mean it and lay a hand against the wall. It's solid, real. If this wall is treated right, it'll stand straight as the stars long after I'm dead. This particular wall is white with blotches of gray from God knows what.

But my wall, the one in my future house, will be blue.

I walk back into my bathroom, the one uglied by water stains and years of neglect, and pull on a black skirt and tee, lace-up heels, and green-and-black-striped tights like I'm the Wicked Witch of the West. Then I hook in my piercings—lip, ears, eyebrow, tongue—and swipe on enough eyeliner and shadow to cause anyone's mama to shiver. Finally…hello, darling…I slip on my pink wig.

My armor is complete. But then I catch my reflection in the cracked mirror. My jaw tightens as I take in what Dizzy saw. The face of an angel, isn't that what they always said?

They. They.

Them.

I see the same inventory Dizzy does: large blue eyes, soft skin, blond hair kept hidden beneath a wig. But there's more than meets the proverbial eye here. There's something else that he doesn't know about. That no one knows about. There's a darkness living inside me. A blackness that sleeps in my belly like a coiled snake.

His name is Wilson.

CHAPTER 3

MONSTERS

It takes us twenty minutes of walking through the sticky night to get to Havoc. Dizzy leads me to the side of a white brick building and into an alley that reeks of spoiled food.

"What's going on, creeper?" I ask him. "Why aren't we going in?"

"We are." He glances around, searching for something. "There." Dizzy half jogs down the alley and then approaches a window. "VIP access."

"We're going through the window?" I ask, wondering why I'm surprised.

"It's packed every night. They can pick who they want to let in."

And that isn't us. That's what he's saying. If bouncers are allowed to pick, they won't pick us. I stumble toward Dizzy, sure my feet are bleeding from the long walk in my ridiculous heels, and stop when something catches my eye. There's a man sitting behind the green Dumpster. He's homeless. A toddler would know this.

His face is mangled in a way that makes my stomach lurch. One of his eyes is missing, a single slash across the space where it should be. His other eye is oozing something yellow. And along his neck is an angry rash that's slowly climbing its way onto his cheeks.

He attempts a smile. "Evening."

His voice is gentle, and I try to return the gesture as Dizzy calls my name.

"Have a good time," the man says sincerely, nodding toward Dizzy.

Before I can talk myself out of it, I dig into my pocket and pull out what little cash I have. I hand it to the man.

"Domino." Dizzy's voice holds a warning.

I move away from the man and toward Dizzy. "Let's go."

"Why did you give that guy our money? Dude looks like a monster."

I eye the man over my shoulder. "I've seen monsters before," I say. "They don't look like him."

They look like me.

There's a *tap-tap-tap* from behind me, and I turn to see a guy standing inside the window, waving. He slides the glass up and reaches out an arm. Music explodes into the alley as if it's offering a hand, too.

"Hey, big man," Dizzy says.

"Hurry up," Window Guy responds. "It stinks of herpes in here."

Dizzy gives me a boost. Using the guy's arm as leverage, I pull myself through the window. It's a perfect opening. My body slides through the square and lightly brushes the frame. I bet whoever put this window here figured it was immune to break-ins, but they never counted on Dizzy and me.

I land in a bathroom that's covered in magic marker.

For a so-so time, call Trini!
Aiden + Amber = Pimp Juice
Jessika is a LIAR and SKANK

I love it instantly. Just a few more streaks of color and—

Window Guy calls for my help and together we drag Dizzy upward. Halfway through the window, Dizzy gets stuck. In an instant, he becomes a kicking, swinging madman, his fear of tight places overcoming reason.

"Calm down, Dizzy," I yell as I tug harder. "Just. Calm. Down."

I pull backward with all my might, and he crashes onto the floor. Then he bounds upright as if nothing happened. As if he didn't just have a completely unwarranted panic attack. Dizzy throws me a grin, and a girl with short black hair and red lipstick swings through the door.

"What's going on in here?" she asks. And then, "No. Never mind. Whatever it is, I'm in. That's how I roll." Except when she says roll it's more like rooooooooll.

Dizzy slams his hand down on the porcelain sink and points at her. "I like you, girl. I'm going to name you Black Beauty."

The girl gallops and slaps her butt as if she's riding a horse. She is, without a doubt, wildly drunk.

Dizzy takes her arm. "I'm also going to let you buy me a drink."

I'm hurt when he vanishes with the girl. Sometimes I feel like our relationship is a close one, or as close as it can be between two homeless people harboring demons. Other times it feels like I'm standing in place as Dizzy walks away, or perhaps trailing behind as he's a step ahead.

I'm overthinking it. Of course I am. Who do we have if not each other?

Window Guy glances in my direction. He's short and thick and built like a closed fist. He smiles with one side of his mouth. "Don't do anything I wouldn't do," he says. And then he's gone, following after Dizzy and Black Beauty.

I quickly recover from being ditched. After all, I enjoy being alone, and there's no better way to be alone than in a place like this. After straightening my pink wig, I walk through the bathroom door to where the music thumps even louder. The room is dark and the ceiling low. A dozen globes hang overhead, lighting up different colors. It reminds me of one of those Christmas houses that times the lights to the music, each strand taking its turn to shine.

The club, Havoc, is packed. Bodies pulse against one another and, as I pass them by, I am forgotten. It's a feeling like no other—to be present and invisible at once. I don't appreciate that the people are so close, that they are everywhere. But they don't see me so it's okay.

It doesn't take long for me to lose myself in the music. I dance alone, and in my head it feels like I'm normal, like all these people are my friends and they give me space, but they care about me, too. My head falls back, and I raise my arms into the air. Music injects my veins and rushes through my body. It takes me away, far away.

Until.

Until someone grows nearer than the others. An arm wraps around my waist and hips brush my rear.

"Back up," I yell, because there's no way he'd hear me otherwise.

He doesn't back up.

I spin around and the guy—tall, broad-shouldered, eyes that remind me of a Sunday school boy but I know better—pulls me tighter. He leans his head down to my ear and tells me I look sexy. Do I want to dance?

We're already dancing, and the answer is no. It's always no.

"Let go of me," I holler. "I won't say it again."

The guy grins so that I can see every tooth in his mouth. His cheeks are bright red, and his brow is covered in sweat. He isn't unattractive, but I can smell what's beneath his sweet cologne. He is ugly on the inside. And his hands are on me.

He spins me around and my stomach clenches.

I'm being pulled backward toward a corner and oh my God no one is seeing what he's doing. Or they see and don't mind. My heart beats so hard it aches, and my breathing comes fast. But I don't care about that. I care about what will happen if he keeps manhandling me.

I fear what I will do.

The guy pushes me against a wall so that my belly touches sheetrock painted black. His hands roam over my body, exploring the curveless shape of my torso. If he only knew. If he only knew he had an explosive in his grasp.

He runs a finger over my lips.

He pulls the clip off the grenade.

He pushes his mouth against the back of my neck.

He relishes the danger of the bomb in his hand.

His palm slides down the flat of my stomach.

Seconds left until detonation. Take cover!

Inside my head, I scream. Outside my head, I scream. I thrash against him but he uses my weakness to his advantage. I am shy of five feet tall, and I am built of bones.

He is built of steak dinners and whole milk.

His hands move lower and lower, and deep inside the recesses of my brain, something sinister yawns awake. No, no, no! Nothing to see here! Go back to sleep!

It's no use.

Wilson stretches tall and smiles to himself.

He looks around like he's amused by what's happening to us.

Hello, Domino, he says. *It's been a while.*

GRAB THE ENTANGLED TEEN RELEASES READERS ARE TALKING ABOUT!

MALICE
BY PINTIP DUNN

What I know: someone at my school will one day wipe out two-thirds of the population with a virus.

What I don't know: who it is.

In a race against the clock, I not only have to figure out their identity, but I'll have to outwit a voice from the future telling me to kill them. Because I'm starting to realize no one is telling the truth. But how can I play chess with someone who always knows the outcome of my every move? Someone so filled with malice she's lost all hope in humanity? Well, I'll just have to find a way—because now she's drawn a target on the only boy I've ever loved…

PRETTY DEAD GIRLS
BY MONICA MURPHY

In Cape Bonita, wicked lies are hidden just beneath the surface. But all it takes is one tragedy for them to be exposed. The most popular girls in school are turning up dead, and Penelope Malone is terrified she's next. All the victims have been linked to Penelope—and to a boy from her physics class. The one with the rumored dark past and a brooding stare that cuts right through her. There's something he isn't telling her. But there's something she's not telling him, either. Everyone has secrets, and theirs might get them killed.

entangled teen

an imprint of Entangled Publishing LLC